DEC   2021

PRAISE FOR *DON'T MAKE ME TURN THIS LIFE AROUND*

"With her trademark wit and charm, Camille Pagán invites us back into the lives of Libby and Shiloh thirteen years after we first met them in *Life and Other Near-Death Experiences*. *Don't Make Me Turn This Life Around* is rich, raw, and real, a new favorite . . . Readers like me can't help coming back for more of Pagán's gorgeously written stories. I loved it!"

—Kerry Lonsdale, *Wall Street Journal* and *Washington Post* bestselling author

"Oh my goodness! Camille Pagán has achieved such an exquisite, delicate balance, writing a profoundly moving novel that expresses both the beauty and heartbreak of loving other people. *Don't Make Me Turn This Life Around* is everything: funny and warm and scary and sad and reassuring—just like real life. I read this in one sitting because I simply couldn't stop."

—Maddie Dawson, bestselling author of *Matchmaking for Beginners* and *A Happy Catastrophe*

"Camille Pagán's latest page-turner brilliantly captures the nuances of marriage and family while tackling the tough challenges along the way. Libby is every wife and mother, and when life throws her a curveball, she finds the courage to keep moving . . . and keep believing. With wit and wisdom, *Don't Make Me Turn This Life Around* will have you laughing and crying along with these perfectly flawed characters and asking yourself, What does it mean to have enough?"

—Rochelle Weinstein, bestselling author of *This Is Not How It Ends*

DON'T MAKE ME TURN THIS LIFE AROUND

ALSO BY
CAMILLE PAGÁN

This Won't End Well

I'm Fine and Neither Are You

Woman Last Seen in Her Thirties

Forever Is the Worst Long Time

Life and Other Near-Death Experiences

The Art of Forgetting

DON'T MAKE ME TURN THIS LIFE AROUND

Camille Pagán

LAKE UNION
PUBLISHING

Text copyright © 2021 by Camille Pagán
All rights reserved.

Published by Lake Union Publishing, Seattle

www.apub.com

Amazon, the Amazon logo, and Lake Union Publishing are trademarks of Amazon.com, Inc., or its affiliates.

ISBN-13: 9781542026468 (hardcover)
ISBN-10: 1542026466 (hardcover)

ISBN-13: 9781542026475 (paperback)
ISBN-10: 1542026474 (paperback)

Cover design and illustration by Micaela Alcaino

Printed in the United States of America

First edition

For my sister, Janette Noe Sunadhar

ONE

I won't say everything happens for a reason; whenever someone said that when I was going through cancer treatment, I wanted to punch them in the mouth, then ask them to give me the reason that'd just happened. As a dyed-in-the-wool optimist, however, I had to believe that getting lymphoma again was a tiny part of some greater plan the universe would later reveal.

Now, technically I hadn't been diagnosed yet. But dread had been sitting like a stone in my stomach for weeks prior to my biennial checkup. Because I knew—the way you just *know* the lurker on the subway is seconds from pulling out something you don't want to see—that it was back.

As my oncologist welcomed me into her office, her outstretched arms were nothing if not a pair of blazing red flags confirming my deepest fears. Then she hugged me so hard I could taste the bagel I'd had for breakfast, which seemed like even more evidence she was about to tell me I wasn't long for this world.

Except she wouldn't try to squeeze the stuffing out of me if my torso were riddled with tumors . . . would she?

"Libby, did you hear me?" Dr. Malone, who had sat back down, was staring at me from the other side of her desk.

"What's that?" I said, blinking hard. I'd just been thinking that if *freedom* was another word for nothing left to lose, then *midlife* must be its antonym. At forty-six, I had nearly everything I'd ever wanted: a happy marriage, two delightful daughters, a meaningful career, a lovely home. I'd basically won the existential lottery.

Well, it had been fun while it lasted.

"Congratulations," she said, beaming at me.

On instinct, I returned her smile. Then I remembered why I was sitting in front of her. I cleared my throat and said, "I'm sorry—why are you congratulating me when my cancer is back?"

She laughed. "It isn't, Libby! I'm sorry if I slipped into medicalese. To be clear, your scans were spotless. There's no evidence of cancer anywhere in your body."

"Are you sure?" I said.

"It's normal to expect the worst," she said, but she had a funny look on her face. "Well, for most patients. Are you feeling all right?"

"Fine," I assured her, because at least my eyes had started leaking a little. I'd live to see my twins, Isa and Charlotte, become teenagers. That was more than my mother, who'd died of ovarian cancer when I was just ten, had been able to say.

"I'm glad, but if you're not fine, maybe this will help," said Dr. Malone, peering at my chart, which was pulled up on her computer screen. She looked away from the monitor and smiled at me again. "Your official anniversary is next month, but I think we can safely call this ten years cancer free."

A full decade. "That's . . ." I was going to say *amazing*, but I couldn't get over the fact that I didn't *feel* amazed. In fact, save the couple of tears that had already escaped, I felt . . . kind of underwhelmed, to be honest. "Time flies when you're still alive," I finally managed.

"Doesn't it? I'm so happy for you," she said, rising from her chair. She came around to the other side of the desk, which was my cue to stand. "This is a big deal, so I hope you find a way to celebrate it."

Dr. Malone didn't have to add what I'd already been thinking about in her waiting room: some of her patients wouldn't have that chance.

"That's a great idea," I told her—and because I'm not a sociopath, this time I was the one to initiate the hugging. "Thank you so much for everything."

"You're so welcome, Libby," she said. "I'm glad you won't have to see me again unless anything changes, but your sunshine will be missed around here."

I thanked her again and fled before she could figure out that my sunshine was hiding behind a rain cloud.

As I escaped the frigid medical building for the sweltering, over-crowded comforts of Manhattan's streets, I wondered why I wasn't hearing birds sing sweet melodies or smiling like a just-burped baby. After all, I was only thirty-four when another doctor all but declared me a goner—but he'd been dead wrong. It took nearly two years of treatment, but I'd gone into remission. Now my lucky numbers had been drawn yet again. Why didn't it feel that way?

No woman is an island, I reminded myself; I probably just needed to share the news with someone in order to get in a celebratory mood. I ducked under the awning of a flower shop and pulled my phone out of my bag. My husband Shiloh, who was a pilot, was in the middle of a flight, so I'd have to tell him later. My finger hovered over my twin brother Paul's number, but it occurred to me that he was probably stuck in a marathon of meetings. Anyway, I could let him know when I saw him for lunch tomorrow.

So I called my father. Paul claims that I inherited my rose-colored glasses from my mother, and she was certainly the more exuberant of our parents. But much of my sanguine outlook was owing to the guy who'd done the job of two parents most of my life. He'd always managed to shine a light on a dim situation by sharing a few choice words or a story that started out completely unrelated to the topic at hand, only to reveal itself as precisely on point. Really, he was the first person I should have reached out to.

But his phone had only rung once when I remembered he would not be picking up. Not today. Not ever again.

Now all of the tears that I'd been anticipating in Dr. Malone's office sprang to my eyes as I remembered that he was dead.

He may be gone, but you are here, I reminded myself, drying my eyes on my sleeve before I descended the stairs to the subway that would shuttle me back to Brooklyn. Rather than wallowing, it was my job to do all the living that my father could no longer do—that's what he would have wanted. How incredibly lucky I was to still have that opportunity!

So . . . why didn't I feel more alive?

TWO

There were years, many of them, when I thought I would never get the one thing I wanted most, which was to be a parent. Finding out that I was pregnant with my daughters was the second-happiest day of my life (the first, of course, was the day they were born). Even so, sometimes mothering felt like being asked to put out a raging fire with nothing but a cape and a pair of pom-poms. It required degrees of grit and patience I could not have imagined possessing before two tiny humans emerged from my body.

It helped to try to be the mother my own mother was to me. There was a lot I couldn't recall about the brief time we had together—but if there's one thing I did remember, it was that she led by example. I couldn't storm around while expecting Charlotte and Isa to act like they were sliding down a rainbow. No, I needed to adopt the same attitude of gratitude I was always telling them to have. And so, on the several-block-long walk back from the subway, I made a point to focus on what I was thankful for. How blue was the sky, how lovely were the brownstones in our cozy Brooklyn neighborhood! How wonderful it was to be coming home to the people who loved me!

My life, I reminded myself as I let myself into our apartment, was charmed.

"No, *you* shut up, you stupid—"

"*You're* the stupid one! I am so sick of your dumb—"

I can't bring myself to relay the rest, but let's just say I can't believe my daughters kiss their mother with those mouths.

"Girls!" I said, flinging their bedroom door open. They were tangled up on the floor like a couple of cage fighters, and the irritation on their faces made me feel—if only for a split second—like I'd interrupted something important.

But I must have been staring back at them just as fiercely, because they quickly released their headlocks and scrambled to their respective beds.

"What," said Isa, who'd tucked her arms into her T-shirt and wedged herself into the corner where her bed met the wall. At least her nose wasn't in a book. She spent nine-tenths of her waking hours reading and pretending the rest of us didn't exist. Ever the pessimist, Paul said it was normal—reading was a perfectly healthy way to cope with the dumpster fire that was reality, he claimed. But lately when I tried to get her to bake or go out with me, even to her favorite bookstore, she had absolutely no interest.

"I told you we need our own bedrooms!" said Charlotte, glaring at me from the end of her mattress. She'd had her hair cut pixie short the month before. She'd always resembled Paul, but now she looked so much like him as a child that I sometimes had to stop myself from doing a double take.

"And I told you that's not happening." I was trying, with only moderate success, to keep my voice from rising. "You know Papi and I are saving up so you can go to college without racking up massive debt. Regardless, I wish you'd try to look on the bright side," I added, ignoring the obvious eye rolls Charlotte and Isa were exchanging. "We gave you the big bedroom. We would be thrilled to have this much space."

We had a nice-sized apartment, at least by New York standards. It occupied the ground and garden floors of a brownstone, and had big bay windows, a second half bathroom that kept us all from murdering each other, and a small stone patio out back where Shiloh and I liked to sit, weather permitting, as the sun went down. We'd been lucky to buy the place during a major dip in the market, though we'd probably pay it off the same week we hobbled into a nursing home. It was worth it. The very first time I visited our neighborhood, Carroll Gardens, I knew it was home. Which was saying a lot for someone who grew up outside of Grand Rapids and once thought Chicago would be her final resting place.

Still. Shiloh and I were jammed into a bedroom that barely fit a queen bed; the closet was so cramped that I kept my clothes on a rack next to the washer and dryer. Our room, unlike the girls', faced the street, and though I knew what I'd signed up for living in New York, the mega grocery store that had recently been erected a few blocks away had more than doubled the traffic volume. Sometimes as I was drifting off at night, I could almost convince myself that the cars whizzing past harmonized with the ocean waves coming from our white-noise machine.

"Whatever. But you can't yell at us when we fight. We need more *alone time*," hissed Charlotte.

I stared at her for a second, willing myself to remember the sweet, pink-cheeked toddler who only wanted to be with me—*on* me, technically, in the koala-style latch she'd been so fond of. What on God's green earth had possessed my daughter?

Oh, yeah—estrogen.

I supposed that wasn't entirely fair. Charlotte had always been small and lean, but last year, she got unusually thin and was constantly guzzling water. It was summer, so Shiloh and I chalked it up to the heat, and that for Charlotte, to be awake is to be in motion. I'll never forget Isa's face peering down at me in the middle of the night. "Mom," she said firmly. "Mom, get up right now. Charlotte's sick."

I denied it for the longest time, but the truth is, twins *do* share a psychic hotline. There's literally no other way Isa could have known that Charlotte was *this close* to falling into a coma, considering they'd both been fast asleep. Charlotte was so asleep, in fact, that we could barely rouse her—and when we finally did, her words were slurred. A few hours later, a physician informed us that our daughter had type 1 diabetes and would need to take insulin every day for the rest of her life in order to stay alive. Carb counting, constant shots, monitoring for any sign that her blood sugar was too high or too low: it was a whole heck of a lot to put on an adolescent whose primary goal had been, up until that point, to ready herself to be the captain of the US women's soccer team. And given how harrowing the situation had been and sometimes continued to be—there had already been a few close calls—I couldn't fault her for being cranky.

"Come on, you guys," I said, softening my tone. "Let's not do this right now, okay? This isn't why I let you stay home." We'd decided to hold off on summer camp because we had yet to find one that truly knew how to handle Charlotte's diabetes, and the girls had vetoed a sitter—they knew how to entertain themselves, they said. I had reluctantly agreed, unaware that by *entertain*, they meant engage in hand-to-hand combat every second I wasn't hovering over them. "Why don't we walk over to Prospect Park?" I suggested. It was a bit of a hike, but I knew spending time with them would lift my spirits.

"I'm going to finish my book," said Isa, turning her back to me.

"I'm going to see if Cecelia can hang out," said Charlotte.

I sighed. "I'll be here if you don't need me."

~

I can't say the girls did wonders for my mood, but as I made dinner, I was mostly able to forget about my blahs for a while. And just as well— Shiloh had been working long hours lately. The last thing he needed was to come home to Debbie Downer.

"Hey, you," I said, kissing him hello after he let himself inside the apartment.

"Hey, yourself," he said. He looked handsome in his crisp, white pilot shirt and navy pants, but there were dark circles under his eyes, and his skin, though naturally tan, looked like it could use more vitamin D.

I followed him into the kitchen. "Long flight?" I asked.

"Yeah," he said, leaning against the counter. "It felt like it took three years."

"I'm sorry." I resisted the urge to mention that he could cut back. He'd worked his way up at the private air carrier where he'd been employed for more than a decade, and now he mostly shuttled executives around the US. It was a solid gig and paid well enough that between that and the modest salary I drew from the foundation I ran, he could afford to take off another day each week. But business was booming and his boss relied on him, so he'd been flying right up to the legal limit.

"It's okay," he said, pouring himself a glass of water. He looked back at me and smiled again. "Any day in the sky is a good day."

"Any day we're alive is a good day," I said, mostly to myself. "Did you eat already?"

He drained his water, then nodded. "Grabbed a sandwich at work."

"There are leftovers if you decide you want something more," I said. He still hadn't mentioned my appointment, but I figured he would as I retrieved a bottle of sparkling wine from the fridge. It had been in there since New Year's Eve; neither Shiloh nor I was big on booze, and we had fallen asleep long before the ball dropped. But if there were ever a time to pop that cork, this was it.

"I'm good," he said as I grabbed two glasses from the cupboard. "But don't let that stop you from having a drink if you're in the mood."

I frowned—had he actually forgotten? The twins didn't know about my tests because I hadn't wanted to worry them. But Shiloh and I had discussed it as recently as that morning. "Then skip it, but first let's toast," I said, filling each flute halfway. I watched the bubbles settle, then finished filling my glass to the top because this was a big occasion, and as Dr. Malone had pointed out, it was cause for celebration.

"Does this mean you got the grant?" said Shiloh as he took the flute I was holding out for him.

He was only human, I told myself, even as I felt nascent tears pricking my eyes. I blinked several times and pushed my lips into a smile. "Try again."

"D'oh!" he said, slapping his forehead. "Your test results. I can't believe I forgot."

He looked so genuinely embarrassed that I immediately forgave him. "Thank you," I said, raising my glass. "Here's to no evidence of cancer."

He brought the edge of his glass to mine and smiled at me. "Here's to you, cutie. I wasn't worried, but this is still a huge deal. I'm so happy for you. For all of us." He looked at me for a moment, then added, "I don't know what the girls and I would do without you."

"Thank you," I said. He'd just said all the right things, but as I took a sip of my wine, I didn't feel any better than I had walking out of Dr. Malone's office that morning. She'd pointed out that it was normal to expect the worst—which explained why I'd had to struggle to keep my mood afloat the last month or two. But what was my excuse now?

He put his glass down, then wrapped me in his arms as if to reassure me that his memory lapse had meant nothing. If that was his aim, it was working.

"I was going to hit the hay," he said, nestling his face in my hair. "Wanna join me?"

For what was possibly the first time that day—really that *week*— I felt a spark of excitement. But that had always been Shiloh's effect on me. While he was unflaggingly kind, preternaturally calm, and wise beyond his years, much of my attraction to him came down to chemistry. There was something about being with him that made me feel alive in a way nothing else could. Even a quick roll in the hay would hit the restart button on my mental state.

We skipped flossing and brushing our teeth and hopped into bed in our underwear, which in and of itself felt like returning to a land before children. "Hello, stranger," I said, curling closer to him. Then I slipped my hand beneath the duvet.

Well, okay, I thought. We weren't spring chickens anymore; it could take a while to get clucking. Anyway, he was kissing me and seemed like he was into it.

But there's a while—and then there's *a while.* "Are you not in the mood?" I finally whispered.

"I'm fifty-five, Libby," he said quietly.

"I'm sorry," I mumbled, my cheeks burning. Age hadn't been an issue last year. Three months ago, even. But this was the second time this had occurred in the past several weeks. And as it happened, we'd only attempted to make love twice during that time period, which meant we were zero for two. "I just thought when you asked me to come to bed with you . . ."

He sighed deeply, then kissed my forehead. "I didn't realize how tired I was. It was a tough flight back and I'm just really fried."

"Oh . . . I didn't realize that. Let's forget this happened."

"Thanks, and sorry." He kissed me on the lips this time, but it wasn't enough to take away the sting. Maybe he sensed that, because he added, "Next time. Promise."

"Don't worry about it," I said, pressing my lids closed. It was one thing for him to have forgotten about my appointment. But to have no interest in intimacy . . . Well, that was another thing entirely. We'd met on the way to Vieques, a tiny island off Puerto Rico's east coast that I'd fled to after my cancer diagnosis; he'd been the pilot on my flight and had saved us both from crashing after a bird flew into the plane's engine. And though I'd been planning to forgo treatment—having seen my mother suffer through chemo and radiation only to die anyway made me resolve to avoid the same ordeal—being with Shiloh had transformed everything, really, right down to my will to live.

Sex was what made us *us*. Who would we even be without that?

We'd be me and my ex-husband—that's who. I'd loved Tom dearly; still did, in fact. But when I'd tried to tell him I had cancer, he'd misinterpreted my distress and revealed that—surprise!—he was gay. Though it took a while to get over his having lied to me for nearly two decades—we'd begun dating as teens—he remained one of my closest friends. Honesty aside, the only thing that had really been missing between us was sexual chemistry.

Stop it right now, I ordered myself. Had my mother moped about the overproducing disease spores that robbed her of her chance to see her children reach adulthood? No, she had not. She had acted like her cancer and the treatment that was supposed to save her but ultimately sapped her body's ability to fight were no more important than the weather—worth an occasional remark, but certainly not something to waste time and energy focusing on. Meanwhile, my circumstances were approximately four thousand times better than hers had been. I was free of cancer and full of life. And didn't Shiloh show me how much he cared every single day?

I waited until he began snoring lightly to slip out of bed and throw on my robe. I didn't bother turning on the lights as I padded into the kitchen, where my sparkling wine was on the counter where I'd left it. Every relationship went through lulls, I told myself as I took a sip. If anything, I should have been cheering about having already enjoyed thirteen passionate years with my husband. Sure, the girls had acted like I was either a maid or invisible all afternoon. But it wasn't news to me that having a family wasn't always kittens and roses.

Tiny beads of air exploded at the back of my throat as I tossed back what was left in the glass, making my eyes water. The byproduct of carbon dioxide: that's all those pesky tears were. Because I was alive and well, and I was *not* about to cry over that.

"I love my life," I said aloud as I raised my glass to the night sky, which was winking at me through the kitchen window. And I did. I did.

I did.

THREE

When I awoke the next morning, Shiloh had already left for work. He often took off before the rest of us were up in order to try to beat the traffic, but I had to wonder if this time it was an attempt to avoid discussing what had happened the night before. Just as well; it wasn't like asking him if he was still attracted to me was going to put the zing back in his thing. More likely it would have the opposite effect. Anyway, it was a new day—another chance to feel like myself again.

Isa was still sleeping, but I found Charlotte sitting on the kitchen counter with a bowl of cereal on one side of her and a vial of insulin on the other. Her shirt was hiked up, and she was sinking a needle into the fold of skin she'd grabbed with her free hand. What a champ—she didn't even flinch anymore.

"Hey, kiddo. You calculated how much you need?" I said, trying to sound casual as I ruffled her hair. As we'd learned over the past year, managing blood sugar was more complicated than just running the numbers. Insulin-to-carb ratios were key, but we also had to figure out how Charlotte's body reacted to heat, physical activity, and even certain foods (pizza, in particular, was a land mine, which she'd discovered one evening when her blood sugar wouldn't come down).

"*Yes*, Mom. Not that I want to think about it, but it's been, like, a year. I know how to count carbs. And yes, I put it in the app," she said, referring to the tracking log she kept on her phone. She held the needle out to me. At least I wasn't so annoying that I'd been banned from menial tasks.

"Great," I said cheerfully, ever cognizant of the fact that Charlotte was influenced by my attitude whether she realized it or not. I deposited the needle into the medical waste box next to the trash can. "You having some protein, too?"

"Milk has protein in it."

Not as much as her dietitian recommended. "Let me make you a crispy egg," I said.

"Gross. No."

Up until a few months ago, "crispy eggs," as she used to call my fried eggs, were her favorite. "Then make sure you track your sugars carefully," I said, switching on the coffee maker. "I'm going into the office this morning and having lunch with Uncle Paul. But I'll be home by five. Can you send me updates every two hours?"

She shrugged, which was not the reassurance I'd been aiming for. "I'll probably go over to LaToya's to see if she wants to play soccer. Or maybe Cecelia's."

"Why don't you hang out with Isa?"

Charlotte looked at me like I'd just suggested she jog down the middle of the highway.

I sighed. "Fine, but please text me to let me know where you're at and when you leave—and tell your sister to do the same. Bring your insulin and meter, okay?"

"Mmm-hmm," she said, shoveling cereal into her mouth.

"Oh, and Char?"

She stopped and glanced up at me, looking so much like the sweet, funny girl she'd always been that I almost blurted out my test results. But all these years, I'd been careful not to make too much of a big deal about my having had cancer, as I knew all too well how awful it was to worry about your mother dying. Yesterday's appointment was a conversation that was best dressed up in casual clothing and trotted out to both girls at the same time.

"Papi should be home by five thirty, so let's all have dinner tonight," I said. "Sixish?"

"Whatevs." She hopped off the counter. "See you later."

"Already looking forward to it. Love you," I called.

I waited for her to say it back, but then the front door slammed and she was gone.

~

"Morning, Libby!" Rupi, my operations manager and all-around MVP, had popped up from behind her computer monitor like a Muppet.

"Morning!" I said, hoping I sounded more chipper than I felt; after all, I was the boss. Twelve years earlier, I'd started the Charlotte C. Ross Foundation, which was named for my mother and funded programs for children who'd lost a parent to cancer. Now we had eight full-time employees, including me. "You sleep here again last night?"

This was our routine: Rupi was always the first to arrive, and usually the last to leave, and I always said something about it. She laughed. "It's going to be a busy day. But before we talk about work . . ." She motioned for me to come closer, even though Kareem was the only other person at his desk, which was all the way across the room. "How did your appointment go?" she whispered.

I smiled—at least Rupi hadn't forgotten. Like me, her mother had died of cancer when Rupi was still young. It was part of the reason we'd grown close over the four years she'd been with the foundation. But even more than that, her unflappable cheer made her great company. In fact, she was probably exactly who I needed to be around right now.

"Great! I'm cancer free yet again—and in fact, next month marks a decade."

"Oh my gosh! That's amazing." She jumped up and hugged me. Unlike Dr. Malone, Rupi didn't try to squeeze the stuffing out of me. She had the kind of motherly hug that gave me the warm fuzzies. Except today I didn't feel much of anything, which was almost as alarming as my nonresponse at the doctor's office. "I had a feeling it was good, or I wouldn't have asked," she added.

"I love your optimism," I said, but this time I had to remind myself to smile back.

"Takes one to know one. Hey, do you have a minute?"

"Of course," I said, because I'd much rather chat with Rupi than read through the several dozen emails that had probably landed in my inbox since I'd checked it in bed that morning.

"Your office?" she said.

I tried not to look surprised. "Sure," I said, motioning for her to follow me. She pulled the door closed behind her, which was doubly curious—we weren't really a closed-door kind of operation. "You're not leaving the foundation, are you?" I said.

I'd been joking, but when she responded by laughing nervously, I wondered if maybe I shouldn't have been. "No, no, it's nothing like that," she said, her voice an octave higher than it had been a moment ago. "I just wanted to bring something up."

"I'm listening."

She sat in one of the two aging armchairs on the other side of my desk. "I'm wondering if you have any plans to evolve the foundation beyond . . ." She motioned to the rest of the office behind her. "What we're currently doing."

"Do you think that we're not doing a good job?" I asked, working hard not to frown. "We gave away five million dollars last year and only directed eighteen percent of donations toward overhead. As you know, that's half of what most nonprofits spend."

"I know, and we're all super proud of that." Rupi was twisting her hands in her lap. "I just think CCRF would benefit from some new initiatives. Maybe even our own program."

I don't know what I'd been expecting, but this was not it, and I felt myself growing irrationally upset. Yes, I'd built this company out of nothing but an idea and the firm belief that I would find a way to make it happen. Yet I knew Rupi wanted it to succeed as much as I did, and she had every right to make suggestions about the future of the foundation. Even if said suggestions were as logical as trying to burn extra calories by leaving brownies in the oven too long.

"We fund programs, Rupi—we don't *run* them," I said, careful to keep my tone in check. "Creating and running a program would take resources we don't have, and I don't know how realistic it is to think we can shift from something that's super successful to something completely unknown."

Rupi sat up straight, and I had the distinct impression whatever she was about to say had been prepared in advance. "I think we *do* have some of those resources. As you know, I implemented several programs at Lighthouse," she said, referring to her previous employer, which had been devoted to the needs of adults. "Kareem has a background in events—"

"And he does a wonderful job using that background to set up our donor banquets," I pointed out. *Same team, Libby,* I reminded myself. "Respectfully, Rupi, we're a child-focused organization, which Lighthouse isn't."

"Exactly!" she said, all big eyes and earnest nodding. "Which is why I think we should open a summer camp upstate for kids who've recently lost a parent. I mean, wouldn't that just be incredible? You always say that good ideas start as a desire, right? And that when you add hard work into the mix, you can figure anything out?"

I guess I *had* said that, but now that I was hearing someone else repeat it, I wanted to reach back in time and slap myself for mistaking a motivational poster–worthy slogan for business acumen.

"And this one is just screaming my name!" she continued, oblivious to my internal debate. On the one hand, she was literally my most valuable employee, and I wanted to support her. On the other, I was ready to run out of the door and tell her to call me when she was back to being dependable, right-sized-idea-generating Rupi. "I still remember not being able to talk to anyone about my mom dying, and how isolating that was," she said, her dark brown eyes brimming with tears.

"I know the feeling," I admitted, because although I had Paul, he was *all* I'd had; for the longest time other kids had treated us like our mother's death was something their parents could catch if they spent too much time around us.

But mostly I was thinking: *A camp?*

A camp involved buying or leasing land. Buildings. More staff, all of who would have to be trained in dealing with kids who were grieving. And loads and loads of cash.

"I love that you're going out of the box for this," I said—except I didn't sound even remotely convincing, even to myself. I tried again. "I agree that it's a wonderful idea, and I would have loved something like that when I was a kid, too. But I thought you were going to suggest doing a one-day event, maybe, or a conference. This is a huge initiative, Rupi. A summer camp requires so many things we simply don't have."

"I totally get that, which is why I'm willing to figure out a lot of the logistics before we discuss it again. I know it's not something we could pull off this year, or maybe even next. But three years from now, Camp Charlotte could be open and operating," she said.

Camp Charlotte had a lovely ring to it; my mother would've been thrilled with it. Which meant I should have been, too. But mostly it felt like *one more thing.*

And what was wrong with that? After all, I wasn't about to start cancer treatment again, as I'd been secretly preparing myself for since Dr. Malone's office called to say I was due for another CT scan. Charlotte's diabetes was relatively well managed, even if I wished she'd take it more seriously. And I'd gotten through the worst of grieving over my dad's death. Wouldn't a new project be just the thing to reinvigorate my career zeal, if not my lust for life?

"Please say you'll at least think about it, Libby?" said Rupi. "I know it's wildly ambitious, but I'm more excited about it than I've been about anything in a long time, and I really believe we could get buy-in from the whole team."

I was glad someone was excited. Because after I promised Rupi that I would be happy to review her proposal when it was ready, then watched her bounce down the hall toward her desk, a terrible thought kept echoing through my mind: *I don't really want to do this anymore.*

FOUR

Paul had already been seated when I arrived at the restaurant. He slid out of the booth and stood when he saw me, then gave me the twice-over.

"You know I stopped dyeing it a few months ago," I said, referring to my curls, which were threaded with silver. I didn't really like it myself—it was less *Steel Magnolias* and more steel wool—but I didn't want *Paul* to dislike it. Especially when I had zero motivation to make an appointment with my colorist.

"No, I actually love it," he said, still eyeing me. "There's just a lot more contrast than when I last saw you."

Translation: I looked awful.

"You can pull off anything," he added as he sat down again.

"You're lying through your teeth, but I appreciate the intention behind it," I said, sliding into the booth across from him. "Now if only I had your immunity to grays." Boyishly lean with a full head of brown hair, my brother usually passed for a decade younger than he was. But as I examined him more closely, I realized the bags under his eyes were even darker than Shiloh's, and his skin was just as sallow as mine had been in the mirror that morning. Forget wrinkles; apparently the true marker of middle age was looking like you were in immediate need of a blood transfusion.

He slid back into his side of the booth. "So your tests came back clear." He said this as a statement rather than a question.

"What if they didn't?" I said, but I was smiling.

"I would have picked up on your distress—but I also know you would have called me immediately," he said, arching an eyebrow. When I'd first been diagnosed with cancer, I'd hid it, telling myself I was protecting him and our father. No surprise, that ended up causing more pain than it spared either of them.

"Learned that lesson the hard way." I hesitated, then said, "I did call Dad by accident."

"I'm sorry, Libs," he said, frowning. "Did you end up listening to his voicemail?"

I shook my head. "No, I hung up before then, thank goodness."

"Thank goodness for what? I call his number all the time just to hear his voice. I suppose at some point I'll have to stop paying his cell phone bill, but for now, that's a hundred dollars a month well spent."

"That's nice of you," I said, not adding that it was also a bit morbid, if not downright depressing. "Now that you know my news, how are *you*?"

He held up a finger to me, then motioned for the waiter. After he'd ordered a glass of wine for himself and club soda with lime for me, he looked at me intently and said, "So when are we burying Dad?"

I blinked—and here I thought we were going to have a pleasant conversation. "Soon."

"Define *soon*. Next month?" said Paul, pulling up a calendar on his phone.

Our father had died five months earlier. Long after Paul and I reached adulthood, our father had admitted that seeing our mother in a coffin had been one of the most traumatic experiences he'd lived through. "She looked like a complete stranger, a melted wax version of herself," he'd told us. Which is why he'd asked to be cremated and have his ashes beside her in the cemetery just outside of Detroit where the rest of her family had been buried. We'd followed his wishes on the first part and had held a small memorial dinner with Paul's and my family and Aunt Patty, my father's sister, and her husband a week after he died. But we had yet to make it out to Michigan; his ashes were still sitting in an urn over my non-functioning fireplace.

"Next month is nuts for me," I said. "Half the office is on vacation."

"Most of North America is away in August, including all the wealthy people who would otherwise be inclined to write you checks," he said. Of course Paul would know this—his net worth was that of a small developing nation, and he'd made many insanely generous donations to the foundation over the years.

"Maybe September? The weather will be cooler."

He leaned forward. "I recall you saying, 'Maybe April' and 'Maybe June.' Should I plan on doing this myself?"

"Don't be like that. Work has been really busy."

"Libs," he said sternly. "You can't pull the workaholic card on someone who wrote the book on living in the office. It's a ten-hour drive to Michigan. We could get it done in a single weekend."

Could and *should* were two different things. Our father had died in February, right after the twins' twelfth birthday, and I'd spent the rest of that month, and all of the following, bursting into tears in inappropriate places. I knew that the minute I saw my father's headstone next to my mother's, I'd revert to sobbing violently every time I saw a nice old man at, say, the bodega down the street. Thanks, but no.

Our server had returned. "We're not ready to order just yet," said Paul as she placed our drinks in front of us.

"Actually," I said, "I'm ready."

He sighed deeply. "Go ahead."

"Caesar salad with chicken," I told the server.

"Same, but no croutons or dressing," said Paul.

"Hold the joy," I remarked.

"Nothing tastes better than being thin. So! Weekend in Detroit!"

"Shiloh often works Saturdays or Sundays. You know that." Paul was still looking at me like he was expecting me to say something else, so I added, "I'll talk to him about it and get back to you, okay?"

Now both of his eyebrows shot up, and he was staring at me so intensely that I had to look away. "Libs, I say this as someone who adores you and loves you more than anyone else in the world: Have you been screened for depression?"

I turned back to him so quickly it's a wonder I didn't give myself whiplash. "That's not something to joke about."

"You know full well that I wouldn't joke about that." Paul had struggled with depression and anxiety most of his life. "I'm being dead serious."

"Har."

"Again—not joking."

"Neither am I," I told him. "I know the signs: I'm not hopeless, I don't spend twelve hours a day in bed, I don't want to hurt myself or anyone else, and I haven't lost interest in sex." It was a shame I couldn't say the same of my husband.

Paul held up a hand. "While I'm glad you know what to watch for, I didn't need to know that last one."

"You asked."

"I suppose I did." His face was pained as he glanced across the restaurant. "Speaking of depressing things, I do have news."

My stomach sank. As kids, Paul and I had our own language; I guess we still kind of did, because I'd secretly known he was going to tell me something I didn't want to hear from the moment I'd spotted him at the booth where we were now seated. But after being wrong about my cancer returning, I'd been hoping this was one more thing I'd gotten messed up in my head.

"Is it the boys?" I said.

"No, they're great."

"Work?"

24

He shook his head, then leaned across the table and said quietly, "Charlie and I are divorcing."

I stared at him blankly. So much for that shared lexicon—he may as well have just spoken to me in Urdu. "I . . . um . . . *what*?!"

"We've been mulling it over for months, but we finally came to an agreement yesterday."

I felt like he'd just socked me in the gut. "But you and Charlie are the happiest couple I know!"

"No," said Paul slowly, the way I sometimes did when the twins were being dense, "we're your closest couple friends."

"Siblings can't be friends," I said, as if this had anything to do with anything. Regardless, he was right. Though Shiloh and I had a small but tight social circle, we spent the most time with Charlie and Paul; the four of us, I'd always thought, balanced each other. They'd been a major deciding factor in our moving out of a charming house with three large bedrooms in suburban New Jersey and into the city. They couldn't just *ruin* that.

"My point is, you think we're happy because you want us to be," said Paul.

I winced.

"We've been growing apart for years now," he added.

"So grow back together! Go to couples counseling! Don't . . ." I was getting choked up. Bad enough that our father had died. Now Paul was telling me he was purposefully widening the crack in our family's foundation? "Just don't *divorce* after more than a decade of marriage," I whispered. "I've already done that, and let me tell you, I wouldn't wish it on my worst enemy."

He patted my hand. Why was he so *calm*, when I was having to work hard not to cry into my club soda? "I know, and I'm sorry, Libs. I knew you'd take this hard, which is why I didn't tell you about it until we were sure."

I sniffed. "Me taking it hard? What about *you*? And Toby and Max?"

"We've actually been going to therapy as a family. They knew it was a possibility, and I think they're as okay with it as they can be."

"You're saying you told your teenaged sons, but you didn't tell me," I said, dabbing at my eyes with my cloth napkin.

"Should I have asked you to join us in therapy?"

Yes. "No."

He sighed deeply and didn't speak for a while. When he opened his mouth again, I wished he hadn't. "I had an affair."

"You did *what*?" I said, so loudly that the couple seated at the next booth immediately turned to stare.

"It was an emotional affair," said Paul in a low voice. "I didn't touch him. It was just a friendship that accidentally turned romantic."

"Oh, that's a relief!" I said sarcastically, though it was, a little bit. If spit and communicable diseases had not yet been swapped, maybe there was still hope for Paul and Charlie to save their marriage. "What were you thinking?"

His brown eyes were flashing with anger, and something else I couldn't readily identify. "You wouldn't understand."

"Try me."

"Fine. It was right after Dad died, and I felt . . . well, dead inside. Charlie was in the middle of filming and he wasn't around a lot. When he was, he was tired, and mostly I felt like he didn't get it. He's never lost a parent. So I started going to a grief support group."

I startled. "You did?"

Paul took a sip of his wine, then said, "There's a reason I asked you if you were depressed. *I* was, and meds weren't cutting it. My therapist suggested the group, and I decided to give it a try."

"Which is where you met—what's this guy's name, anyway?"

"Andy," he said, wrinkling his nose like it was a bad word. "His wife had just died and, well, I guess the whole wife thing made me think it wasn't a big deal when we grabbed a drink after the group was over."

"Paul Ross! Didn't Tom coming out teach you anything?"

"I know!" he said, throwing his hands in the air. "But it was just so nice to talk to someone who listened and understood. Then one night, Andy and I ordered a second round of drinks and he told me I had nice eyes. Before I knew it, we were texting several times a day."

We sat in silence, and not the comfortable kind. I wasn't sure if I was more upset that I was just hearing this now, after the decision had already been made, or that he wasn't trying harder to save his marriage. "Oh Paul," I finally said. "I'm sorry."

"Thank you. Obviously, it's over with Andy—I cut it off once I realized that I was in too deep."

"I'm glad," I said. "But I don't really understand how you got to that point in the first place. You and Charlie love each other!"

"We do," he said morosely. "But our chemistry just isn't there anymore, though."

My face grew warm as I thought of the previous night. "How can it be if you're paying attention to other men?"

"Touché. Still. Chemistry isn't something you can fix with willpower or wishing—which, by the way, I know you're going to suggest. I know things look fine from the outside, but that's because we thought we could fake it until we made it. The truth is, we've been unraveling for a very long time."

Maybe I *would* have suggested willpower, even if I would have phrased it differently. But mostly I was too shocked to form an articulate sentence. Shiloh and I had dinner at their place not two weeks earlier, with all four of our kids there, and they'd seemed like any other long-married couple. Were they playing footsie under the table or meeting in the middle of a strand of spaghetti? No—but they weren't hollering at each other, either. Faking it or not, as Paul's twin, I should have been able to sense this so-called unraveling.

"Holy Shih Tzu," I muttered. "This makes zero sense to me. If you still love each other, why don't you find a way to make it work? Isn't love about compromise?"

He pursed his lips and looked across the restaurant for a moment before responding. "Our compromise is to divorce amicably. We're even going to both stay in our place until next year when the boys are in college. Honestly, Libs, I've been thinking about this since Dad died. Life is so stupidly short."

"Are you trying to tell me you're having a midlife crisis?"

He shrugged. "Did you know that a recent study revealed that existential dissatisfaction peaks at forty-seven?"

We would be forty-seven in two months. "Is that factoid intended to spark joy? Because it sounds more like a self-fulfilling prophecy to me," I said, even as I considered my flatlined emotional state at Dr. Malone's office. Was my ennui age related? Maybe that was also what was going on with Shiloh. How long until we, too, decided that the only way to deal with our existential dissatisfaction was to ditch our hard-earned union? But no, that was ridiculous. Emotional states were contagious— I'd seen the studies myself. And I was in the middle of catching a case of the Pauls.

"Personally, I think it's great to know, because we can prepare for it," said Paul.

"I don't need to prepare for anything. My life is already good, and I intend for it to stay that way."

He lifted his glass to me. "Please don't stop snorting fairy dust on my account."

I knew he was trying to get me to laugh, but I couldn't. All I could think about was how absolutely heart-wrenching it had been to separate from Tom, even though our marriage truly wasn't salvageable.

He took another sip of his wine, then said, "I, for one, am not leaving my future in the hands of fate. I'm going to take action even though it's going to be hard, because I want to be happier than I am while I still have the chance."

"Define happiness, please. Because from where I stand, your life checks all the boxes. I fail to see how you're going to be 'happier,'" I said, putting the word in air quotes, "by leaving your partner of nearly twenty years."

He eyed me. "You should want the same thing for yourself. Happiness, I mean."

"I want what I already have," I said evenly. "That's the definition of *happiness*." Then I reached across the table and helped myself to his wine. It was as dry as a camel's back and made me cough a little, but I took another swig after I'd swallowed the first.

Paul, who hadn't even blinked at my pirating his booze, said, "Libby, it's not just that Charlie and I aren't on the same page. It's like we're not even reading from the same *book* anymore. Listen, if anyone's immune to divorce, it's you and Shiloh. But don't make the same mistake we made, okay?"

I was almost afraid to hear what he was going to say next, though I wasn't sure why. "And what's that?"

He turned toward the window at the front of the restaurant. On the other side of the glass, a couple was making out. And by making out, I mean they were really going at it—right in front of the restaurant in broad daylight. And they weren't even young!

Paul turned back to me. "We coasted," he said quietly. "And it turns out that coasting is just quitting in slow motion."

FIVE

I've heard divorce described as a slow death. Mine was more like a spontaneous amputation. When I'd tried to tell Tom that I'd just been diagnosed with cancer, he'd mistaken my sobbing for a sign I'd figured out what he'd been working up the courage to tell me for months: he wasn't actually attracted to women, including but not limited to me. As such, we went from being what I'd thought of as deliriously happy to a complete farce in the span of mere minutes. So when Paul referred to the "unraveling" of his relationship with Charlie, I didn't really know how that worked. If a marriage unspooled itself over time, didn't that mean there were ample opportunities to rein it back in? I had a strong suspicion that it wasn't something that had just *happened* to them. It was a decision that Paul had made—again and again and again.

Now he needed to decide to reverse it while he had the chance.

I was still stewing when Shiloh got home from work that night. The girls were eating dinner at their friend Cecelia's, so I'd made a quick salad, knowing that Shiloh would grab something from his work cafeteria.

"Hey, you," he said, kissing me. "How was your day?"

"Interesting," I said, following him into our bedroom.

"Interesting good, or interesting bad?"

"Maybe a mix?" I admitted, watching him unbutton his shirt. I didn't really want to tell him about my conversation with Paul. Saying it aloud would make it . . . real, I supposed. And the more I thought about it, the more I was convinced that it was only a matter of time before my brother saw the error of his ways.

"Rupi proposed a new project," I said, my eyes still on him. Now he was in his boxers, looking far fitter than a fifty-five-year-old man had any right to. "She wants us to do a camp for kids who've lost a parent to cancer."

"Really?" he said, running a hand through his curls. Like mine, they were partially gray, but it looked good on him.

"I know," I said. "I told her it's the opposite of what the foundation does. But she thinks we're in a rut, and apparently some of the other employees do, too. I told her I'd think about it."

"It's not a bad idea," he said, reaching into the dresser for a T-shirt and a pair of shorts. "But do you think that's true about being in a rut? You guys have been doing so well."

That's what I'd thought about my brother's marriage. "I don't know," I confessed. "I'm not super jazzed about the idea, but Paul tells me that coasting is just quitting in slow motion."

Shiloh smiled. "You know I love him, but I'm not sure you should be taking business advice from an avowed pessimist."

It was the perfect opportunity to tell him that Paul and I hadn't been talking about my career, but I couldn't make myself say it. Yes, Shiloh and I had both been through a divorce, so I knew that sometimes an ugly ending could blossom into a beautiful beginning. That didn't mean I wanted to so much as utter the *D* word in our bedroom.

"I do worry I'm in a rut, though," I admitted.

He sat beside me on the bed. "At work, you mean?"

"Well, maybe," I said, thinking about how lately it had taken every ounce of willpower I possessed to open my inbox each morning, knowing I would have to spend the next hour or three responding to emails. "But I've been feeling . . ." I wasn't sure how to describe the weird funk I'd been dealing with. I hadn't told Shiloh that I'd been worried about a recurrence, because I didn't want to spread doom and gloom any sooner than I had to. But now that I knew it had been a false alarm, why didn't I feel better? I'd had time to process my clean bill of health.

"It's more than that." I took a deep breath, then added, "I'd actually been worried my cancer was back."

"Oh, Libby," he said, looking at me with a mix of tenderness and surprise. Then he kissed my forehead, and my eyes welled with tears. "Why didn't you tell me?"

"I didn't want to get you worried," I said, sniffling. "Anyway, Dr. Malone said it was normal to expect the worst."

"Maybe for other people. But that's not really your style."

"I know," I said, though I didn't add that Dr. Malone had made a similar comment. "What's even weirder is that after she told me I was healthy, I should have been jumping up and down and feeling alive. Except I didn't feel much of anything."

As he pulled me close, I realized this was the entire reason I'd just confessed this to him. Just the warmth of his body and the weight of his arm around my shoulders were enough to make me feel better than I had in days.

"Hey," he said softly. "That's normal, too. Remember how I told you how depressed I was after I went into remission? My dad had to remind me to eat and shower."

"Well, your wife had just left you," I pointed out.

"Sure, but wife or life? I'd argue that I got the better reward—not to mention a fantastic upgrade on the spousal front," he said, pulling back to wink at me.

I laughed. *See?* I told myself. *He adores you. Don't mistake a defeat or two for having lost the battle.*

"Anyway," he added, "all I'm saying is you can feel incredibly grateful without being overjoyed."

"What is it?" I asked, because his smile had just morphed into a full-on grin.

"You want to feel more alive?"

"Yes . . . ," I said hesitantly, still thinking about what had happened when I'd come on to him.

"I think I can help. You have plans tomorrow night?"

"Thursday?" We never went out on school nights, even during the summer.

He nodded. "We haven't been on a date in weeks."

It had actually been months, but who cared? My husband was taking me out for a romantic evening. I was getting flutters just thinking about it.

"I'm off all day, so say we leave after you get home?" he said.

My smile fell. "I'd love that, but what about the girls?"

"Cutie, they stay home by themselves all day."

That was true, and I fretted about Charlotte's blood sugar the whole time—in hindsight, I really should have hired a sitter after we ended up canceling their camps. "I guess I can make them dinner before we go, and ask Isa to keep an eye on Charlotte," I conceded. "Where are we going, anyway?"

"It's a surprise."

"I do like surprises."

"Liar."

I laughed and nestled into his side again. "You got me. But I'm game for whatever you have in mind."

"I was hoping you'd say that," he said. "I'm sorry we haven't even had a chance to celebrate your scans being clear. That's a big deal."

"It's okay," I said, because even though it still stung, saying it was all right made that feel closer to true. Anyway, we were going on a weeknight date—and if that wasn't the opposite of coasting, I didn't know what was.

SIX

Had I survived cancer only to meet my bitter end in the middle of New Jersey? Had I narrowly escaped a brush with death in one propeller plane, just so I could crash in another?

No. No, I had not.

But apparently my husband had not gotten that memo.

I'd first realized I was in trouble when we merged into the Brooklyn-Battery Tunnel. "We're leaving the city?" I'd said, like he'd just suggested a jaunt to North Korea. "But we never leave."

Then I realized this wasn't true at all. Shiloh made this drive several times a week on his way to the Teterboro Airport. By the time I fully gathered what was happening, we were pulling into the employee parking lot. I considered flinging myself out of our moving vehicle and running in the opposite direction, but then I remembered what Paul had said about coasting. Didn't I owe it to my marriage to try something new?

"Are you sure this is safe?" I yelled. There were just two seats in the whole tin can of a plane, which was far smaller than the ones he flew for work, so I was seated to his right. However intimate the setup, the acoustics weren't so hot, so I had to attempt to blow out my vocal cords in order to be heard.

"Don't worry, I would never do anything that wasn't safe, and conditions are perfect, Libby—that's why I wanted to go out today!" Shiloh yelled. "And you've been fine on all the other flights we've taken!"

Sure, on large commercial planes manned by not one but two pilots, just in case. This was not that.

"Wait until we're up a little higher," he added. "This will be fun!"

Fun? Who'd said anything about fun? I'd wanted romance. *Not* an activity that was best experienced wearing a panty liner.

But at least he was trying, I reminded myself. He looked so happy, and it would be over soon; there was absolutely no reason to burst his bubble.

"You okay?" he hollered.

"Great!" I said through gritted teeth, but that's about as far as I could get because my breath started getting shallow and ragged. When I'd said I wanted to feel alive, I hadn't meant by being reminded that I was going to die—and soon. "Oh, sweet Cheez-Its!" I yelped as the plane began to dip. Had I given a copy of our will to Paul? How would Charlotte manage her diabetes without me?

"Libs? Do you want me to take us back down?" he said, glancing over at me. "We're about to hit smoother air, but say the word and we'll be on the ground in five."

I was staring at him, and even though my parasympathetic nervous system was seconds from blowing a fuse, he looked so handsome and hopeful that I just couldn't bring myself to tell him I hated everything about this experience.

"I'm fine!" I gasped. "Just find that smoother air, okay?"

To myself, I thought: *Well, if this is how it ends, at least I'll get to see my parents again.*

Seconds later, the ride did get noticeably less choppy. And knowing Shiloh would ask me the minute we were on the ground, I made sure that I found something to like. It wasn't impossible: To my right was the Hudson River and New York's jagged skyline, which never failed to dazzle me. In front of us, there was an expansive forest filled with oaks and evergreens—this, just a few miles outside of the city!—and to my left, a small town that looked absolutely idyllic, at least from the sky.

But as I dug my nails into my thighs, all I could think about was whether this flight was a sign that maybe my husband and I weren't actually on the same page.

~

"I'm sorry, cutie. It wasn't that bad, was it?"

"It was fine," I said, even though my hands were still trembling a little. I'd tried to skirt the subject on the drive back to Brooklyn, since I hadn't wanted to make him feel bad. Now we were home and sitting on the patio, sipping the prosecco he'd bought. Though he hadn't said as much, I knew it was a do-over for the other night. The thought alone counted for a lot. And who knew—maybe a glass of bubbly or two would be just what we both needed to move our party into the bedroom.

"I'm sorry," he said, looking so bummed that I had the urge to comfort *him*. "I know you don't like to hear about bad flights, but I honestly had no idea you were really afraid of flying."

"I'm not," I assured him. Shiloh, who'd been my pilot on the flight I took from San Juan to Vieques thirteen years earlier, had narrowly pulled off an emergency landing on said flight. But thanks to Paul's proclivity for reciting random statistics, I knew a person was more likely to die eating barbecue wings than in a plane (not that this had alleviated Paul's flying phobia). "I just think I'm not cut out for small planes."

He frowned. "Yeah, but now that I'm thinking about it, you never say yes when I ask if you want to go flying with me." He put his palm to his forehead. "Rookie move, Velasquez."

"Hey," I said, reaching across and touching his arm. "Don't beat yourself up. I really appreciate you trying. But maybe we go to the movies next time?" I said, even though I was on record as this being the adult version of parallel play; whether we saw a rom-com or one of those war films where no fewer than twenty-eight people are blown to smithereens in the first five minutes, one of us was bound to suffer.

Now that I was thinking about it, why *couldn't* we agree on a movie?

"I'll do better next time. But for now, let's finally celebrate." He lifted his glass to me. "To love, life, and your continued good health. *Salud*, Libby."

It was a lovely sentiment, even if I might have overheard the same toast at, say, a business dinner. "*Salud*," I said, forcing my lips into a smile.

"When I met you nearly thirteen years ago, I had no idea that we'd be sitting here together one day, let alone celebrating your complete remission," he said, staring into my eyes.

Okay, I thought. *This is an improvement.*

"I'm so happy for you," he added. "For *us*. You're the glue that makes this family stick together."

Yes, I was—and I was glad he'd reminded me of that. It was time to stop nitpicking and start being grateful for the experience I was literally in the middle of. "Me, too," I said. Then—and I'm still not sure why—I blurted out, "Paul and Charlie are getting a divorce."

Shiloh, who'd just taken a sip of his wine, coughed so hard he nearly choked. "Pardon me?" he said when he'd recovered.

"Sorry," I said with a grimace. "Bad timing. But yeah. He told me at lunch yesterday."

He looked incredulous. "Where is this coming from? They seemed fine."

"That's what I said. He claims their chemistry isn't there anymore," I said, watching Shiloh to see if his expression changed.

"Huh," he said. "I guess that can happen, but is that really a reason to end a good marriage?"

It was all I could do not to wince. Was he trying to tell me something?

He continued, oblivious to the fact that all of the rejection and disappointment I'd been attempting to hold down had just floated right back up to the surface. "But it's not like chemistry is some fixed entity. You have to work at it. Anyway, every relationship has its ups and downs."

It did, and hearing him say that instantly lifted my mood. "That's what I told Paul."

"Great minds," he said, but then his face grew serious. "Did he say anything else, though? They really don't seem unhappy together."

"They don't," I agreed. Not two years earlier Charlie had finally won a best actor Emmy for his long-running role on a popular TV police procedural show. And in his acceptance speech, the first person he'd thanked was Paul—the father of his children, he'd said tearfully, the man who had helped him realize his full potential, the love of his life.

If that wasn't enough, what *was*?

"He didn't elaborate, but between us I have to wonder if Charlie even wants this. Paul's the one who initiated it," I said. I didn't add what he'd told me about his emotional affair, since that seemed like a secret he wouldn't want me to share, even with Shiloh. "I don't understand why he can't just be grateful for what he already has instead of thinking he should try for something different or better."

"Yeah, but that's kind of the human instinct, isn't it?" said Shiloh, reclining in his chair.

I frowned, recalling what Paul had said about Andy's attention. "Is it, though? Or is that just what people who don't want to stay married tell themselves?"

"I'm not saying it's a good excuse. But novel experiences are what get people out of bed in the morning. Maybe that's what's going on with Paul."

"Maybe," I allowed, even as my mental wheels began spinning. If that was true, why hadn't our flying excursion made me feel any better? However terrifying, it *was* novel. "He says it started around the time—" My voice caught. "Around the time my dad died."

Shiloh leaned forward and took my hand. "I'm sorry, Libby. Grief can do weird things to people. I bet he'll realize he's making a mistake and try to reconcile."

"I hope so," I said softly. "What will Christmas and birthdays and family dinners be like without Charlie?" I shook my head. "You know, I can't believe I'm saying this, but I'm actually a little glad Dad isn't alive to see this go down."

Not half a year earlier, my father had come to visit. He and I were cleaning up after dinner while Shiloh and the girls went to the bodega to get ice cream—a rare treat since Charlotte's diagnosis. My father, who'd been up to his elbows in sudsy water, had looked over at me and remarked apropos of nothing, "You and Paul are incredibly lucky."

"How's that?" I said, drying off the pan he'd just handed me.

"Well, Libby Lou, it's one thing to truly like your spouse, and another to share that special spark. But to have both: that's like the holy grail right there. Your mother and I had that. And now both of you do, too."

"Yes, we do," I told him, smiling to myself. "We're lucky."

And we *were*. Except as my eyes landed on Shiloh again, I suddenly felt almost as fearful as I had when we'd been zipping over New Jersey in a deathmobile. Because as handsome as my husband was as he lounged in his shorts and T-shirt and two-day scruff, I realized that the sparkling wine was not the liquid courage I'd been hoping for. In fact, I was afraid to suggest that we head to the bedroom, lest he confirm that our chemistry really had gone missing. Then there was the issue of his idea of a hot date, which was a hundred and eighty degrees away from what actually would have made me feel better.

You're making melanoma out of a mosquito bite, I told myself.

But was I? Or was the doom and gloom I'd mistaken for a cancer recurrence actually my intuition trying to tell me that my marriage, like my brother's, was in the midst of unraveling?

SEVEN

"Hey—I'm sorry about last night."

I'd just started cooking dinner when Shiloh joined me in the kitchen. He'd returned from a bike ride and was still dressed in the ratty T-shirt and athletic shorts he'd worn out; his skin was coated in the thinnest sheen of sweat, and his cheeks were pink. At any other time I would have thought he looked edible. Now I was afraid to even let myself get the tiniest bit tingly, knowing that I'd only be setting myself up for disappointment.

I glanced down at the pan I'd been using to sauté spinach before addressing him. "You can stop apologizing, you know. I'm not traumatized from the flight or anything."

He shook his head. "I didn't mean flying. I meant—you know."

I glanced over my shoulder to make sure the girls weren't nearby. "The non-bonking?" I said, resisting the urge to throw in the word *again*. This time, we hadn't even tried—just crawled into bed beside each other and quickly kissed goodnight.

His face twisted up. "Yeah."

I'd already decided not to ask him if he wasn't attracted to me anymore, but the question kept inching its way toward my lips. *Stop it,* I commanded myself. *Do not make him feel worse than he already does.*

After a moment, he said, "I think that because things didn't go well the last time we tried, I was feeling kind of . . . pressured."

"Whoa," I said, holding up my spatula in protest. "I deliberately *didn't* bring this up so you *wouldn't* feel pressured."

"No, I get that," he said quickly. "I didn't mean you did anything. It's just . . . a guy thing, I guess."

This seemed like a cop-out answer to me. "We don't have to have sex, you know," I said quietly. I thought of the couple I'd spotted outside the restaurant where I'd had lunch with Paul. "But I have to ask—when was the last time you *had* to kiss me?"

He frowned. "I kiss you all the time."

Technically, this was true. But I wanted . . .

Well, I wanted us to go at it like we were the last two survivors of the apocalypse and it was up to us to repopulate the planet (never mind that given our ages, we were now statistically more likely to get hit by an asteroid than to have another child). But if I couldn't have that, some super passionate kissing—the kind that's so good that when you finally stop, your lips look like they've had a close encounter with a swarm of yellow jackets and your face is half-coated in saliva and you don't even care—would be just the thing.

"I don't want to argue," I said. "I'm not upset about—you know. So we don't have to talk about it again."

He looked at me like he was trying to figure out what to say. After a moment, he sighed and said, "Fine."

"What are you guys fighting about?" said Isa. She'd just wandered into the kitchen with a book in front of her face.

"Sweetie, I've asked you a hundred times not to walk and read at the same time," I said. "You're going to trip and hurt yourself."

"Agreed, and your mother and I aren't fighting," said Shiloh. "We're having a discussion. A *private* one."

"If it quacks like a duck . . . but yeah, okay," said Charlotte, who'd appeared behind Isa. "Mom, I'm starving. When's dinner?"

"In ten," I said. "Didn't you have a protein bar an hour ago?"

"Those things are disgusting," she said, making a face.

"Then you *didn't* eat it?" I said with alarm.

"Relax, Mom."

"Here we go again. 'Let's see your food log, Charlotte! Let's check your sugar! Let's watch another episode of the Charlotte show!'" said Isa, who was still behind her paperback.

"*Isa*," warned Shiloh.

"You think I like this?" said Charlotte, glaring at her. When Isa didn't respond, she knocked the book out of her hands.

"Hey!" yelled Isa as the book hit the tile with a thud. "You just made me lose my place!"

"That is *enough*," I said, so sharply that I startled myself as much as I had the girls. "Your father and I were in the middle of discussing something."

"How you're divorcing?" said Isa, bending down to grab her novel.

She might as well have just kneed me in the gut. "Isabel Milagros Ross-Velasquez, what on earth would make you say something terrible like that?" I hissed.

She stood and shrugged. "I don't know."

Shiloh's eyes flashed with anger. "If you don't know then don't say it."

"You don't have to hide it from us," said Isa. "Everyone gets divorced nowadays. Like, look at Uncle Paul and Uncle Charlie."

"Excuse me?" I said, staring at her. "How did you know that?"

Isa shrugged again and opened her book.

"Toby told us they were probably going to when we were over there for dinner," said Charlotte, peering into the cupboard.

Now Isa piped up. "And *probably* means *wait for it*. Anyways, I just read, like, three books where the main characters' parents divorce. It happens." She looked back and forth at me and Shiloh.

"Yes, it does," I said. "But *not* to me and your father."

"Oh, I can tell," said Isa.

44

"That's enough," said Shiloh.

"Let's talk about something else, okay?" I said, eager to keep this from turning into a four-person fight.

But Shiloh's mouth was a taut line, and Isa, who was glaring at Charlotte like she'd just tossed her books in a bonfire, said nothing. Then Charlotte slammed the cupboard door closed and stormed off. And I stood there fighting back tears as I wondered if my daughters had already picked up on what I was just now opening my eyes to.

~

You've never seen four people eat a meal faster than we scarfed down dinner. *The twins were probably right about needing alone time,* I thought as everyone scattered to different corners of the apartment. And maybe Shiloh and I did, too. After all, there was a good reason that the adage wasn't "Being under the same roof makes the heart grow fonder."

Still—the thought of putting more distance between us gave me a terrible pang, because I couldn't see how that could possibly be an improvement. Our ill-fated date aside, when was the last time we really connected? Not binge-watching British TV shows before bed together. Not folding laundry side by side as we discussed Isa's preference for the fictional world and Charlotte's annoyance with our monitoring her health. Real. Quality. Time.

Blame my sex-starved state, but every time I tried to recall some point in recent history that we'd really enjoyed each other's company, I wound up remembering our whirlwind romance in Vieques.

After the one-two punch of my cancer diagnosis and Tom's marriage-decimating confession, I'd intended to head to Mexico to live out my final days. But when my father told me that my mother had loved Vieques, I'd abruptly changed my plans. I met Shiloh on the flight to the island, and though I'd initially found his pithy humor and hands-off approach grating, his quick thinking had allowed him to safely land our plane after a run-in with a bird destroyed its engine. And minutes later, he talked me down from the panic attack I'd suffered after realizing that whether from cancer or a crash, I was about to exit life stage left. Before I knew it, we were spending time together in the way that only two naked people can.

Though I'd decided to forgo treatment, Shiloh confessed that he'd had cancer himself in his twenties. It took some doing, but he eventually convinced me to give survival—and yes, love—another shot. Still, neither of us had expected our fling to go the distance. But once we were apart, it had been impossible to stay that way, and he'd moved from Puerto Rico to the East Coast. Despite being told I was infertile, I'd gotten pregnant with the girls; Shiloh and I married a few months before they were born. What had started out as the most disastrous time in my life soon became the most magical.

Thinking about Vieques made me think of Milagros, too, which was infinitely more pleasant than wondering why my present relationship bore so little resemblance to its past. Milagros had been my landlord during the month I'd spent there, and in spite of our four-decade age difference, we'd hit it off. I'd only seen her a few times since then. But we'd stayed in close contact over the past thirteen years, and she'd become a dear friend. A mentor, even. As I'd learned after my mother died, the desire to be comforted by your parents never really went away, even when you had children yourself. But at least Milagros was still there when I, say, wasn't sure what to do after I'd stuck my foot in my mouth with a neighbor. Or when I just wanted to chat.

I was about to start scouring the pots and pans when it hit me that she was exactly who could pull me out of my doldrums. I abandoned the dishes, grabbed my phone, and went out to the patio to call her.

She picked up right away. "Libby?" she said, half laughing my name. "So happy to hear from you." We usually spoke every week or two, but I'd stopped calling as frequently since . . . well, around the time my dad died, to be honest, even if it hadn't been intentional.

"Hi, Milagros," I said. And then I burst into tears.

"Oh, *mija. ¿Qué es?*" she said, meaning, "What is it?"

"I'm sorry," I said, still crying. "It's just been a rough day and I needed to talk to someone."

"Don't apologize—I'm glad you called me! I've got nothing but time," she said, and although I knew she was trying to reassure me, hearing her say this made me cry even harder because that's probably what my father, who'd been seventy-four when he'd passed, had thought, too. While Milagros was in great health for a woman in her eighties, time was arguably not on her side. "Now, what's going on?"

I took a deep breath and wiped my eyes. "I don't even know," I said, my voice quavering. "I went to the doctor the other day, and I thought I had cancer again. But I don't. In fact, next month is my ten-year anniversary. And even though I know that's the best possible news a person could wish for, I feel . . . well, not like myself," I confessed, and even just saying this was like having a boulder lifted off my chest.

"Oh Libby," she said kindly. Some tropical bird cawed in the background, and I could just picture her sitting on her palm tree–canopied patio, which was right beyond the guesthouse in her backyard. As much as I liked my own patio, I would have given a pinkie toe to be there next to her, listening to the waves hit the shore and feeling like everything was right with the world. "You don't have to feel good all the time, *tú sabes.*"

"I know." I glanced over my shoulder to make sure the double doors to the apartment were still closed. "But I don't like feeling like this."

"*Lo sé,*" she soothed, but then I heard a man calling her in the background.

"Who's that?" I said.

"My lover, Hector," she said with obvious delight. "He came over to move furniture for me and ended up moving in. Life is never boring for a moment, *mija.*"

I wanted to laugh and be happy for her—but hearing her call some man "lover" only reminded me of all the naked Twister I'd not been playing. If I was envious of an octogenarian's love life, things were even worse than I'd thought.

"Libby?" said Milagros. "You still there?"

"I'm here," I said, looking up at the sky. The sun had just begun to set; above me a pair of airplanes were heading in opposite directions, leaving white trails in their wakes.

"How's Shiloh?" said Milagros, who seemed to have read my mind.

"Fine," I sniffed. "Busy lately, but fine."

"You're lucky to have a man who loves you. That's more than I can say for at least five of my seven ex-husbands. Or maybe there were six—it's a little fuzzy now. But if I know anything, it's that you have yourself a winner."

I did; I really did. And wasn't knowing that I'd married someone I truly loved, and who loved me, enough?

"Hector, amor, un segundo," she hollered. "Sorry, Libby," she said. "I'm telling you, the man is insatiable!"

I managed a laugh.

"¿Y las niñas? When are you going to bring them to Vieques to see me?" she asked.

Though our family visited Puerto Rico at least once a year, getting to Vieques was time-consuming and logistically complicated. So we'd only taken the girls there once, when they were two, and too young to remember Milagros. Shiloh and I had planned to return last summer but canceled after Charlotte's diagnosis; everything had seemed so overwhelming at the time. We'd discussed going for spring break instead, but then my father had died.

"I know we're long overdue for a trip. But the girls are doing great," I told Milagros. "Charlotte's blood sugar has been under control, which is the most important thing. Granted, they're fighting more than I'd like because they don't have camp this summer. They don't realize what a privilege it is to be bored."

Milagros cackled. "Kids never do! But if they're bored, why don't you bring them here for a week or so? Hector just made some updates to the guesthouse, and they didn't take as long as we thought, so the month of August is open. It's hot, *tú sabes*, but I can't imagine New York will be any cooler. Celebrate being cancer free for ten years—my treat."

"That's so nice of you, but I don't think we can pull it off," I said, even as I imagined lounging in the hammock outside her guesthouse. It wasn't just the idea of taking a break that was so appealing; Vieques was where I'd pieced my life back together and found peace and clarity at a time when both had seemed impossible. And given the week—heck, given the *month*—there wasn't a single thing that sounded better than sticking my toes in the water and feeling like everything in the world was going to work out just fine. "Shiloh has been working a ton."

"Then it'll be even easier for him to ask for time off," she said matter-of-factly.

"You're funny."

"*Pero* I'm also right. Come back to the place where you two started. And bring those gorgeous girls of yours so I can see them again before I croak."

She was kidding, but her words pierced me. What if the twins never really got to know the woman who'd mothered me all these years?

"I miss you, Libby," she added.

Here came the waterworks again. "I miss you, too, Milagros," I told her, wiping away a tear. "I'd love to come, but I don't know if I can make it that soon. Let me talk to Shiloh and get back to you."

"That's all I ask," she said, and I could just see her grinning. "I'd say the door is open, but we're booked solid from September through the second week of January."

I sniffed. "Noted."

"Of course, old Milly understands if you can't visit. Either way, hang in there, okay, Libby?"

"I'll try, Milagros. Thanks for helping me feel better."

"Any time, *mija*, and I mean that."

I knew that she did. Which is why I was going to find a way to see her again—and soon.

EIGHT

After I finally dried my eyes, I went into the living room and pulled my Vieques photo album from the bookshelf before heading to our bedroom. Still fully dressed, I got under the duvet, then opened the album.

I ran my finger along the edge of the first page. At the top, there was a photo of palm trees against a bright blue sky; I'd taken it shortly after arriving at the airport in San Juan. Just below that was a snapshot of the plane I flew to Vieques with Shiloh, who was barely visible in the background. Of course, at the time, I had no idea that the maddening if highly attractive stranger would eventually become my husband.

On the next page, Shiloh and I were at our favorite restaurant in Vieques, the one with twinkle lights and the open-air bar that looked like a movie set. It was where we went on our first date, which ended with us fighting about why I wasn't planning to get treatment—not that that had been enough to prevent us from finding our way right back to each other.

And there I was, lying on a towel on the beach in my bathing suit and a wide-brimmed sun hat, smirking at Shiloh, who was taking my picture. I wanted to reach through the page and shake thirteen-years-ago me. Forget that I had no clue that just a few years later I would have traded a kidney for skin that supple and unlined. What I *really* didn't realize was that what I'd thought was a low point was really one of the highest of my life.

New tears sprang to my eyes, because I'd just realized how much I looked like my mother in that photo. Specifically, I looked like the photo of her that my father had sent me right before I decided to flee Chicago, where I'd lived with Tom, for Puerto Rico. They'd been on the beach in Vieques, and she had been pregnant with me and Paul; she had been so luminous and filled with joy that I knew I had to see that place for myself and had ditched my plans to head to Mexico. In spite of my tumultuous emotional state, I, too, looked luminous and joyful in the photo Shiloh had taken. The island was magical that way.

I kept flipping and reminiscing until I reached the last page, which held a picture of me and Milagros standing in front of her pale pink guesthouse. I remembered how scared I was—of officially ending my marriage; of taking a chance on Shiloh, who was practically a stranger to me at the time; and yes, naturally, of dying. But none of that fear was evident on my face. Instead, I was wearing the smile of someone who knows she's just made a lifelong friend. Beside me, Milagros was grinning like she had it all figured out. Which, of course, she did.

I really missed her. She was already getting up there in years when we'd taken the photo, and now she was . . . eighty-three, I determined after doing the math in my head. The last time Shiloh and I had been to visit her, she'd been bounding around like a woman half her age, but that was five years ago. And if my décolletage was any indication, a lot could change in that amount of time.

Shiloh stuck his head in the door. "Hey, I was going to join you on the patio, but you weren't there. What are you up to?"

"Just looking through old photos," I said, hoping I didn't look like I'd been crying. "I talked to Milagros for a little while."

"Oh yeah? How is she?"

"Good . . . but old." I'd already made up my mind but wanted to take the opportunity to gauge his mood before determining how I'd ask him about going. "She asked us to come stay at the guesthouse, so she can meet the girls before she, quote, croaks."

He laughed lightly from the doorway. "Let's hope it doesn't come to that."

It always came to that, not that I said this to him. "We *are* overdue for a trip, though. We've been telling Charlotte and Isa that we'd take them back to Vieques for years now."

"It has been a while for us, too," he said. When the girls were seven, Shiloh and I left them with Paul and Charlie for a week and flew to Puerto Rico for our first and only solo vacation. That time we'd gone to Vieques for a quick overnight trip. I thought we'd begin to visit more regularly after that, but in the following years, something had always seemed to come up. "What about the week between Christmas and New Year's? I should be able to take it off if I give Kasey enough notice," he said, referring to his supervisor.

The holidays were only five months away. It might as well be a decade. "Milagros said the guesthouse is available in August, and it's ours to use—her treat for my ten-year cancerversary," I told him.

"Next month?" he said, running his hand through his hair. "As in August, which starts next week?"

"Yes," I said in a tone that was bordering on defensive. There were a dozen different reasons we couldn't make it work—last-minute tickets would be a fortune, Shiloh probably couldn't get the time off, and so forth and so on. Not a single one of them mattered. Visiting Vieques the first time had allowed me to figure out what seemed like an impossible situation. Surely now—*when nothing was actually wrong with me*—I'd get my head screwed on straight within minutes of setting foot on the island.

But I wasn't the only one who needed transformation. If the past several weeks were any indication, Shiloh and I needed a serious dose of the island enchantment that brought us together in the first place. And while I wouldn't describe my family as coming apart at the seams, spending a week away from the stressors of our everyday life might be just the thing to help remind us how lucky we were to have each other.

He was frowning like I'd just told him we'd won a free night at the Bedbug Motel. "You know it's hot as hades in August, right? And that it's hurricane season?"

"New York will be just as hot, except without the ocean breeze," I said, but as soon as I heard myself, I realized I was going to need better ammunition. "Hey—we're talking about Puerto Rico. As in your homeland. Don't you want to visit?"

"I do," he said slowly. "The question is, why do you sound upset?"

"I'm not." More like desperate. "Anyway, remember when we were supposed to be in San Juan last August? You'd said then that hurricane season is several months long and it didn't make sense to plan around it."

"True . . ." I could all but see the wheels turning in his head. I just hoped they were turning in the right direction. "I'm not sure I'll be able to get off work."

Now I had to resist the urge to throw up my hands in exasperation. This was a man who said yes first and figured out the details later. What was his hang-up?

But then I looked at him again from across the room, and unlike me, he wasn't irritated at all. He just looked . . . tired. My annoyance immediately disappeared. "Hey, you need a break as much as I do," I said softly. "You've been working a ton, and we missed two vacations in a row. Add Charlotte's diabetes to the mix and . . ." I exhaled. "It's a lot."

"You're right, cutie," he said, his face softening. "I've been kind of stressed."

He had, I realized. And I didn't need WebMD to tell me the effect stress could have on a person's libido.

"I'm sorry," he added.

"Don't be sorry." *Just say you'll go.* "Will you at least see if Kasey will give you the time off?"

He came and sat beside me on the bed. "Sure, I'll ask. August is probably the least busy we've been all year, so I might be able to switch shifts with a few people if there's an issue with my schedule." He brushed a stray curl from my cheek and I felt my spirits rise. Just the *mention* of Vieques and we were already headed in the right direction. I could only imagine what might happen once we were actually on the island. "What about the tickets?"

"I haven't searched yet," I admitted. "But it's off-season and we have a million miles on our credit card."

"You sure about this?" Shiloh was looking at me like he couldn't figure out if I was a lunatic or a genius.

"Yes," I said, even though I was well aware that I'd just made major plans in the time it took to pack a suitcase. It was half-baked and impulsive—but hadn't my first visit to Vieques been, as well? Even if this vacation were only a fraction as successful, I'd still end up becoming reacquainted with my enthusiasm for life.

And if my husband and I had a chance to relax and remember how we came together—rekindling our spark in the process—who was I to complain about that?

NINE

As it turned out, the cheapest tickets had been the ones that required us to leave a week and a half later. Shiloh wasn't sure he'd be able to get the time off on such short notice, but apparently all the extra hours he'd been putting in had bought a whole lot of goodwill with his boss. Meanwhile, I'd left Rupi in charge in my absence, and though I could tell she was disappointed that we'd have to delay our meeting about the camp, she'd told me she was excited to hear the fresh new ideas she was sure I'd come up with the minute I wasn't glued to my desk.

I'd sooner volunteer for a colonoscopy than devote precious brain cells to "fresh" and "new"; I just wanted to get out of there. I'd hoped my mood would lift at the prospect of visiting my favorite place—and I *had* been momentarily elated after calling Milagros to tell her we were coming. What I hadn't anticipated was that instead of making normal life more tolerable, it immediately felt like twice the drag. Had there always been so much laundry to do, so many emails to answer, so many people to weave through just to make it to the subway?

A week in paradise couldn't come soon enough.

But as our plane descended over San Juan, I was reminded of the beating our paradise had taken. We usually visited Shiloh's father, who lived outside of Fajardo, at least once a year. After Hurricane Maria hit in September of 2017, though, he'd urged us to stay home. Even after the airports had reopened, many of the roads had remained torn up from the floods, and some hotels and restaurants were shuttered indefinitely. The island slowly began to recover, so we thought we'd visit the following summer, but then came Charlotte's diagnosis, and seven months later, my father's death. So it had been two and a half years since our last trip, which had been over winter break. And as it happened, a lot had changed since then.

My stomach sank as I peered through the small plane window and saw one building after another with a bright blue tarp for a roof.

"Why do the houses look like that?" whispered Isa, leaning over my lap to look down at San Juan.

I wasn't sure how to answer. Puerto Rico as a whole had been given a fraction of the assistance other hurricane-stricken areas in the continental US had received for similar natural disasters, and the little they had been granted had been shamefully slow in arriving. On top of that, the island itself was still struggling from decades of debt, and since the economy relied so heavily on tourism, that debt had only grown after Maria. "Puerto Rico didn't get the help it needed after the hurricane," I told her. "So they've still got a long way to go. But it's good for us to be here. The more visitors, the more money people on the island can make, and that can help them make repairs."

She was frowning as she turned to me. "I hope it looks better once we're on the ground."

"I do, too," I agreed.

But after we landed, gathered our suitcases, and got in a taxi, I saw that "better" was relative. Some buildings were fully intact. As we sped down the highway, however, we saw many others that were missing their facades or had windows blown out; sometimes whole walls had caved in. Equally jarring, it was clear that people were still living in some of those buildings. And for every one tree that was green and flourishing, another was still stripped of its leaves and either dead or dormant. "I can't believe how much destruction there is, even two years later," I said quietly to Shiloh.

"It's hard to see," he said, staring out the taxi window forlornly. "The island has always had its problems, like anywhere else. But you have to wonder how long it will take to recover from this."

If it does at all, I thought, only to cringe at the thought—where were my rose-colored glasses when I needed them? After all, this was my husband's birthplace; though he'd shuttled back and forth between Puerto Rico and the states for several years after his parents divorced, it had been home for most of his life, right up until he moved to the East Coast to be with me. "It'll recover," I said, as much to myself as him as my eyes landed on another swath of land that had once been lush and verdant but was now dry and brown. "It has to."

~

Our flight hadn't arrived until late afternoon, so instead of rushing to try to make the last ferry to Vieques, we'd decided to spend a night in the Condado neighborhood of San Juan, where Shiloh had lived before we got married. I sighed with relief when we pulled up to our hotel, not because the hotel was in good shape—though that didn't hurt—but because I'd spotted the ocean on the other side of the building. Just the sight of it made me feel like somehow, some way, everything was going to work out.

Charlotte and Isa had always loved the water, too; I could still remember the way their faces lit up the first time they dipped their tiny toes in the Atlantic on our first trip to Puerto Rico. I wasn't surprised that as soon as we dropped our bags in our room, they ran out to the beach.

Shiloh and I followed them to the shore, then stood back watching them splash each other and dive into the waves. From a distance, they could almost pass for children who hadn't spent the past several days complaining about having to leave their friends for a *whole week* (never mind that half their friends were at camp). I wasn't about to complain about that.

"Things are looking up," said Shiloh.

"I mean, I don't want to say I told you so, but . . ."

"But you totally told me so," he said, bumping my hip with his own.

I grinned. An hour in the land of palm trees and piña coladas and we were flirting like a couple on their third date! I had half a mind to call Paul and tell him that I'd found a cure for coasting, and that he and Charlie should hop on a plane immediately and try it for themselves.

"It's so good to be here," I told him.

"It really is," he agreed. His hair was blowing in the wind, and even from behind his aviator glasses he looked awfully darn content. Which was a relief—even though he'd *said* he wanted to go on this trip, he'd been so busy with work the past week that I hadn't gotten a sense as to whether he really meant it. *"Aquí, me siento como yo mismo,"* he added.

"You feel like yourself here?" I said, attempting to translate. My Spanish had improved a lot over the past thirteen years, but I still managed to say things like "I have poop!" when I was actually trying to say, "I'm afraid." No surprise, I left the talking to Shiloh when it came to anything important.

"Yeah," he said, smiling at me.

"Do you *not* feel like yourself when you're in New York?" I asked, thinking of how I hadn't felt right lately, either.

He looked from me to the water and back again, and I could tell he was trying to work out how to respond. "I do," he said slowly, "because that's where you and the girls are, and that's where my home is."

I exhaled a breath I hadn't realized I'd been holding. "Thank you," I said softly.

"You don't need to thank me. But I should thank *you*. I'm glad you wanted to come."

It felt good to hear him say this. In fact, I could almost ignore the tiny nagging voice deep within me saying that if I'd only done this sooner, I could have avoided flatlining when I should have been hollering hallelujah. Maybe next year we'd leave in June, as soon as the girls were done with school, and make it an annual trip. Heck, maybe at some point we could even spend the whole summer here. It was probably an impossible idea. But as I stared out at the ocean as the sun warmed my skin, I realized an impossible idea was a massive improvement over the Nancy Nostradamus persona I'd been sporting the past couple of weeks.

"Mom! Papi!" Isa was flapping her arms and jumping up and down. "Come in the water!" she said. "Come on!"

My children were inviting me to join them without being bribed or guilted? Score. "Coming," I called. "But don't get me wet. I'm not wearing a suit under my sundress."

"So?" said Charlotte. She motioned to the running shorts she'd worn in lieu of a bikini bottom. "The water's *so* warm right now. You have to try it!"

"Okay, okay. Just a little," I said, putting a foot in the water. It *was* warm, and the sand was soft beneath my feet. "Hey," I said to Shiloh. "If I'm doing this, you are, too."

He grinned and shrugged, then rolled up his shorts and waded in.

"There you go," teased Isa.

"Was that so bad?" said Charlotte, who looked at Isa and laughed.

"Listen, you two," I said, splashing them.

"This is war!" said Charlotte. "Isa! You know what to do!"

Isa grinned. "*Get her!*"

"Not while I'm in my dress!" I protested, but it was too late—they were on top of me, pulling me down into the ocean.

Salt water seeped into my mouth and burned my eyes, which I'd closed a second too late. I didn't care. I resurfaced with a big smile on my face. "You'll pay for that!" I yelled before dunking a screaming Charlotte.

Isa attempted to run through the waves away from me, but Shiloh was faster. "Don't worry, Libby—I've got her," he said, grabbing Isa as she squealed. He lifted her as though she was no lighter than a doll and tossed her into a wave. Seconds later, she popped up, laughing gleefully like she had when she was a toddler.

"Team Parent for the win," said Shiloh, winking at me.

I winked back, though I was on the verge of weeping with happiness. My family was actually enjoying each other's company! This was the best idea—

My thought was interrupted by a stun gun hitting my calf. At least, that's what it felt like.

"Oh sugar," I said, lurching forward to clutch my leg. "Oh, mother plucking sugar."

"Libby?" asked Shiloh, who was standing a few feet away. "What's wrong?" He'd been holding Charlotte over his head, but he took one look at my face and let her go.

There was a smacking sound as her torso hit the water, and I swear I could hear her yelling before she even surfaced. "*Papi!* Ow!"

"Sorry, *niña*, that was an accident. But Mami's hurt," he said over his shoulder. He put his arm around me gently. "You okay?"

No. "I will be."

"I'm sorry," he said, kissing the top of my head gently. "Come on, let's get to the shore."

Surely the pain will ease up once I'm on land, I told myself. But no— as Shiloh helped me limp back to the beach, the pain only intensified. I took a few steps before throwing myself down on the sand, even though I hadn't made it to the towel. Crap. Was our vacation over before it even began?

"Uh-oh," said Shiloh, examining my leg. There were several long strings of welts up and down my right calf. Each welt was circular and perfectly spaced from the next, like beads on a necklace. I would have appreciated the artistry if it hadn't felt like hundreds of shards of glass implanted in my flesh. "Looks like you had a run-in with a jellyfish," he said.

Isa, who was standing over me, started to scream. And I mean really scream. "There are *jellyfish*?! In *the water*?!"

"*Con calma,*" said Shiloh. The girls weren't fully fluent in Spanish, which I knew was my fault; everything I'd read said it took both parents speaking around the clock to really immerse children in a language, and I'd not been capable of that. But he'd always used Spanish phrases to soothe them. To me, he added, "That's really unusual for this part of the Atlantic, especially so close to the shore. Although maybe global warming . . ."

"Honey," I said, but then I had to squeeze my eyes closed because my leg had just started throbbing. "It really hurts," I said through gritted teeth.

"Pee on it!" said Charlotte. "That's what you're supposed to do for jellyfish stings—I saw it on YouTube!"

Isa's face brightened. "Pee on it! Pee on it!" she yelled.

"Pee on it! Pee on it!" chanted Charlotte.

Every beachgoer within a half-mile radius had turned to stare at us. Really, I wouldn't have been surprised if someone walked over and offered to empty their bladder onto my leg just to shut my children up.

"No one is peeing on anything, now knock it off," Shiloh told them. "Libs? Can you stand on it?"

I could, but it hurt. A lot. "Do you think I need to get to the hospital?" I whispered, one arm slung over his shoulder. I was starting to feel kind of woozy. "What if it's poisonous?"

"Luckily, the kinds of jellyfish you find in this part of the Atlantic are perfectly harmless. Well," he said, glancing at my leg, "not harmless, but not poisonous, either. Let's get back to the hotel so we can clean it out. Girls, grab our towels."

"But we just got in the water!" said Isa.

Charlotte put her fists on her hips. "We want to stay. I'll keep an eye on Isa and she can watch me."

I remembered how Milagros had practically hauled me out of the Caribbean when she saw me swimming alone in an area that hadn't been designated for swimming. Unlike then, the four of us had been wading in a roped-off part of the ocean, but the receptionist at the hotel had warned us that the current had been particularly strong over the past week. "Until both of you are trained as lifeguards, no one is swimming without us," I said. "Now please come with me and your father."

"This always happens," said Isa, trailing behind us.

I didn't fully catch Charlotte's response, but I heard her say, "Lame start to our vacation."

My heart sank. Not because I disagreed—but because she was right.

TEN

Imagine my relief when the concierge at our hotel informed us that vinegar, not urine, was the best way to treat a jellyfish sting. Shiloh plucked a few stray pieces of tentacle from my skin with a pair of tweezers, which is every bit as repulsive as it sounds, then attempted to pickle my calf with the vinegar he'd bought at a convenience store. Afterward I took a warm bath, which reputable online sources said was helpful for easing pain. Not so much—but it was nearly dinnertime, so I tossed back a handful of ibuprofen and pasted on my best poker face.

We'd intended to eat at the Parrot Club, which had been one of our favorite spots in Old San Juan. But when we arrived there, we learned that it had been permanently shuttered several years earlier, though it wasn't clear if that was a business decision or a result of the hurricane.

"I can't believe how much of the island has been affected," muttered Shiloh as we stood in front of another restaurant across the street. The building had a gaping hole in its roof that looked like it had been there since Maria hit. "I should have expected it, but still."

"Maybe we'll find something even better," I suggested, trying to keep the disappointment out of my voice. I knew we had almost the whole vacation ahead of us, but as my throbbing calf was intent on reminding me, we were already seriously off course.

"When?" demanded Isa, leaning against a tree in front of the restaurant. "I'm starving."

"I am, too," said Charlotte, who was sitting in a heap on the concrete, not far from Isa's feet.

"Good, because now they'll actually find food for us," muttered Isa. "If I'm hungry, it doesn't matter. If you're hungry, stop everything! You might die!"

"Isa, for the love of all that's good and holy, please knock it off," I pleaded. "Can we be nice to each other tonight? We're on vacation."

"Are we, though?" said Charlotte, rolling her eyes, and Isa laughed.

"I'm glad you're at least agreeing on something. Why don't I call the hotel concierge to get a suggestion?" I said. "I bet a good meal will have us all feeling better."

After a few minutes on the phone, we ended up back in Condado at a restaurant that served traditional Puerto Rican food. Shiloh immediately decided on mofongo, a dish made of mashed, well-seasoned plantains topped with meat or seafood, while I settled on the *ropa vieja* with a side of red rice and beans. But Isa had abandoned her menu in favor of her novel without choosing a meal, and Charlotte was scowling off into the distance.

"What is it, Char?" I asked.

"I don't like anything they have," she said, still looking at the wall. "Can't you just ask them to make chicken fingers?"

"No," said Shiloh. "You can find something on the menu to eat, or you can go hungry."

I glanced at him, wondering if he was hangry; he didn't usually snap like that. "Actually . . . ," I began. Actually, she couldn't skip meals without risking a serious dip in her blood sugar—which he knew. "What about the grilled chicken with rice and beans?" I suggested.

"Whatever," she muttered.

"Is this about the beach earlier?" I asked.

"No."

"It's about you being spoiled, *Charlotte*," Isa said, not glancing up from her novel.

I could feel something stirring in me. It wasn't strong enough to qualify as anger, but it wasn't mild enough to be mere irritation. In fact, if I didn't know better, I would have diagnosed myself with a raging case of disappointment. Was I the only person on this vacation who remembered how fortunate we were to be able to hop on a plane to spend a week on not one but two tropical islands?

I opened my mouth, then clamped it shut just as fast, because I'd just remembered that my own mother had never broken up my arguments with Paul by telling us which one of us was in the wrong. She'd figured out early on that it was far more effective to play head cheerleader than referee.

"Isa, chicken with rice and beans work for you, too?" I said pleasantly.

"Fine," she said from the other side of her book.

"Great!" I said, waving our server over. He took our order and asked if we wanted anything to drink. I glanced at Shiloh, who hadn't seemed relaxed since . . . well, since the jellyfish incident, come to think of it. In fact, unless my eyes were playing tricks on me, he looked just as tense as he had in New York. I needed to turn this ship around, and fast.

"A piña colada for both of us," I told the server.

Shiloh arched his eyebrows.

"The ibuprofen's not cutting it," I explained, "and hey, we're in Puerto Rico."

"Thank you . . . I think."

"You're welcome, I think. Hey, remember when you took me out for piña coladas when we went to San Juan together?" I said, hoping the reminder of those heady days would make him smile.

He broke into a grin. "You didn't believe me, but they really were the best, weren't they?"

"They were," I agreed, grinning back at him.

"I heard from my buddy that the place is actually still there," he said. "I wish our trip was a little longer." We were spending five nights in Vieques, then another night in San Juan before flying home.

"Maybe we can come back with just the two of us," I said, eyeing the girls. From the way they were slouched down in their chairs, you'd think we were making them sit through a trigonometry lesson. I had to remind myself that I'd planned a family vacation on purpose; they needed this as much as the rest of us did.

"What are you both looking forward to?" I asked them after the waiter delivered our piña coladas. It was a question my father used to ask Paul and me at dinner; he'd believed that even if we were just having microwaved lasagna, meals were for interacting with each other.

"Going home," said Charlotte.

"What she said," said Isa.

"That's enough," said Shiloh. His voice was low, but all business. "We're on vacation and we are *going* to have a good time."

"Aye, aye," said Isa as Charlotte pretended to salute him.

For a second, I was on Team Twin. Forced fun—sign me up!

Then I remembered that this whole thing had been my idea.

"Let's change the subject," I said before taking another sip of my drink. "You still think we'll have time to see your dad on the way back from Vieques?" I asked Shiloh, who was staring at the television over the bar. A soccer match was on, and although he was a fan, I suspected Isa and Charlotte's behavior was the real reason his eyes were trailing a bunch of soccer players on teams he didn't follow.

"It'll be tight, but we'll manage," he said, glancing at me quickly before looking back at the screen.

"Maybe we can look for souvenirs for your friends after we get settled at Milagros'," I said to the girls, but now they were watching the game, too. I sighed; what was wrong with good old-fashioned conversation?

A whole lot, based on the little my family said to each other after our meals arrived. Maybe that's why, when our server appeared to see how our food was, I ordered a second drink, which I drank with gusto as everyone else continued to vegetate.

"You're in rare form," whispered Shiloh as we made our way back to the hotel.

"Are you suggesting I can't walk in a straight line?" I joked, leaning against his arm. In truth, I didn't actually like feeling tipsy, but it *was* easier to harness my inner Pollyanna when the world around me was all soft and fuzzy. "Anyway, I need to let my hair down at some point, right?" I said, looking over my shoulder to make sure the girls were still straggling behind.

"I guess so. I know things have been pretty intense for you lately."

I frowned. "For all of us."

"But your brother and Charlie's divorce, and your dad . . ."

Boy, he really knew how to accentuate the positive. "My dad's been dead for six months now," I said, watching a lizard dart along the side of a wrought-iron fence.

"Do you want to talk about picking a date for the burial? We never did that before we left, you know."

"While we're on vacation?" I said, looking at him quizzically. "Not really."

"Fair enough," he said quickly before turning back to the girls. "You two coming?"

Isa nodded. But Charlotte, who was a few steps behind her, said nothing, and there was nothing behind her glassy eyes.

I was stone-cold sober and at her side faster than you can say *helicopter parent*. "Char, what is it?" I asked.

But I already knew that it was exactly what I'd been most afraid of since the moment she'd received her diagnosis. Her blood sugar had plummeted and was continuing to drop. Her face was pale, and she was shivering as I put an arm around her and guided her into the hotel. "How much insulin did you take?" I asked.

"The usual," she mumbled. "I think . . . I didn't eat enough."

My heart was galloping in my chest. "But your plate was almost empty."

"She put it in her napkin," said Isa.

"Oh Charlotte," I said. "You can't do that."

She started to say something but gave up before the first word came out.

"It's okay," I told her as we got on the elevator. "We're here now. It's going to be fine."

In fact, I didn't know she'd be fine any more than I knew how to stop elephant poaching and cure cancer. This had happened to Charlotte once before, after a soccer game. She hadn't eaten as much as she should've beforehand, and she'd been running so hard that her blood sugar had dipped perilously low before she even realized it was happening. It was quite possibly the most terrifying thing I had ever lived through.

And now it was happening again.

The elevator opened and let us onto our floor. I motioned for Shiloh to unlock the door to our room.

"Isa, glucose gel—it's in my purse. Now," I barked, making a mental note to apologize to her later. "Shiloh, please get some orange juice from the vending machine, then get the test strips. Go!" Charlotte was like a rag doll as I guided her to the bed. "Stay here, love," I said, willing myself not to cry. "This is just going to take a minute, and you're going to feel better."

Isa, God bless her, was back in a flash with the tube of gel. I pulled the lid off with my teeth and told Charlotte to open her mouth. *Please be okay, please be okay,* I prayed, watching her glassy eyes as I squirted it onto her tongue. She claimed to hate the way it tasted, but now she didn't protest at all. In fact, she didn't really do anything.

"Sweetheart," I said, trying to keep the panic out of my voice, "I know you feel terrible, but please try to swallow." Her eyes had just closed but her throat had moved, so I told her to open her mouth again, and I emptied the tube.

"How is she?" said Shiloh, who was at my side, holding a bottle of juice out to us.

"Definitely hypoglycemic," I said.

"Crap," he said, frantically trying to unscrew the top of the juice bottle. "Try this."

"Just a little," I said. "The gel should be kicking in soon, and we should test her sugar before we go too far." I tried to hoist Charlotte up. "Some juice, Char. Open up for me."

Shiloh held the juice to her mouth. She startled slightly, but then sat up and took the container from him and took a sip on her own.

"There we go," I said as the light began to return to her eyes. I smiled, even though I wanted to sob, because I needed her to see that she was going to be okay.

"You scared us, sweetheart," said Shiloh quietly, putting his arm around her. To an outsider, he would have looked oddly calm, but I recognized this as his version of coming down from fight-or-flight mode. "Thank goodness we caught that in time."

I knew what he was thinking but hadn't said—because I was thinking it, too. Even a few minutes longer and she could have slipped into a coma.

"You okay?" asked Isa, her hand on Charlotte's arm.

Charlotte nodded weakly. "I'm sorry," she mumbled. "I didn't mean to do that."

"I know you didn't." I was so overcome with relief that it took me a minute to be able to speak again. "We're all learning here. Let's check your blood sugar and get a little more food in you, and then what do you say we hit the hay for the night?"

"Yeah," she said. "I'm really tired."

Dear dog almighty, I was, too. So tired that when Shiloh and I crawled into one of the room's two double beds an hour later, I didn't even wonder when he'd finally make love to me, or think about my daughter's latest brush with death, or wish that my vacation had not gotten off to such a disastrous start. Instead, Vieques, in all its verdant, tropical glory, appeared like a mirage behind my closed eyelids, and before I knew it, I had fallen into a deep, dream-filled sleep.

ELEVEN

"That was way too close." Shiloh and I were side by side in front of the sinks in the hotel bathroom while the girls changed into their bathing suits. He met my eyes in the mirror. "I know we didn't have a chance to talk about Charlotte last night, but we need to. I don't want that to happen again."

"I know. We should talk about a new plan when we get home. Maybe even get Dr. Ornstein involved," I said, referring to her endocrinologist.

"Sure, but what about the rest of the vacation?" he asked, frowning as he reached for a towel to dry his face.

"I think we got all of our bad luck out of the way for this trip," I said, adjusting the straps of my sundress.

"Hmm," he said, sounding unconvinced. "I hate to say it, but maybe this is how she learns. Maybe this scared her into never pulling that again. I know it's not great to have to eat your food whether you feel like it or not, but if she doesn't . . ."

Was he kidding right now? If she didn't, she could slip into a coma and die. "That cannot possibly be an option," I said firmly.

"I know that it feels better to think that way, but we need to make sure Charlotte understands the risks," said Shiloh, still watching me in the mirror. "If last night is any indication, she isn't taking this seriously."

"So, we take it seriously for her. I want her to have a childhood. I don't want her to spend every waking moment worrying about her blood sugar."

"She has a childhood," he said, frowning. "A really good one. Kids deal with hard things all the time, and you know what? They grow up to be adults who are good at dealing with hard things. Look at you and Paul."

He was trying to be kind, but he couldn't have picked a worse example if he'd tried. If I thought about it—and I mostly tried not to—there was a reason Paul and I had turned out the way we had. Yes, I was a natural-born optimist, while Paul had emerged from the womb expecting the sky to fall. But over time I'd come to understand that our personalities had probably been dialed up a dozen notches in direct response to our mother dying. I didn't want that for Charlotte.

"You guys almost done in there?" yelled Isa. "We're ready to go to the beach."

"Let's finish talking about this later, okay?" said Shiloh, and I nodded.

"We're done, but you're absolutely eating breakfast before you go anywhere near the water," I announced as I emerged from the bathroom.

"Thanks a lot, Charlotte," muttered Isa.

"What did *I* do?" she growled back.

"You need to *eat* so your *blood sugar's* okay before we can go have fun," Isa said, rolling her eyes.

"Isabel Milagros, I hear one more comment like that from you and you've lost your phone until October," snapped Shiloh.

Neither of us raised our voices at the girls very often, but honestly? Isa had deserved it.

"You think Charlotte chose to get diabetes?" I said to her. "Or that this is fun for her or any of us?"

"Thanks for reminding me that I ruin everything, Mom," said Charlotte before opening the glass double doors and walking out onto the patio.

I felt like someone had just tied a cement block around my waist and tossed me overboard. My mother would never have phrased it like that—and come to think of it, my father wouldn't have, either. So if my daughters were fed up with me, I couldn't blame them.

I was, too.

~

After a terse breakfast we headed to the beach. Even at nine in the morning it was already blazing hot, but the sun was hidden by a cluster of ominous-looking clouds, with more rolling in by the minute. "Think that'll pass by the time we're on the ferry?" I asked Shiloh.

He grimaced. "I'm guessing now's not the best time to tell you there's a tropical storm watch in effect."

"Since when?" I said with alarm. As a pilot, he had access to weather data that put the app on my phone to shame, so I barely bothered checking it myself.

"This morning, apparently—last night they were just predicting showers."

"But a watch isn't the same as a warning, right?" After the argument I'd had with the girls that morning, I really—really—needed to get to Vieques so we could hit reset on this vacation. "Do you think we should be worried?"

He shrugged. "Watch, warning: none of it is great. I mean, there were half a dozen storm warnings every hurricane season when I was growing up, but I can only think of a single one that ever actually materialized into something truly dangerous. Since Hurricane Maria, though, I worry more than I used to. The weather patterns are more severe than they've ever been, and it's only getting worse. You saw the shoreline." He gestured to our right, where an entire stretch of beach we'd loved had disappeared into the ocean.

"I hate to even suggest it, but do you think we should stay in San Juan instead of going to Vieques?" I asked, crossing my fingers that he wouldn't say yes.

"I'm not sure," he said, his eyes following Isa and Charlotte. "I think we check the weather again before we head to Fajardo and make the best decision we can at that point."

The horizon was a deep gray. I had a sinking feeling in my gut, but I reminded myself that the same feeling had told me my cancer was back. Maybe I was wrong about this, too. "I bet it'll pass," I said.

And to my surprise, it did. Within the next hour the sky had cleared and the storm seemed to be petering out, so we decided to proceed as planned.

I'd vetoed flying; after our near crash on our first trip to Vieques, the ferry seemed like a far safer option. Except maybe it wasn't, because as our boat began to cruise away from the marina in Fajardo, the waves grew higher and higher. One after another, the waves slapped against our ferry, which was bouncing with such vigor that I was certain we were catching air. Normally, I wasn't afraid of the water. But right before I'd gotten up that morning I'd had a dream about Charlotte. She'd been drifting away from me on a life raft, and I'd stood on the shore, paralyzed and unable to swim to her. I'd awoken coated in sweat, my heart pulsing with panic.

"You okay?" Shiloh whispered beside me.

"Yes," I quickly replied, pushing away the image of my daughter desperately waving for me even as she went farther out to sea. But it was probably just leftover anxiety from her hypoglycemic incident playing tricks on my mind. "I didn't sleep great," I added. "It's making this feel worse than it is."

"Worse?" said Isa, who'd been listening to our conversation. She clung to the arms of her seat as we hit another wave. "Not possible. This *is* the worst."

"It's okay," Shiloh assured her. "They wouldn't take us out if it wasn't safe."

"Really? Because if we don't die first I'm going to hurl, and I'll probably choke on my vomit and die anyway," said Isa. "Tell me how that's safe."

"Let's not joke," I said, glancing at Charlotte, who looked awfully green. "Did you check your blood sugar?" I asked quietly.

"Before we left," she said, and I was grateful that the edge I'd heard earlier was missing from her voice. "I feel fine, Mom. Just tell me when it's over."

"Soon," I promised. Through the window, frothy waves were cresting nearly as high as the ferry. But if we could all just hang in there a little bit longer, the ocean would calm and Vieques would appear before us like a glittering promised land. And then, finally, things would take a turn for the better.

TWELVE

"*This* is it?" said Isa, pressing her face to the window as the ferry approached the shore.

Through the glass, the dock was a bit more weathered than I remembered, and the overcast skies were making the marina look especially dingy. Yet the sight of the island's northern coast filled me with excitement. It was a good feeling, one I hadn't had since . . . well, roughly a minute before the last time I realized my husband wasn't going to be making love to me after all.

"Hold tight," I told Isa. "You're going to love it."

But as we shuffled to the back of the boat to collect our luggage, Charlotte whispered, "I thought you said Vieques was magical."

"Sweetheart, please don't be so quick to form an opinion based on the first thing you see," I said, resisting the urge to sigh as I glanced around. Vieques had been one of the last areas to receive aid after Hurricane Maria. Maybe that explained why the garbage cans at the marina were overflowing and the chain-link fence around the waiting area was in desperate need of replacing.

"I hope you're right, Mom," said Isa, trailing behind me. "Because this place? It's kind of a dump."

If they were trying to bleed my enthusiasm dry via a thousand tiny cuts, they were doing a bang-up job. "Please find something nice to say, and if you can't, bite your tongue. Look—chickens!" I pointed to the fence, where several hens pecked at the ground as their chicks swarmed behind them.

"You know they're chock full of salmonella, right?" said Isa.

Charlotte eyed them skeptically. "What about the horses?" she asked, referring to the couple thousand horses that roamed the island.

"We'll see them soon enough," said Shiloh, shooting me a look of solidarity. I smiled at him. The kids were just kids; maybe they wouldn't enjoy themselves, but he and I definitely would. "Happy to be here?" I asked.

He smiled back at me. "You know I am. You?"

"Never happier," I said, because although that wasn't technically true, I knew it wouldn't be long before it was.

After Maria hit, Shiloh and I had read the news reports and watched videos of the destruction in Vieques—hundred-year-old trees that had been completely uprooted, the promenade that had crumbled after being battered by record-breaking waves, entire neighborhoods flooded by water or worse, mud. Over time, those reports and videos—as well as Milagros' updates—assured us that the island was on the mend. Still, hearing that wasn't the same as seeing it for ourselves. After we picked up our Jeep from the rental agency and headed out, I nearly wept with relief as the countryside came into view. The rolling hills were lush and green again; the winding roads were paved and clear. The same pastel cinder-block homes dotted the landscape, and in the distance, the Atlantic met the Caribbean, forming a swath of bright blue beauty. It was almost exactly as I'd remembered it.

We'd just passed a schoolyard when Shiloh hit the brakes.

"What is it?" I said, but just then four horses emerged from the field to our left and began ambling across the road. There were two adults and two foals, all brown except for one of the mares, who was cream colored with a dark mark on her nose. The island was teeming with horses—some wild, others fed and groomed by locals who let them roam free. Though we'd seen dozens, if not hundreds, on previous visits, they never ceased to steal my breath.

The girls were quiet, too. I swiveled around, excited to see the wonder on their faces.

But there were no faces to see—just the top of their bent heads as they moved their thumbs with the frenetic energy of a couple of professional gamers (or, you know, twelve-year-olds).

On instinct, I snatched their phones out of their hands.

"Hey!" protested Isa, crossing her arms over her chest.

"That's *my* phone!" said Charlotte, glaring at me. "Give it back!"

"Oh, I'm going to give it to you, all right!" I hissed. I don't know what had come over me; it was like all of the negativity I'd been keeping bottled up was slithering right out of a tiny crack I'd forgotten to seal shut. "And when I'm done, you're going to be begging to have *my* phones back, because guess who pays for them? Now look. At. The. Gosh. Darn. *Horses.*"

I was staring right at them, but I'd forgotten how blinding rage can be; it took a few seconds for my eyes to inform my brain that my daughters were staring back at me like I was the ghost of Joan Crawford, waving a wire hanger at them.

Beside me, Shiloh looked nearly as shocked. And no wonder—one tiny disappointment and I'd instantly morphed into Momzilla. I needed to pull myself together before my daughters started making the kind of memories that they'd later parse with a mental health professional.

"I'm sorry," I said immediately. My father had always said that the faster you apologized, the faster you moved on. "I didn't mean to snap. It's already been a long day, and I just wanted you to pay attention and look at the horses."

But as I pointed out the window, the only horse left to look at was a foal's backside, disappearing into the wooded area on the other side of the road.

"We'll see more," Shiloh assured me, but before I could respond, raindrops started to ping the Jeep.

Behind me, Charlotte sighed deeply. "So much for the horses."

"And so much for the beach," muttered Isa.

"It'll pass," I said, trying to make up for having spewed acid all over everyone's mood. "Storms never last long in Puerto Rico."

But as we drove south to Milagros', the rain grew heavier and heavier until the windshield wipers could barely keep up. I wish I could say that's why we drove straight past Calle Rosa, the dirt road Milagros' house was off of. The truth was, we were looking for a picturesque dirt road with a handmade wooden sign—and it never appeared. It was only after we rerouted using our GPS that we realized the road had been coated with asphalt, and the cute sign was now a standard metal plaque. If he noticed it, Shiloh didn't say as much, so I decided not to share that I sure hoped it was the only thing that had gotten a charmless makeover.

I sighed with relief as we pulled into the driveway. We were finally here.

Milagros' house was still the same shade of pale pink, and her yard was dotted with the plastic flamingos that had been there on our last several visits. Except she wasn't waiting for us on the porch, as I guess I'd been expecting her to. In fact, only a rooster seemed to notice our arrival as the four of us clambered out of the Jeep and ran through the rain.

Shiloh knocked once, twice, and then a third time. I was just pulling out my phone to call her when a man appeared in the doorway.

He had deeply tanned skin and a gleaming white smile; if I had to guess, he couldn't have had more than five years on Shiloh. His guayabera was starched, and his slacks were pressed. He smelled of cologne. Milagros didn't have children, but maybe this was a nephew or some other relative who'd come in from the big island to visit.

"You must be Shiloh and Libby," he said in a booming voice. *"Mucho gusto."*

"Mucho gusto," said Shiloh, reaching out to shake his hand.

"I'm Hector."

"You're—" I stopped myself before I could say what I was thinking: *This* was Hector? He was too young and too good-looking, and . . . well, not what I'd envisioned when Milagros said she'd taken a lover.

Shiloh didn't blink an eye before he began chatting with Hector in Spanish. But where was Milagros?

Then I heard her yodel my name from inside the house and I smiled. A moment later, she appeared on the porch, whose broad awning was shielding us from the rain.

"Mija," she said, opening her arms to me.

"Milagros." All of my troubles evaporated as I inhaled her citrusy scent. Her arms were tight around me, and though I normally didn't like prolonged hugs from anyone other than my nuclear family, I could have stayed there all day. Milagros would know how to fix me, just like she had the last time I'd been here. In fact, based on the way my mood had lifted, she was already working on it.

As she let me go, I stepped back to examine her. My initial reaction was worry, because her legs, which were sticking out of the bottom of her yellow dress, were as thin as a small child's, and her face was more lined than it had been the last time I'd seen her. But as I looked at her pink cheeks and shining brown eyes, I realized she was glowing . . . the way people glow when they're in love.

Just for a moment, I had the most terrible, sinking feeling.

I was *jealous.*

Get a grip, Libby Ross-Velasquez, I commanded myself. Milagros had four decades on me, and after so many unsuccessful relationships, wasn't it wonderful that she'd found love and all the energy and enthusiasm that comes with it while she still had the chance?

Hector smiled at us, then said, "Milly, do you want me to get your glasses?"

"Hector, you know they don't make a difference. *Estoy ciega*," she said, batting a hand in his direction.

"Blind?" I said with alarm. I knew she'd been having vision problems, but she'd said she'd been taking eye drops that were helping. "Milagros, are you serious?"

"Legally, *sí*. It's just the glaucoma—I can see *un poco* right in the middle of things, but not on the sides." She laughed and looked up at Hector as he linked his arm through hers. "But I can still see what's important."

"Milly," said Hector, bending to kiss her.

"I'm sorry, Milagros," I said, glancing at Shiloh. If he was surprised by their May-December romance, he didn't show it; instead, he stood there like he didn't have a care in the world. *Good!* I thought. Vieques was working its magic on him, which meant it wouldn't be long before we embarked on the Libby and Shiloh reunion tour.

"Don't be sorry," she scoffed. "There are worse problems to have. *Y dónde está* Charlotte? And Isabel Milagros?" she said, smiling at her namesake.

The girls stepped forward. "Hi, Milagros," squeaked Charlotte.

"Hi," said Isa, standing there like a deer in headlights. I nearly leaned in to whisper for her to be warmer to the woman from whom she got her middle name. I knew she and Charlotte were too young to remember their visit to Vieques, but they'd heard me talk about Milagros for years, and they'd spoken with her on the phone many times. And though Shiloh and I had probably made a whole host of parenting mistakes, one thing we'd taught them was to hold their own during conversations with adults. Especially adults as important as Milagros.

But now they were staring at Milagros and Hector like they were dumbstruck. I was about to nudge them when Charlotte blurted, "You guys are in *love*?"

Milagros laughed and gazed at Hector adoringly before turning back to Charlotte. "*Sí, amiga.* It's the most wonderful thing in the world. Ask your parents—they fell in love right here," she said, gesturing toward the guesthouse. "Isn't that right, Libby?"

"That's right," I said, meeting Shiloh's eyes.

The rain had slowed, and he was standing at the edge of the porch, leaning against a dry section of stucco. Warmth spread through my body as he smiled at me. How silly of me to worry. *Of course* he was still attracted to me, just as I was to him. And if all went according to plan, we'd soon have an opportunity to act on that attraction, just like we had thirteen years earlier.

THIRTEEN

Milagros had told me that they'd updated the guesthouse, but I'd be lying if I said I wasn't gobsmacked when I walked inside and saw that the kitschy island decor had been replaced by myriad shades of gray. Gray sofas, gray walls, gray rugs—and for a little variation, a trio of white glass vases on the gray stone counter, which Charlotte and Isa would be sure to shatter at their earliest possible convenience. Didn't anything stay the same?

"*¿Qué te parece?*" asked Milagros, who had followed us inside. "Hector's been working on it. We just put posters up, and our rentals are almost back to what they were before Maria."

I couldn't bring myself to tell her that I felt like I'd just stepped into a rain cloud, so I glanced at Shiloh. "It looks great, Milly," he said, taking the hint. "And I'm glad business is booming."

"Me, too," I managed, because at least Hector'd had a solid financial motive for erasing all semblances of whimsy and personality. I shook my head; it wasn't my guesthouse, so what did I care? It was like I was turning into . . . *Paul*, I thought with a shudder. As much as I loved my brother, I had no interest in taking a page from his worst-case-scenario handbook.

"Libby? You okay?" said Shiloh.

"Great," I said. "Tired but thrilled to be here."

"We're happy you're here, too, *mija*," said Milagros. "I'll let you get settled, but you holler if you need anything, okay? Oh, and drinks are at six—rain or shine."

I smiled, because at least her old ritual remained. We'd spent many a happy hour on her patio, talking about love and life and making the most of the hands we'd been dealt. "We wouldn't miss it for the world," I assured her. "You sure you don't need me to help you back?"

Milagros, who'd already retrieved her umbrella and opened the door, turned to look in my direction. "*Gracias, pero no.* I know every step like my own face." She smiled broadly and said, "That's why I'm leaving this place in a body bag."

"Milly," I said, laughing nervously. "Don't even say that."

"No one makes it out of this life alive, *mija*," she called as she stepped outside. "Not saying that doesn't make it any less real."

Maybe not, but I still couldn't bear the thought of losing her—not so soon after my father.

After Milagros was gone, Charlotte threw herself down on an armchair. "This place is *so* small, Mom."

"It's not huge, but it's lovely." At least, it had been. Were it not for Milagros herself and the beach just outside our door, it could have been any rental in any town. *But how lucky you are to be here,* I reminded myself. *And you're not even paying for the privilege.*

"Just look at that view," I said, pointing through the large windows of the sunroom, where Isa and Charlotte would be sleeping on a pull-out sofa.

"I'm not going anywhere near 'that view,'" said Isa, using air quotes. The water on the south side of the island was no less choppy than the north side had been, and the sky was almost as dark as if it were sundown. She scrunched up her nose. "I wish we were still at the hotel, so we could go use the pool. Jellyfish don't do chlorine."

I would have scolded them for complaining if I hadn't been partially to blame. There was no way that my little meltdown in the car hadn't left a dent in their mood.

"Please find something—anything—to like, okay?" called Shiloh, who'd just opened the side door that let out onto the patio. He glanced over his shoulder at me. "The patio's wet, but the outdoor shower's still here."

"Oh yeah?" I said, smiling at him. "How soon do you think we can use it?"

"Not anytime soon, unfortunately," he said, pulling the door closed. "The storm's picking up and they're predicting more of the same for the next few days."

"It could change, though."

"Definitely," he said, finally smiling back at me. "And if it does rain, we'll just have to find ways to stay busy."

This was a welcome one-eighty. "Want to go nap before we head to Milagros' for drinks?"

He tilted his head. "You know, I'm suddenly bone tired."

My stomach did a little jump. "Girls," I called, following Shiloh as he headed for the other room, "your father and I are going to lie down for an hour. Find something to do that doesn't involve trying to murder each other."

The bedroom had been subjected to the same monochromatic makeover as the rest of the place, but Hector hadn't replaced the old rattan bed frame. This struck me as a good omen, as it was where Shiloh and I had conducted the first of many chemistry experiments. I lay across the mattress, watching him undress on the other side of the room. "You remember that night after the bay?" I asked. Vieques' bioluminescent bay was one of only a few in the world; Shiloh had taken me to it thirteen years earlier so I could see the water, which was filled with tiny organisms that lit up when they were disturbed. It was the first time after my diagnosis that I'd felt truly hopeful about my future—and not coincidentally, it was also the night I'd realized just how strong my feelings were for him.

"Of course." He tugged his T-shirt over his head and discarded it on the dresser. "Like it was just yesterday."

"Me, too. Do you remember what you were thinking?"

He grinned at me. "If I had a thought in my head, I couldn't have identified it. Well, other than maybe that it was totally unexpected."

"Unexpected! You left Milagros' but then came back to kiss me! You knew exactly what you were doing."

He held my gaze, and all my worries disappeared. How ridiculous, how shortsighted, how very pessimistic of me to think that after thirteen years he'd suddenly lost interest. "I knew I wanted you," he said in a gruff voice.

I was trembling with anticipation, and sweet mother of pearl, was it ever a wonderful feeling. It was almost as though someone had turned back the clock, and I was falling for him all over again. "I wanted you, too," I said. "I may have told myself otherwise, but I did."

"Hellooooo!" Isa sounded so close I wouldn't have been surprised if she emerged from beneath the bed. "I thought you guys were sleeping!"

I giggled and held a finger to my lips. "Shhh, don't disturb the children."

Shiloh was not amused. "Did you lock the door?"

"It doesn't have a lock, but I put a suitcase in front of it."

"Better than nothing. Still, I wonder if we should have looked for a larger place."

No, no, no. We were not debating our lodging choices right now; we were preparing to throw ourselves at each other with the wanton abandon of two carnal creatures who had no recollection of the petulant tweens they were responsible for keeping alive. "We're here now," I said, beckoning for him to join me on the bed. "Let's enjoy ourselves."

"You're right," he said, lowering himself over me. He kissed me softly, and then not so softly. I would have swooned if I'd not already been horizontal, which was a sure sign I'd been more starved for affection than I'd realized. Here was my husband, with his beautiful body and full attention and wonderful smell, which wasn't really a smell at all, just his natural pheromone cologne that drove me absolutely crazy. And he was going to finally—dear God, *finally*—make love to me.

"I've missed you," I murmured as his lips made their way down my neck.

"I haven't gone anywhere," he said from my collarbone.

"You know what I mean," I said softly, trying to reroute him.

He looked up. "Things have been kind of stressful lately."

Sure, but was this the time and place to rehash that? "I was just trying to let you know that I've been looking forward to this," I said.

"Me, too," he mumbled, or at least I think that's what he said; his mouth was blessedly on my skin again. I didn't respond, because I don't know what sound would've escaped if I'd tried.

Then he said, "Like this?"

Had it really been so long that he'd forgotten what did the trick? I was about to say yes when something in the living room came crashing down. Many things, I should say; rather than the three vases I'd been worried about earlier, it sounded like someone had just thrown a basket of toys across the room.

I froze and held my breath, praying that the silence that followed the crash would last. Alas—Charlotte had already started howling like a hound on a hunt.

Still, she wasn't calling for me, or for Shiloh. And if whatever had happened was really serious, Isa would have been pounding on our door. Which meant we could go back to what we'd been doing.

But Shiloh, who had just sat up, sighed wearily.

"They're fine!" I said as he rose from the bed. My desire was very quickly being replaced by desperation. I wanted—no, I *needed*—to know that he still wanted me, that we still wanted each other, that the rest of the world, including our daughters, could cease to exist for just two stinking minutes. Because I was more than willing to have a quickie if that's what it took to break the seal. "No one's hollering for us."

"I'm not going out there," he said, which was when I realized he'd actually been heading for the dresser, not the door. He pulled his shirt back over his head and sat on the end of the bed.

I felt as crushed as though he'd just pointed out the dimples on my thighs. "I don't understand," I said to his back.

He didn't turn around. "It's just distracting, with the girls being right there and wide awake."

I could remember when he and I had made love on the floor in the middle of the twins' nursery while they babbled beside us in a crib. And what about the time we'd sneaked off to the bathroom for a spirited make-out session in the middle of their tenth birthday party? Distractions were no match for our passion.

Or so I'd thought.

He glanced over at me quickly and said, "We can try again tonight when they're sleeping."

"I don't want to get my hopes up," I said, but the humor I'd been shooting for landed with a thud between us.

"Libby."

As I pulled the sheet up to my neck, I felt as vulnerable as if I'd just had my mammogram broadcast on network television. "Since you're dressed, would you please go see what happened out there?" I said in a low voice.

His expression told me he wanted to say something but couldn't manage to dislodge the words.

Good, I thought. Because I was tired of excuses and explanations when the facts were all there in front of me. My husband had lost interest in me. I had lost sight of the woman I used to be.

There was no way those two things weren't related.

FOURTEEN

"Libby! Libby, wait!"

I'd just reached the beach when Shiloh came running out of the guesthouse after me. Though he'd said he wasn't going to check on Charlotte, my sullen silence must have changed his mind because he excused himself moments later. I'd quickly gotten dressed, and after overhearing that Charlotte had been howling because she'd stepped on one of the board-game pieces that had tumbled out of a cupboard, I slipped out the side door.

"You're upset," he said when he reached me.

The sun had reemerged, and the pale sand was already hot beneath my bare feet. "I'm fine," I told him, shifting from one foot to the other. "I just wanted to call Paul before we met Milagros and Hector for drinks."

"You'll talk to your brother but not to me?" he said, frowning.

"I promised him I'd let him know we got here safely," I said, but it sounded lame. I sighed and tried again. "Listen, I just need to cool off, okay? I don't think there's even anything to talk about. We tried to sleep together, but the girls were too distracting. End of story." I shrugged.

Shiloh was staring at me, but I couldn't tell if he was angry, upset, or grappling with some other emotion I wasn't picking up on. "Given how touch and go things have been with Charlotte's health, I was a little surprised you didn't want to stop and find out what had happened," he finally said.

For once, that hadn't occurred to me. "Call it mother's intuition, but I had a feeling she was okay. Her blood sugar doesn't usually make her scream like she's just seen a little green man."

He lifted a hand to his forehead to shade his eyes from the sun. "Okay, but I wish you wouldn't read into what happened. It didn't mean anything."

Right, because I'd never heard that one before.

"We can try again tonight," he added.

"How do you know I'm reading into anything? And if it's all the same to you, I don't want to make a plan for tonight, or any other night." This was starting to feel like a fight, so I tried to soften my tone. "You already told me you felt pressured. I don't want to add to that."

"Hey," he said, frowning. "That's not what I meant."

Was there another meaning for *pressured* that I was unaware of? "Listen, I know this has a lot to do with me." Possibly everything to do with me, not that I said that. "I've been kind of off lately. I'm trying to get my head on straight instead, so we can all move forward." I sighed, thinking about how I'd erupted in the car earlier. The last thing I wanted was for that to happen again. "Do you mind holding down the fort for just a few?"

His shoulders lifted, then sank as he sighed. "Sure."

"Thank you." Even though I knew it would look as disingenuous as it felt, I smiled anyway because it was better than bursting into tears. We'd spent more than a decade side by side, raising our daughters and building a life. Why did it feel like there was a chasm between us that was growing wider when it should have been closing? "I love you," I added.

"I love you, too," he said.

I could feel him watching me walk to the ocean and down the beach, but I didn't turn around. Instead, I pulled my phone out of the pocket of my shorts and hit Paul's number. I expected it to go to voicemail, but he picked up right away. "You rang?"

"I know you're probably in the middle of something—"

"While you may not be vying for Mary Kay marketer of the year, you might want to work on your sales pitch."

The laugh I attempted got stuck in my throat. I swallowed hard and said, "Do you have a minute?"

"For you, dear sis, I have all the minutes. How's Vieques?"

"Great," I said, but I had to take a second before continuing. "So far we haven't seen as much hurricane damage as we did in San Juan. And it's really good to see Milagros."

"So why do you sound like you're about to go in for a root canal without anesthesia?"

I sighed even as I could feel the tears rising from deep within me. "You know I hate it when you poke around in my thoughts without permission."

"I'm not the one who called to chat."

"Your point. It's just . . . when you said you and Charlie coasted, what did you mean?"

"Ruh-roh!"

"*Paul*," I warned.

"Oh Libby, you know I can't digest hard conversations if I don't season them with a little humor. Now as to your question: I meant that neither of us did anything different for a long time, and then one day we looked up and realized we'd faded into the wallpaper."

"What do you mean?"

"Like, we became the background of each other's lives, you know? We liked the way it looked, but it wasn't particularly functional or important. Our therapist told us we should start dating each other, which sounded absolutely ridiculous to me at the time because—*hello!* You try being all romantic and spontaneous with two teenaged sons. But now I wonder if maybe that was better advice than I thought."

"And yet you're not asking Charlie on any dates, are you?"

"Too late for that now."

"Is it, though?" I said, but at least I'd turned off my tears.

"Hey, lady, we're supposed to be talking about you, not me. Are you worried about you and Shiloh coasting?"

I looked out at the ocean, wishing I could dive in, but the waves were too high and choppy for anything other than wading in the shallow surf. It took me a moment to respond. "A little bit, yeah," I finally said.

"What's going on? The last time I saw you guys, you seemed like your usual lovebird selves."

Had we? When I thought back to our last dinner together, all I could picture was how Paul and Charlie had been interacting. In fact, I barely remembered anything about what Shiloh and I were doing that night.

"I seem to recall saying almost that exact thing to you."

"I'll allow it."

"He . . ." I wrinkled my nose. "He just doesn't seem that into me anymore."

"Are we talking about carnally?" asked Paul in a gentle tone.

"Yes," I whispered.

"I see. And have you mentioned this to him?"

"Sort of? He said that it didn't mean anything, and that he felt pressured the second time we tried."

"Ahh, ye olde sexual pressure. I bet you a Benjamin that it has nothing to do with you."

"How can you say that?" I said, thinking about how weird I'd been feeling lately. "I was the one trying to—you know."

"I do know, and let's just say I have experience in this realm."

"You and Charlie?" I said with surprise.

"At the end, yes."

"That's not reassuring, Paul."

"You're not us, and we're not you. You can still fix this."

"How? Every time I've tried, I've made things worse."

I could hear him sigh through the phone. "I'm not sure, actually, but being in Puerto Rico is probably a good start."

"I thought you knew everything," I joked, though the truth was, I was a bit disappointed he didn't have an answer at the ready.

"I am indeed a pantomath."

"Panto-who?"

"Pantomath," he repeated. "That's someone who wants to know everything and mostly does. So, thank you for the compliment."

"You're incorrigible," I said, looking out at the ocean. "All the same, I wish you were here."

"I do, too."

"You could come, you know," I said suddenly. "I know you can afford it, and we'll be here for another five days."

"Honestly, getting out of this asphalt jungle sounds amazing, but the boys are doing an SAT test prep course for the next few weeks, and Charlie is going to Fire Island to stay with a friend."

"A *friend*? That sounds less like coasting and more like riding a tsunami."

"Moving right along! I wish we could join you guys, but the timing is rotten."

"We *are* going to discuss this," I warned, trying not to get upset. Here I'd been blaming Paul, but if Charlie was seeing other men . . . well, they were in even worse shape than I'd allowed myself to admit.

"And we will—later. For now, go put on your sexiest sarong and do your best to be adventurous. A little adrenaline is often just the thing to kick-start passion."

"I think it works a little differently for women," I said.

"As loath as I am to discuss this particular aspect of your health and well-being any further, do recall that we're not targeting your libido."

"Right," I said. What I didn't say was that I suspected Shiloh's waning sex drive was probably a direct reaction to me—*not* a lack of adrenaline.

The clouds that had looked miles away were suddenly cloaking the sun again. I'd intended to walk a little longer, but with the sky looking ominous I turned to start back toward the guesthouse. "I'd better get going," I told Paul. "Thanks for talking me down."

"Anytime. Hang in there."

"I will," I said, because at least I felt better than I had before I called. "Love you."

"Love you more and no take backs." And then, because this had always been our game—to try to get the last word—he hung up.

When I returned to the guesthouse, Shiloh was helping the girls pick up the board games. He looked up and shot me a closed-lip smile, probably for the girls' benefit, but I managed to smile back at him. "Almost ready for drinks?" I said cheerfully.

"Yes," he said, looking at me quizzically. "You're feeling better?"

"I am!" I wasn't, actually, but the more I thought about it, the more convinced I was that the only thing to do was throw everything at our marriage and see what stuck. I would try adventure and adrenaline, per Paul's advice, because it couldn't hurt. But I was also going to double down on relocating the real me—the one I'd found thirteen years earlier on this very island. Because that was the woman Shiloh fell in love with.

~

It had begun to drizzle when we headed to Milagros' for drinks, so instead of meeting on the patio, Hector ushered us into the house. I steeled myself for more of his signature achromatic style but was relieved to see that little about Milagros' home had changed. There were the same paintings of fruit trees and the Puerto Rican countryside on her pale peach walls; here was a familiar basket full of orchids swinging over the kitchen sink. And there was Milagros, sprawled on one of the two weathered velour sofas she and I had spent many an afternoon gabbing on back when Shiloh was still just my vacation fling. It felt like coming home.

"*Bienvenidos!*" she said, rising. "Let me get you a drink!"

"Please, sit. We can do it," I told her.

"You're my guest, Libby. Let me. And don't worry about my eyes!" she squawked, already reaching for the pitcher on the coffee table.

"Milagros, *amor*, let me," said Hector, gazing adoringly at her.

I couldn't help it; seeing Hector look at Milagros like she was the best thing that ever happened to him made me glance at Shiloh, who was on a chair across from the sofa, saying something to Isa. The last time I could remember him looking at me like that had been at Rupi's wedding the summer before. She and her husband, Trevor, had just kissed and were strutting down the aisle as newlyweds. It was one of those moments when everything up ahead seems to be brimming with promise, and Shiloh had kissed the back of my neck softly before meeting my eyes. "I love you even more than the day we married," he'd whispered, sending goose bumps dancing up my arms. That night, we'd made love like a couple of teenagers, and I remembered thinking that although we were heading into the autumn of our lives, maybe we were in the midst of a sexual spring.

If only I'd known it was more like a short-lived heat wave that would be followed by an arctic blast.

"Okay, *amor*," said Milagros, beaming at Hector. "As you like it. I'm going to go get something from the kitchen."

"So how did you and Milagros meet?" I asked as Hector handed me a glass of something bright red and, from the smell of it, highly flammable.

His smile was dreamy. "I've known Milagros since I was a kid. But I moved away after high school, and then worked in Florida for a long time. A little over a year ago, I came back to Vieques with my wife—well, ex-wife now," he said, somewhat sheepishly. "We'd only come to check on her parents, but we'd ended up buying a home and staying. But our marriage was already falling apart—running into Milagros again on the island only made that even clearer to me. To make a long story short, we separated and now here I am," he said, gesturing to the house. He grinned at me and Shiloh. "How about you two?"

"We met in Vieques, actually," said Shiloh.

"Technically, we met in San Juan," I said. "He was flying the plane I took from there to here."

I'd expected Shiloh to chime in with more details, but he just nodded. I was about to fill in for him when Milagros appeared, carrying two glasses teeming with electric-pink liquid.

"Mocktails!" she announced, shuffling across the tile toward Isa and Charlotte, both of whom looked bored but at least had the good sense not to say as much. *"Sin rum."*

"That's so kind of you, but they'll have to pass," I said. "Charlotte can't have sugared drinks." I glanced at Isa. "And in the interest of fairness, it's best if Isa doesn't, either."

"I can so—I just need to adjust my insulin," said Charlotte. She'd been examining the framed photos Milagros had displayed on her tiered television stand. I sent photos every Christmas, so we were in several of them, but seeing them now made me realize that holiday cards were a lousy substitute for time together. I would have to talk to Shiloh about how we could afford to make this summer trip an annual event. After all, he'd said he felt more like himself here. And I had to believe that soon I would, too.

"We've talked about this. Remember how shaky you were after LaToya's?" I said, referring to the time she'd decided to sneak a jumbo-sized soda.

"I know how to manage my blood sugar now," she said, throwing herself down on the end of one of Milagros' two sofas.

"So what happened after dinner the other night?" said Isa.

Charlotte swiveled and gave her a look that could have sunburned Satan.

"Don't blame me for your broken pancreas," Isa volleyed back.

If she weren't being so childish, I would have commended her for correctly identifying the root cause of Charlotte's condition. "Isa, please," I said, hoping to nip their bickering in the bud before it got worse. I glanced at Shiloh, who shook his head in frustration.

"Try to be more compassionate, okay?" he said.

"This is me being compassionate," she retorted. "Otherwise, I would have said that I'm tired of the world revolving around Charlotte. Or at least my food revolving around her. Stop lumping me in the same category as her, Mom. I'm sick of it."

"You guys," said Shiloh wearily. "Knock it off."

At this rate, we were going to need a vacation to recover from our vacation. I glanced back and forth between the three of them, silently pleading for everyone to act normal. We had so little time to spend with Milagros; I didn't want her and Hector, who'd been watching us from the sofa, seeing us at our very worst.

"Charlotte!" said Milagros. I hadn't realized she'd disappeared again until she reappeared in the doorway, holding two more glasses. "I'm sorry that I forgot you have to be extra careful about what you drink. Do you want to try this? It's sparkling water with just a tiny splash of sugar-free lemonade. No sugar."

I braced myself for Charlotte to say something else that would embarrass me, but she reached for the glass Milagros was holding out to her. "Thank you," she mumbled. She took a sip and looked up at Milagros. "This is really good."

"*Bueno*! I'll make it anytime you want, so don't be afraid to ask. Now Isa," said Milagros, sitting beside her on the other sofa. "I made you one, too, but that doesn't mean you have to have it. Would you like the first one with sugar, provided that's okay with your parents?"

"Oh," said Isa softly. "No, I'll try the one Charlotte's having."

"I was hoping you'd say that, because it's *delicioso*. But if you change your mind, you tell Milly, okay?"

"Thanks, Milagros," said Isa, smiling shyly at her.

"Yes, thank you," I said. I wasn't sure how she'd just sucked the tension right out of the air, but the girls were contentedly sipping their drinks, and Shiloh had begun chatting with Hector in Spanish. Maybe Milagros could give me a few pointers later on.

"No need to thank me!" she protested. "Now, *niñas*," she said to Charlotte and Isa, "it's been years since I've seen you. Tell me everything."

FIFTEEN

"Morning, sleepyhead." Shiloh was standing next to the bed with a small ceramic mug of espresso. Birds were chirping just outside our window, and sun had begun to spill through the gaps in the wood blinds.

"I'm still dreaming, right?" I murmured as I pushed myself into a sitting position and accepted the mug from him. It had been years since I'd woken up on my own, without an alarm, and had my husband present me with fresh coffee before I'd even thrown the covers off. "Leave me here."

"Not dreaming," he said with a smile. His hair was wet, and he smelled ever so faintly like soap, which told me he'd just gotten out of the shower. "Happy cancerversary. How do you feel?"

"Good," I said, because it was true for a change. The rest of the night before had been blessedly uneventful; to my relief and delight the girls had talked Milagros' ear off over drinks; then the six of us had gone out to a nearby restaurant for dinner, during which no one had stared at the television (because there hadn't been one, but all the same). I'd been so tired—and yes, relieved that the day had gone well—when we finally crawled between the sheets that I'd immediately fallen asleep, negating any worries about whether Shiloh would attempt to be amorous.

But even more than my relief over finally having a calm and uneventful evening, I was happy because today was *the day*: exactly ten years earlier, Dr. Malone's predecessor had informed me that the war being waged inside of me had been won.

"Thank you for remembering," I said, smiling back at him.

"No need to thank me," he said, touching my arm gently. "Do you remember the doctor's office?"

Of course I did—we'd jumped up and down, crying and kissing like we'd just won the jackpot (which I supposed we had). On the ride from Manhattan to New Jersey, where we lived at the time, we couldn't keep our hands off each other; as soon as we paid the sitter and made sure the girls were still napping, we'd stripped down in the middle of the living room and gone at it in a way that still made me blush, even all these years later. That time, I hadn't had to tell myself to feel alive or be grateful. I just *was*.

"That was one of the best days of my life," I told Shiloh.

"Mine, too. But let's make today rival it. I know we have the bay trip planned for tonight, but what else do you want to do?"

"Oh, gosh," I said, because I hadn't actually put much thought into it. "How about the black-sand beach if the weather's good, and maybe lunch at El Chinchorro?" I said, referring to our favorite restaurant in Vieques.

"Sounds perfect," he said, bending to kiss me softly.

My mouth felt like it had been stuffed with cotton, and my eyes were still hazy with sleep; my hair, no doubt, was sticking up in every which direction. But I forgot about all that as Shiloh's lips met mine.

"I love you," I murmured.

"I love you, too," he said. "So—"

"I was here first!"

"But I *really* have to go!"

The girls were on the other side of our door, bickering about who was going to use the bathroom.

"I'll take care of it," Shiloh said before I could spring out of bed. "Relax, go for a walk if you want. Today is for you."

"Thank you," I said again, feeling awash with appreciation. Who cared if we weren't having sex? Okay—I did. But he was being so loving and thoughtful that it seemed to me I'd gotten it all wrong. We weren't unraveling. We'd just needed a break. *I'd* needed a break. And now that I was getting one, our family was finally starting to gel again.

I threw some clothes on and slipped out the door before Isa or Charlotte could spot me and make me play judge in the ongoing trial that was their relationship. Instead of heading to the beach, though, I hoisted myself into the hammock strung between a pair of palm trees. The breeze was strong, and I could hear the waves slapping against the shore. Above me, a couple of blackbirds were twittering back and forth, and I'd just been wondering if they, like my daughters, were bickering but in a better-sounding language, when I suddenly remembered something I must have pushed into the distant corners of my memory.

All these years, I'd only ever focused on my initial response to being declared cancer free—especially since the oncologist I'd initially seen had predicted I'd have six months, if that, to live. But now it occurred to me that my euphoria had actually worn off pretty quickly after getting an all clear. In fact, after the heady rush of those first few days, I'd spent the next couple of months feeling . . . not unlike I'd been feeling lately, actually.

Underwhelmed. Anxious. And so very, very tired.

At the time, I'd been able to chalk it up to having two very active toddlers and a new business to tend to. Moreover, I was sapped from undergoing treatment on and off for nearly two years. But in retrospect, it cut deeper than that. Surviving is inherently performative; not only do people want to see how you'll react to this wonderful thing that's just happened to you, they want to be a part of your good luck—enhance it, even, by reminding you that it could have turned out oh so differently.

I could barely buy toilet paper without bumping into an acquaintance who felt the need to inquire about my health—and before I'd even managed to complete a sentence, proceed to tell me (insert sad face here) how their cousin's best friend's ex-girlfriend had recently had a recurrence or was in "a better place"—never mind that if this alleged place was so much better, they themselves would dispense with seat belts and health insurance.

I know how great I have it, I wanted to interrupt. *Please don't remind me that it could all go away in a second.* I learned that earlier than any person should ever have to.

But they were hurting, too, so I smiled and wished their loved ones well . . . and walked away feeling like a little more of my hope had just been stolen from me.

Still, it wasn't long before my blues gave way to blue skies and my old sunny outlook. And though I had seen a social worker a few times, I hadn't done much of anything other than to just keep reminding myself of who I was—a mother, a wife, a survivor.

An optimist, just like my mother before me.

The hammock rocked gently as I stared at the sky, which was framed by palm trees. For a second, but only a second, I wondered what I would do if reminding myself wasn't enough.

∼

Just knowing that things would eventually be all right made everything feel more that way. And apparently my newfound lightness was contagious, because the girls got into their bathing suits and cover-ups without being asked or raising their voices at each other, while Shiloh whistled as he loaded a backpack with snacks and supplies.

"Should we tell them what today is?" Shiloh whispered after we parked the Jeep near the trailhead leading to the beach.

"Later," I said, because I was anxious to preserve the morning's good vibe. "I want to tell them but feel like that's a longer discussion. Right now, let's just have fun."

A frown flitted across his face so quickly I wasn't sure I hadn't imagined it. "Okay," he said. "Maybe at lunch."

"Perfect," I agreed. The girls had already begun down the trail, and their heads were bent in conversation. The fact that they still weren't fighting confirmed my decision to wait. "Let's get going."

The half-mile trail to the beach was steep and muddy; some sections were so flooded that we had to step into the thick brush along the side of the trail. We'd managed to make it about two-thirds of the way down when I miscalculated and stepped into a giant puddle. I yanked my leg up, but my foot wouldn't move. I pulled again, even harder this time, but it was no use.

"Ugh, Mom, I'm beginning to think you're cursed," said Isa, but she was looking at Charlotte. They did this sometimes—had an entire conversation with a single glance. I knew what they were up to because Paul and I had been doing the same thing all our lives. I was willing to bet whatever they were saying had something to do with their mother being a master at manifesting disaster.

"Your vote of confidence is much appreciated," I said to Isa. "And no, I don't need help, but thanks so much for asking."

"Libs?" said Shiloh, who'd stopped beside me. "You okay?"

"Peachy," I said, like I wasn't slowly being swallowed by a flesh-eating puddle. I tried again, and when my foot still wouldn't budge, I said, "Actually, can you give me a hand?"

"Of course," he said, looping his arm through mine. As he tugged gently, the earth finally let go of me.

"Mary and Joseph," I muttered. Because the top of my foot felt like it had just been skewered like a shish kebab and stuck on a flaming grill.

"You're hurt," said Shiloh, which was when I realized I was grimacing.

I quickly fixed my face. "Only a little," I told him, but there was a lump between two of my toes that was growing from a pea to a grape to a genetically engineered cherry tomato before my very eyes.

He whistled. "That doesn't look great, cutie. Think you broke something?"

As I stepped gingerly on a less muddy part of the trail, pain shot from between my toes straight up my ankle. "Just pulled a tendon," I said through gritted teeth. "Or maybe broke a blood vessel."

His forehead was etched with concern. "We can head back."

"No," I said quickly. Things had *just* started getting better. There was no way that I was going to let a little tiny thing like childbirth-esque pain ruin our adventure. "I'll be fine," I said, trying not to visibly limp as I started on the path again.

"Listen, we really can come back another time. It's not a big deal," he said, giving me a sympathetic smile.

"Another day won't be my cancerversary," I said in a low voice, because I knew that was the one thing that would put an end to the discussion. I took another step to show him I meant it. "Let's go see this mystical beach."

The beach was set behind a red, rocky bluff, and the dense sand, which stretched for at least half a mile to our right, was the color of charcoal. It was beautiful to the point of being almost otherworldly.

The girls had been up ahead of me and Shiloh, and now they were running in the surf, squealing with glee. Tears sprang to my eyes, and not because of my foot. Maybe all this time, I hadn't been looking for my own happiness at all, but for my daughters'. No wonder I'd been struggling so much—I'd been thinking about myself instead of what was most important.

"They love it," I said to Shiloh. "Aren't you glad we didn't head back?"

He laughed. "You're incredibly stubborn sometimes."

"You're welcome," I quipped.

Most of Vieques' beaches were speckled with pastel shells, but this one was dotted with tiny rocks. Shiloh squatted to examine a clay-colored stone. "You know, I haven't been here since I was young," he said, chucking the stone into the ocean.

"You're still young," I said, looking at his muscled back. "Or at least, you're young-passing."

"Thanks, I think?" he said with a laugh. He stood and put his arms around me. "So what does young-passing get me?"

I laughed with surprise. "Who wants to know?"

"Your husband," he said in a saucy voice.

Just for a second I had a pang, because it had occurred to me that if we were actually younger and here without children, we might have ducked into a secluded area along the path and acted on our more primal urges. But a moment of spontaneous connection was nothing to scoff at, I reminded myself.

Then his shorts started to vibrate.

"Leave it," I murmured, pulling him closer.

"If I leave it, it's going to keep buzzing," he said, already reaching into his pocket.

The screen was lit up, but he silenced the call before I could see whose name was on the display, then switched his setting to "Do Not Disturb." He tried to smile again as he slipped the phone back into his pocket, but it was as authentic as a Rolex someone was selling out of their trench coat.

"Who was that?" I asked.

"No one," he said. "Don't worry about it."

I immediately began rationalizing. He had his arms around me again, and we weren't in the habit of keeping secrets from each other. Maybe he had a surprise planned. After all, it was my cancerversary!

But it was too late; my buoyant bubble had already burst. Paul had probably told Charlie all those text messages he'd gotten were from no one, too. I felt queasy. I'd never once worried about Shiloh cheating on me—he was as loyal as they came. But as Paul had reminded me, people did change.

And sometimes their partners were the reason.

Before I could press him further, he let me go and shielded his eyes with his hands. "Hey, I don't see the girls anymore. I think I should go try to catch up with them before they get too far."

"Sure," I said. My voice warbled ever so slightly, but he didn't seem to notice.

"Should be back in five—hold tight," he said, pecking me on the lips.

"Will do," I said. Now my foot wasn't the only thing aching as I watched him jog down the beach.

So much for turning things around.

SIXTEEN

When Shiloh returned with the girls a short while later, he acted as though nothing was amiss. In fact, he was so casual as he took photos of Charlotte and Isa building a sandcastle that I almost convinced myself I'd imagined the whole thing.

Almost.

I was still trying to come up with plausible explanations for his secrecy when tiny bugs began jumping from the sand onto our feet and ankles. One minute the girls were digging a moat; the next, Isa was jumping into it and screaming bloody murder while Charlotte ran in circles slapping at her skin.

Shiloh, who was already scratching his calf, glanced up at me. "And . . . scene."

"I'm ready," I said. The beach was beautiful, but between Shiloh's phone call and my throbbing foot, which was now a bunch of bugs' lunches, I was ready to get out of there. Anyway, the girls were already running toward the trailhead.

The trail was steep, and it hurt to climb it, which made it difficult to hold a conversation. "You okay?" Shiloh kept asking me.

I had half a mind to yell back, "What do you think?" But yesterday's Momzilla moment was still fresh in my mind, so I told him I was hanging in there—because after all, wasn't I?

"Lunch will be good," he said as we piled into the Jeep. "We ready for some food?" he called over his shoulder to the girls.

"Always," said Isa.

"I don't really care," said Charlotte.

"You have your kit, right?" I said to her.

She held up her nylon bag. "In here, Mom. Stop worrying so much."

Right—because the only thing I'd been waiting for was her permission to relax about the chronic health condition that had nearly killed her the other day. "Thanks for being on top of it, honey," I said pleasantly, stealing a glance at Shiloh. He still looked calm, which was somewhat reassuring. But a few minutes later, his expression clouded over.

"You've got to be kidding me," he muttered as we pulled up to the restaurant, or what was left of it.

The place had never had an official name, so the locals referred to it as *El Chinchorro*—The Shack. That was part of the charm; it was slapped on the edge of a hilly side road, and you had to know someone who knew about it, or just stumble across it, as Shiloh had years before we met. The food was so-so, truth be told, but the dining area was open air and surrounded by lush vegetation. Twinkle lights were strung over booths and tables, and the bottles lining the oval tiki bar were lit up like jewels. Shiloh and I had our first date here and had returned several times afterward. It was one of the spots I'd been most excited to revisit on our trip.

But now the roof was caved in, and vines had roped their way around the bar; the turquoise paint was peeling off the sideboards of the facade.

I tried hard not to let my face reveal my disappointment. "You think this is from Maria?" I asked after I'd gotten out of the Jeep.

"No doubt," said Shiloh, surveying it from where we were standing on the side of the road. "This is . . . depressing."

I didn't bother trying to find the silver lining, because there wasn't one. As awful as it was to see a place that had been part of our story decimated, it was far worse to know that good people had worked there; good people had eaten here, and one storm had taken all that away. As I watched a pair of stray cats scurry through a gap between two rotted planks of wood, I was struck by how insignificant, how petty, truly, it was to worry about a stupid phone call, or obsess over a few botched attempts at intimacy. I was healthy and whole. We had so much more than a roof over our heads. The building my charity was housed in was intact, and my employees didn't have to worry about whether their next paycheck would show up on time—or at all. Suddenly my face was burning, and not from the heat.

I was a walking, talking first-world problem.

No more, I vowed. From here on, I was going to view everything through my old rose-colored, gratitude-tinted glasses.

"I'm sorry, Libby," said Shiloh, who was standing beside me on the side of the road. "I know you were looking forward to this, and so was I."

"Don't be," I said, shaking my head. "Not for me, at least. What a loss for the island."

He looked at me, and even though he was wearing his aviator glasses, I could tell he was sad. "Yeah," he said quietly. "It is."

The girls had stayed in the Jeep, but Isa had just stuck her head out the window. "Mom! Papi! Come on!" she yelled.

"Is Charlotte okay?" I yelled back.

Isa rolled her eyes. "I'm fine—thanks so much for asking!"

"Charlotte can tell us if she's not okay," Shiloh said. "It's not Isa's job to monitor her. I don't want to give her a complex."

"Do you think that's what I'm doing?" I said, but just hearing myself say it made me realize that of course he did, and Isa probably did, too. "Never mind," I said quickly. "I'll try to work on it."

"I didn't mean to hurt your feelings," he said. "Maybe *complex* wasn't the right word."

I glanced back at what was left of the restaurant. "You didn't hurt my feelings." Not that much, at least. "It's a good reminder."

"Okay. Let's go eat before the girls start threatening to revolt." He shot me a small smile, and I found myself momentarily wondering if it was just to appease me. But as we walked back to the Jeep, he added in a low voice, "If it helps, they're driving me crazy. This is the trip of a lifetime. I wish they'd act like it."

Was it the trip of a lifetime, though? I was beginning to wonder. The girls groused at every turn, and now Shiloh had admitted they were getting to him. Meanwhile, I couldn't seem to keep my spirits afloat. Maybe because I'd been counting on the island to do that, even as I kept running smack dab into examples of how it—like me—had changed.

"Girls," said Shiloh when we got into the Jeep, "I shouldn't need to tell you this, but for the love of all that's good and holy, can you please stop complaining and try to enjoy yourselves?"

"Fine," said Charlotte, staring out the window.

"Sure, but I'm starving. What are we going to do now?" said Isa.

I rummaged through my bag and found a couple of protein bars. I usually saved them for Charlotte—since her diagnosis, I was never without bars and some kind of fast-acting glucose. But Shiloh's comment about giving Isa a complex was still at the top of my thoughts, so I handed one to each girl.

"Aren't these for Charlotte?" said Isa, eyeing it suspiciously.

"And you," I chirped.

"Huh," she said, ripping open the wrapper. She took a bite and made a face. "Gross. This tastes like chocolate-flavored sawdust."

"Told you," muttered Charlotte.

"You have it," said Isa, shoving the bar at her.

"Yeah, no," said Charlotte. "Give it to Mom."

I held my hand out and suppressed a sigh; no good deed went unpunished.

"Speaking of food, can we talk about lunch?" said Shiloh. "Since we're a lot closer to Isabela Segunda than Esperanza, I'm going to head that way and see what's available. Sound good?"

"Sure," I said, crossing my fingers that we wouldn't end up at yet another place that had been destroyed.

We found a colorful Mexican restaurant, but it was closed for the afternoon. Charlotte suggested we try a fried-food cart, but her diabetes guide didn't have carb counts for street food, so that was out, too. I was steeling myself for a twin-sized freak-out when Shiloh pulled up in front of a restaurant down the block from the marina. It was painted bright purple and had seen better days, but it looked over the water, and by that point, almost anything that was open would do.

We parked and went inside, where a grizzled-looking bartender told us to seat ourselves. The sky had been light gray just minutes earlier, but by the time we'd taken a four top near the balcony, charcoal-colored clouds were rolling in from the direction of the mainland.

"That doesn't look great," said Shiloh.

It didn't, but did we really have to play I Spy with My Pessimistic Eye? "Maybe we can try to eat quickly," I suggested. We had some food at the guesthouse, but nothing substantial enough to call a meal.

"I think we're going to have to try," said Shiloh. "How about I order a bunch of burgers at the bar, so I can settle the tab right away, and then we head back as soon as we're done?"

"Good plan," I said, ignoring the look of skepticism that both girls were wearing.

They pulled out their phones as soon as he left, and maybe because I knew Isa, at least, was on the verge of getting hangry, I let them be. By the time Shiloh had returned, the sky was dark gray. I didn't need a degree in atmospheric science to know we were about to get stuck in a massive storm.

Sure enough: no sooner had we bitten into our burgers than the sky began dumping rain.

"Yikes—this is a monsoon," said Charlotte, pointing at the street. The restaurant, like much of the island, was on a hill, and water was rushing down the street from gutter to gutter like a waterslide.

Shiloh was staring at his phone, and though I'd been trying not to think about it, I couldn't help but wonder if maybe he was going to check his voicemail to see what the person who'd called him earlier had to say. But then he glanced up at me. "It's a flash flood."

Don't panic, I told myself. "What about the bay tour?" I said. I was coming to terms with our vacation not being the idyllic getaway I'd envisioned, and that so far, my cancerversary had been chock full of disappointments. But if I could just make it to the bioluminescent bay again, none of that would matter quite as much.

The girls were both staring at me with big eyes. "Are we going to be okay?" asked Isa.

"Is there going to be another hurricane?" said Charlotte, gnawing on a cuticle.

"We don't know," said Shiloh, just as I said, "No."

"Great," they said in unison.

"Listen, you two, there's nothing to worry about," I assured them. "It can't rain all day." But as I looked out at the dark clouds rolling in over the ocean, I couldn't help but wonder if I'd just jinxed us all.

~

To my surprise, it stopped raining a few minutes after we finished eating. We decided to head back to the guesthouse so Shiloh could take a nap and the girls could have some downtime (read: play on their phones). After everyone was settled I went out to the patio, where Milagros was lounging in a chair.

"Now, *mija*," she said, waving me over. "Why do you look like someone peed in your piña colada?"

I managed to laugh as I sank into the chair that was next to hers. "No piña coladas for me yet today, but I'm sorry if I look down. I'm just tired, I guess." This was true—between the hike and the heat I was wilted—though I suspected Shiloh's secrecy and the decimated restaurant were as much to blame. But at least my foot had finally stopped throbbing.

She stretched her thin legs out in front of her and leaned farther back. "Eh, I can't see so well. But am I wrong in sensing that you're still having a hard time, like we talked about?"

"You're not wrong," I admitted. "Well, not entirely. I'm starting to feel a little better."

"It's okay if you aren't, *tú sabes*," she said kindly.

"I know." I hesitated, then said, "Today is my ten-year anniversary. Of being cancer free, I mean."

"Felicidades," she said, raising her water glass to me. "I still remember taking you to the doctor the first time you were here. *Ay*, you were in a bad way, *¿recuerdas?*"

"I do," I said, smiling at her. The incision on my abdomen where I'd had part of my tumor removed had gotten infected, but I'd thought the pain was just another sign of cancer. I'd been on the verge of developing sepsis when Milagros had driven me to the health clinic, where another doctor had given me antibiotics. Looking back, Milagros had probably saved my life. "Do you remember what you said to me?"

"Never ask an old woman what she remembers!" she said, swatting in my direction.

My smile widened. "I told you I was supposed to die. You said that if that was true, I'd be dead, and that everyone was exactly where they were supposed to be, even if they didn't realize it."

"And I was right, wasn't I?"

"You sure were." I meant it, even as I wondered what it meant for me all these years later. Cancer—well, that had been a gift, albeit the kind that you'd definitely return, given the option. But I was hard-pressed to see the purpose in this ridiculous midlife funk I was in the midst of. "Hey, Milagros?"

"*¿Sí?*"

"Did you ever have a midlife crisis?"

"*Claro que sí, amiga!*" she hooted. She leaned in conspiratorially. "His name was Nacho."

I looked at her and began to laugh. "Nacho?"

"Short for Ignacio. Now *that* was a man. He had the biggest—"

"Milagros!"

"I was going to say boat!" She grinned. "Anyway. It was a bad idea, and I knew that from the moment I let him put his arm around me."

"Huh," I said, thinking of Paul and Andy. "Then why'd you do it?"

"*Ay*, there aren't many things better than being naked with someone who'd give anything to be naked with you. Why do you think I'm having so much fun with Hector?"

I tried not to wince and ended up wrinkling my nose.

"You think old people shouldn't have sex, eh?" said Milagros, frowning.

"No, it's not that at all." My cheeks were warm. "It's just that Shiloh and I—" I glanced around to make sure no one was in earshot. "Things haven't been going so well for us."

"That hunky husband of yours? He adores you!" she protested.

"I'm sure he does," I said, even as I thought of him silencing his phone on the beach. "I mean . . . *in bed*." Just admitting this, however mortifying, was an immense relief.

"Ahhh." As she pushed herself up and leaned toward me, I was reminded of how frail she was. "Can I give you a bit of advice?"

"Please do."

"Don't try to fix it."

115

"What do you mean?"

She shook her head firmly. "*Mija*, I've had a handful of husbands, not to mention Nacho and Hector and all the others who didn't put a ring on my finger. If there's one thing I know about, it's the bedroom. And believe me when I tell you sex is never about sex. Shiloh loves you. Things will work themselves out, so don't spend all your time worrying about why your fancy underwear isn't doing the trick, *tú sabes?*"

I was wearing cotton briefs and a bra that had seen better days. Still, the point stood. "I hope you're right," I said.

"I'm always right most of the time!" she declared, grinning at me.

Milagros had yet to steer me wrong. But as she began telling me about the gaggle of stray dogs she'd been caring for since shortly after the hurricane hit, I kept thinking about what Paul had said to me. Wasn't letting our marital issues work themselves out the very definition of coasting?

SEVENTEEN

"No flash photography. If you have a phone, we recommend you leave it on the bus, but if you must take it with you, please use one of the sealable plastic bags we provided and place it in a zipped pocket. And again, you are welcome to put your hands in the water, but absolutely no swimming or otherwise attempting to leave your kayaks."

The four of us were standing in a semicircle with half a dozen other people, listening to our guide run through what was turning out to be a very long list of instructions for the bioluminescent bay tour we'd booked. And with every new prohibited activity, my enthusiasm waned a little more.

"Really?" I said to the guide. "We went swimming last time we were here."

He looked at me agog. "Must have been ages ago. All that sunscreen and bug spray is bad for the dinoflagellates," he said, referring to the tiny organisms that lit up when the water was disturbed.

"And hurts the fish," said an older man dressed in khaki cargo shorts and a matching vest decorated with pins shaped like fishing lures. "There are more than two hundred and fifty species in this bay alone."

I frowned. I guess I cared about the fish. No, I *did*, I reminded myself. But . . . what about being able to float beside Shiloh, as we did on our last trip here? I could still remember him reaching for my hand as we stared up at the stars and realizing that my life was about to change in ways I couldn't possibly imagine.

"No swimming? Lame," Charlotte said from behind me.

I didn't bother shushing her. It *was* lame. And judging from Shiloh's tight expression, he thought so, too.

Isa, who was beside him, glowered at me. "You said this was going to be magical," she hissed.

I sighed. "Just wait until we're out there, okay?"

"Questions?" said the tour guide.

"Yeah—what do I do if I have to pee?" called Charlotte.

The guide shrugged. "Hold it until we're back at the porta potties in the parking lot."

"Of all the things he mentioned earlier, you'd think letting the kids know they won't be able to use the bathroom for several hours would have made the cut," Shiloh whispered.

"I know," I whispered back. "But hopefully they'll forget about their bladders once we're out on the water. Remember my reaction?" Shiloh had taken me out on his own—a friend who ran a tour at the time loaned him a couple of kayaks—and hadn't told me what to expect. When I first saw the water glowing, I'd been speechless.

His expression softened. "You're right. I bet they'll love it."

That's what I was counting on. But even more than that, I wanted *us* to love it.

The guide had stopped yapping and was directing us to a bunch of kayaks lined up at the edge of the bay. *Finally,* I thought, as Shiloh helped Isa and Charlotte drag their tandem kayak into the water. Then he and I got into our own single-seaters and began to paddle out toward the center.

"I don't see anything," Isa called to Shiloh.

"Why isn't it glowing?" huffed Charlotte, who was in the seat in front of her.

Had these children not heard of patience? I was about to tell them to keep going when Charlotte swiveled around. "Isa, look!" she called. As she skimmed her paddle over the water, a bright blue-green line formed just behind it.

"No way," said Isa reverently, leaning over the side of their boat.

I laughed with equal parts delight and relief. "See?" I called. "I told you it was amazing!"

"So weird!" said Charlotte, dipping her hand in the bay.

"But good weird, right?" I said, pulling up next to them.

"Definitely," she agreed. "I can't wait to tell Cecelia and LaToya about this."

Still smiling, I ran my fingers along the water's surface. Though the sparkling reflection was no longer a surprise, it was still every bit as incredible as it had been the first time I saw it. Warmth filled my chest. Even more than Vieques itself, this bay was where Shiloh and I had become . . . us. What had started as a conversation about stars—how the light we see in the present is really the remnant of an explosion that happened in the past—ended with us tangled up in bed, having what was the best sex of my entire life. But like Milagros had said, it wasn't even about the sex; not really. It was about realizing that in spite of my grim prognosis and my inability to envision my life without Tom at my side, I still had a whole lot of living left to do.

When I looked up from the water, hoping to paddle over to Shiloh and tell him what I'd just been reminiscing about, I realized he was already several hundred feet away, and traveling fast.

Wait, where was he going?

I looked back and forth between him and the girls. If I tried to catch him, I'd leave Isa and Charlotte behind, and our guide was still near the shore, getting the final few tourists into the water. As I watched the glowing light on the front of Shiloh's kayak grow fainter in the distance, it occurred to me that I didn't want to have to *tell* him to spend time with us. Hadn't he said he wanted to make this a special day?

But that was before he'd gotten the phone call on the beach. I didn't know what or why or how, but that call had changed something.

And honestly, I was a little afraid to find out what.

The girls were splashing each other, but as far as I could tell, they were enjoying themselves for a change rather than attempting to mortally wound one another. So I leaned all the way back in my kayak and looked up. The last time I'd been here, the sky had been a carpet of stars. Now the moon was half-full, and the clouds were dark and heavy, so I could only see a few pinpricks of light. I stared at the ones I could see, wondering if my parents were up there somewhere.

I wasn't sure when, but I'd begun to cry. And I don't mean a few tears here and there—which was starting to be an everyday event for me, even if I didn't like to dwell on that. No, this was the chest-heaving, twisted-up ugly face kind of cry. The only saving grace was that I was so busy gulping for air that I wasn't actually making any noise, so I couldn't freak out the twins or anyone else within earshot. I wasn't even crying because Shiloh had abandoned me in the middle of what was supposed to be a rousing rendition of our greatest hit.

I just really missed my father.

My mother was always with me—not so much a voice in my head telling me which battle to choose and how to fight it, but rather a soft hand on my back, subtly guiding me in the right direction. The last time I'd been at the bay, I'd felt her looking down on me and sending her love. And I guess deep down I'd expected that, once I was out here again, my father would make the same sort of appearance. After all, I'd waited six whole months for some sign he'd made it to the other side, wherever that was.

Now I felt . . . a whole lot of nothing. In fact, it was not unlike the doctor's office: I'd been expecting a thunderbolt but had barely registered a slight breeze.

"Mom? What are you looking at?" said Charlotte. The girls had just paddled up beside my kayak.

I swallowed hard and pushed myself into a seated position. Thank goodness it was too dark for them to tell I'd been sobbing my face off. "I was trying to see the stars, but it's too cloudy for that."

"Yeah," she said, glancing overhead. "It's still nice here, though."

"I'm really glad you think so."

"Thank you for bringing us," said Isa. "This is really nice."

"It really is," I agreed, trying not to think about how I wished I were having this conversation with Shiloh, too. After all, my mother would have given anything to have had this experience with me and Paul. Having Isa and Charlotte with me was enough. "I'm so glad you two are here," I said.

"Me, too," said Isa softly.

I blinked several times, trying to keep my tears at bay. So much had been riding on this trip—and so far it had been a bust. But at least one day Charlotte and Isa might look back on the tour and feel the same sort of reverence I felt about this place.

The guide was in the middle of the bay, calling for everyone to join him, so I motioned for the girls to follow me. Together we cut through the water, our paddles softly slapping the surface and sending sparkling ripples out to the sea.

In the moonlight, I saw that Shiloh was making his way back.

"Hey," he said when he reached us. "I just followed this huge school of fish around the bay. They were right near the surface, so some of them were making the water glow—it was incredible. I wish you'd seen it."

"No kidding," I said. But inside, I was thinking: *Fish? Fish?!* Bad enough that we would not be swimming side by side in the water tonight—or if our tour guide was to be believed, ever again. Now Shiloh was trying to explain his fifteen-minute absence as a nature excursion? There wasn't a lens of gratitude from here to Mongolia that was going to make the truth any more palatable: this truly *wasn't* about sex.

Because Shiloh and I?

We had far bigger fish to fry.

EIGHTEEN

"Well? What did you think?" asked Shiloh.

The tour guide had just returned us to the parking lot, and we'd toweled off and piled back into our Jeep. It was after eleven p.m. already, and although I was still raw about Shiloh's disappearing act—particularly since the rest of the tour had required us to follow the guide, who yapped like he'd never heard a lovelier sound than his own voice—I was so exhausted that I'd resolved to deal with it tomorrow.

"It was good," I said, fastening my seat belt.

"Are you disappointed that it was different from last time?" he said, glancing at me briefly from the driver's seat.

Of course I was; that he didn't know this was yet another reminder of how out of sync we were. "Weren't you? Actually, never mind," I said as I remembered that I'd already decided against airing my grievances. "It doesn't matter."

"What's that supposed to mean?" he said in a low voice. The girls, who looked as tired as I felt, were silent in the backseat.

"It doesn't mean anything except that it's over now, so there's really no reason to discuss it."

I could just barely make out the taut line of his jaw in the moon-light. "Libby, would you just tell me what you're thinking for a change?"

"For *a change?*" I said, jerking my head back. "I tell you what I think all the time. I don't even know what you mean right now."

"Don't fight," said Isa groggily.

This was rich from someone who practiced mixed martial arts on her sister at least twice a day. "We're not fighting, but you're right, Isa. This is a discussion best had another time."

"Fine." Shiloh sounded irritated. Well, I was, too. How could I keep my mood afloat when my husband kept reminding me that he was drifting away from me?

I turned away from him to stare out the window. "We're all beat. Let's just get back and get some sleep."

Neither of us said anything more the rest of the drive, though I kept stealing glances to see if Shiloh's expression softened. It didn't—nor did he ease up on his death grip on the steering wheel. *So now we're both angry,* I thought as we pulled into Milagros' gravel drive. It was a fitting cherry to top the poop pie that was my cancerversary.

"Charlotte, check your sugar and let me know your numbers. Then both of you brush your teeth and hop in bed, okay?" I told the twins as I unlocked the guesthouse. Behind us, Milagros' place was dark, save a dim light coming from her bedroom. For all I knew, Hector was up reading, but the thought that Milagros might be getting lucky made me feel even bluer than I already was, which was saying a lot. I blinked back fresh tears as I remembered what had happened after the last time Shiloh and I had been to the bay. We hadn't hit our stride at that point, so we exchanged awkward goodbyes—but then he'd driven back to the guesthouse and kissed me with ferocity before making love to me in all the ways that my gay husband had been incapable of. Though I wasn't aware of it at the time, it was the point at which my life finally began to turn around.

I didn't need a crystal ball to know that would not be happening again tonight.

Shiloh was standing at the counter now, drinking one of the soft drinks Milagros had put in the fridge for us. "Libby," he said.

When you've been married to someone long enough, a single word can contain a soliloquy. He wanted to know if we were okay.

"Shiloh," I said, looking pointedly at the bathroom, where the girls were getting ready, to make sure he understood that this really, *really* wasn't the time to talk.

His eyes washed over me. "I guess we should go to bed," he said after a moment.

I nodded and headed to the bedroom. *Good,* I thought. I hated that I was glad the day was nearly over—but I was. I'd never been big on my own birthday, and Christmas had been anticlimactic since my mother had gotten sick (though I was sure to throw on my elf hat and a big, eggnog-guzzling grin every year, so my girls didn't inherit my secret holiday humbug). Yet clearly, I had given my cancerversary—and really, the entire vacation—too much significance. No wonder I felt like a child who'd expected Santa to gift her a real live pony, only to find a lousy toy horse under the tree.

After I'd changed into my nightgown, I returned to the sunroom to tuck the girls in. Isa was already snoring softly, and Charlotte, who was lying on her stomach, had an arm slung over Isa's back, just like she used to do when they were babies. As I kissed the top of their heads, it occurred to me that they had barely argued all day. Maybe they'd leave this vacation on better terms than they'd started. Someone had to.

Shiloh was in bed when I let myself into the bedroom. "Sorry," he said quietly as I slipped beneath the covers and pulled them up to my chin.

"For what," I said, but as soon as I heard how wooden I sounded, I felt terrible. Were we acquaintances running into each other at a coffee shop, or two people who'd vowed to love each other through good times and bad, so help us God? "No, I'm sorry," I said quickly. "Today has been tough."

"Sorry," he said again. "I knew we couldn't swim in the bay anymore, but I didn't think to mention it to you."

"Telling me wouldn't have changed anything," I said, blinking up into the darkness.

"I know, but still. And I'm sorry about taking the kayak so far from you guys. I didn't realize how long I'd been gone, or that we wouldn't have another chance to go off on our own without the rest of the group."

"It's fine." For a brief moment I considered asking him about the phone call. Then I realized I didn't want to know. Not tonight. "If it's all the same to you, I'd rather not try for a big talk when we're both tired and cranky."

I waited for him to tell me it was okay, or at least say goodnight. But the next minute passed in silence, then the next, and I realized that even though I was right beside him, I was alone—again.

The worst part was, I didn't even know how we'd gotten here. Everything I'd tried to do to feel like myself had been a spectacular failure. But the past twenty-four hours had made me realize that this just wasn't all on me. It took two to talk turkey, as my father, who'd been famous for mangling aphorisms, had liked to say. Something was amiss with Shiloh, too.

I squeezed my eyes shut. What if that "something" was that he'd fallen out of love with me? As Paul had reminded me, it happened.

It happened all the time.

"Hey," he said, reaching for my hand. "Can we start over tomorrow?"

I opened my eyes. The alarm clock on my nightstand read 12:02; it was already tomorrow. I opted against mentioning that we'd already missed our shot, lest that turn into another conversation I didn't want to have.

"Okay. I love you." And I did. Wasn't that what was most important?

"I love you, too," he said, leaning over to kiss me. But his lips were on mine so briefly that I almost wondered if I'd imagined it. Then he rolled over to face the wall.

My husband's back was barely visible through the bit of light streaming in through the shutters. I stared at it for a very long time, trying to convince myself that this was all unfolding exactly as it was supposed to. As I'd learned the first time I'd been in Vieques, sometimes you have to hit rock bottom before you can bounce back to where you're supposed to be.

But as I finally closed my eyes for the night, I had a terrifying thought.

What if this wasn't rock bottom at all, but rather the very beginning of our fall?

~

I was dreaming. Shiloh and I were at Tom's apartment in Chicago, and Charlie was sitting at the end of the dining room table. "Hey, Libby," he said when he saw me. "You should probably know that Tom's the friend who took me to Fire Island. He's why Paul and I are divorcing."

"You can't do that," I said, turning to Tom. "You already broke up our marriage. Don't break up my brother's."

"Sure, I can," said Tom. "You of all people should know that happy marriages never stay that way. That's life, Libby."

But now Shiloh's voice was pulling me back to reality. "Libby, wake up."

Good, I thought, only semiconscious. *I don't want to have this dream, anyway.*

"Libby."

"Hmm? What is it?" I must have been even more upset than I'd realized if my subconscious was sending my ex-husband to inform me that a happy long-term marriage was an oxymoron. But I was mostly alert now, though I felt like my head was filled with wet sand.

I pushed myself into a seated position and glanced at the clock. Four in the morning! "Is Charlotte okay?" I said, already scrambling out of bed because if Shiloh was waking me at this hour, it had to mean she was in trouble.

"She's fine," he said, but I realized then that he was dressed in a T-shirt and shorts and looked like he'd been awake for more than a few minutes.

"What is it?" I said, wondering if he was so upset about our fight that he'd been unable to sleep.

Just then the room, which was dimly lit by the lamp, became blindingly bright for a split second. A moment later, a crack of thunder rang out and I jumped.

"*That's* what woke me up," said Shiloh. "I'm actually surprised you slept as long as you did, and that the girls aren't in bed with us right now. We're in for a bad storm."

I was about to ask him how bad when it hit me that he'd never been one for hyperbole. In fact, he was probably downplaying the severity of whatever was headed our way.

He rubbed his forehead as he looked at his phone. "This weather pattern's been upgraded to a tropical storm again," he said, answering my unspoken question. "And . . ." He was staring at me like he wasn't sure he should continue.

"What is it?" I pressed.

He grimaced. "There's a hurricane watch in effect."

He might as well have injected espresso directly into my bloodstream. "Hurricane? Why aren't there any alarms going off?"

"I don't know—I guess it's possible the alarm system isn't working. The storm was headed east, but from what I can gather it looks like it was in the middle of the Atlantic when it boomeranged back to us. Storms do that sometimes."

"How far out is it?" I said, sounding every bit as panicked as I was. I couldn't hear rain yet, but the wind was picking up, and the waves slapping against the shore could have been just outside our window.

"A couple hours at most," he said. "What do you think we should do?"

Should? I had no idea. But what I *wanted* to do was call my father. Whether it was dealing with a flooded basement or trying to figure out why our car wouldn't start, he always had an answer, or at least an idea as to how to find one. My throat constricted, and I had to swallow hard before responding. "I think we should ask Milagros. I hate to wake her at this hour, but she's lived through this more than a few times. I feel like we should find out what she has to say."

I wondered how much of the stress on his face was weather related and how much was the aftereffect of the conversation we'd had, oh, four hours earlier. "Good call," he said after a moment. "Let's go."

The girls were still fast asleep, so after I threw on some clothes, I scribbled a quick note on a notepad and left it under Charlotte's phone. The wind was bending the palm trees as we ran through the patio to Milagros', sending images of Hurricane Maria flashing through my mind. Were we about to live through that? Would we even be *able* to? More than three thousand Puerto Ricans had died as a result of the storm. I wanted to tell myself I was overreacting—but I'd just spent several days witnessing the aftermath of this exact scenario.

What fresh hell had I dragged my family into?

"Eh? Libby, is that you?" said Milagros when she came to the door. She was wearing a nightgown and fluffy slippers, but she didn't look like she'd been asleep.

"I'm so sorry to pull you out of bed at this hour," I said.

"You didn't," she said, ushering us inside. "Now that I'm old, I can't sleep more than a couple hours—I'm up by four most days. So Hector and I were finding ways to pass the time."

Hector, clad in a silk robe, appeared behind her. His cheeks, like Milagros', were flushed, and there was a faint sheen of sweat on his brow.

They didn't look embarrassed, so I wasn't sure why I was. But at least I wasn't envious for a change.

"*¿Qué pasó?*" said Hector, slipping his hand around Milagros' waist.

"*Viene una tormenta tropical,*" said Shiloh—there's a tropical storm coming.

"And a hurricane watch is in effect," I added.

Milagros' smile evaporated, and she shook her head. "I used to like a good storm. *Pero ya no.* Maria ruined them for me."

I winced. "I'm sorry, Milagros. We were wondering what you think we should do. Do you think it's safe to stay here?"

"Safe? There's no such thing," she scoffed. "We're on the water, *claro*, but so is everyone else on this island."

My mind was racing. We couldn't evacuate if we wanted to—there was no plane or boat that was going to go head-to-head with a tropical storm. But what if Milagros' house flooded? What would we do if Charlotte's blood sugar tanked and we needed to get to the hospital?

Before Milagros could answer, the porch lights, along with the rest of the house, went dark.

"*Ay,* I'm not so blind that I didn't just see all the lights go out," said Milagros. "*No es bueno.*"

If Milagros was saying this wasn't good, we were screwed. "We need to go get the girls," I said to Shiloh.

"Let me grab the flashlights first," said Hector from somewhere behind me.

"I appreciate that, but I don't want to wait in case they try to come out and find us in the dark," I said.

"I'll go, Libby. You follow when you have a flashlight," Shiloh told me.

"Be careful," I said, reaching out to touch his arm. I'd always thought that the advice not to go to bed angry was ridiculous—who had the energy to stay up and argue, when a good night's sleep would fix most everything on its own? Now I saw the wisdom in it. What if our last real conversation ended up being the one I couldn't manage to have? "I'll be right behind you," I told him.

Hector, who had already disappeared, was muttering to himself in Spanish and English from the other room. It wasn't until he'd gotten quiet again that the hum of the refrigerator, now gone, drew my attention to another problem.

"Charlotte's insulin," I said immediately.

"Eh?" said Milagros. "*¿Qué es?*"

"Charlotte's insulin and test strips need to be refrigerated when it's this hot out." I sounded frantic—because I was. This was so much worse than I'd even allowed myself to imagine.

I could barely make out Milagros' outline in the darkness. "Don't worry, *mija*," she said. "The fridge will stay cold for at least a day if we don't open it. And the storm won't last more than a day or two."

That had been true of Maria, too, but the electricity had been out for months afterward, and access to the island had been blocked for weeks. Who was to say that this wouldn't be the same?

"Here we are," replied Hector, who'd reappeared. He handed me two lit-up flashlights.

"Thank you so much," I said to him.

"*De nada.* I'm sorry the storm picked this week to arrive."

"Bad timing on our part." The worst, in fact—but now wasn't the time to split hairs. "I'm going to go check on Shiloh and the girls. We'll be back as soon as possible."

"Be careful," said Milagros. "Mother Nature isn't messing around today."

As if to reiterate her point, a large piece of plastic flew past my face as I opened the back door. I tucked my chin to my chest, covered my head, and ran for the guesthouse.

Shiloh had just woken the girls up when I let myself inside.

"Didn't I say we were doomed?" said Isa. When I shone the flashlight on her, she was looking at me like I'd conjured the storm just for her benefit. "Didn't I say that jellyfish was a sign?"

"Knock it off. You sound like Uncle Paul," I told her, even as my pulse whooshed in my ears. I handed one of the flashlights to Shiloh, already running through a mental inventory of what we needed. "Help the girls get ready while I get the snacks and Charlotte's insulin and kit," I told him. She would need both in a few short hours, and I didn't want to have to run back to the guesthouse again—though with the way the wind was wailing, I wasn't sure that would even be an option at that point.

"This sucks," muttered Charlotte, pulling on a pair of shorts. "I want to go back to sleep."

"Me, too. I was having the best dream," said Isa, who'd fallen back on the sofa and draped her arm over her eyes.

"Were you dreaming that you were home?" said Charlotte.

"How did you know?"

"Because I happen to be with you on the . . ." Charlotte started doing jazz hands.

"Worst vacation . . . ," said Isa in a show-tunes voice.

"*Ever!*" said Charlotte.

"Not funny," I said firmly. "Not funny at all."

"We're totally doomed, aren't we?" said Charlotte.

I shone the flashlight in their direction so that they couldn't see my expression. "No," I said firmly. "We're going to be fine."

But for all I knew, this would not only be the worst vacation ever, but also our last—all because I'd insisted on trying to re-create an experience that was impossible to replicate.

What had I *done*?

NINETEEN

Outside, the wind continued to howl and rattle Milagros' metal-slatted shutters, while rain pummeled the roof. The weather was just the start of my worries. Charlotte's insulin and test strips would stop working if they sat in the heat for too long. With the fans off and the windows closed, the house was already sweltering; it was only a matter of time before the fridge would be, too. We'd need to find either a health clinic or a place with a generator and a refrigerator as soon as we could leave the house.

And I had no idea when that might be.

In spite of the racket, Milagros and Hector went back to bed; she was concerned about being able to see with only a flashlight to light her way. Likewise, Shiloh was drifting in and out of sleep on one of the sofas, while the girls were dozing beside me on the other. I was glad someone was able to rest, because I sure wasn't. I knew I'd need my energy soon, but I was so wired that every time I closed my eyes I kept imagining the roof flying off, trees hitting the house, water rushing at us.

And Charlotte, shaking, sweating, unable to get her blood sugar under control, as the rest of us looked on, helpless.

"Mommy?" she said. She'd been asleep, too, but her whole body had just jerked suddenly, like she was dreaming about falling, and now she was awake.

"What is it, love? Are you feeling okay?" I asked, trying to keep the concern out of my voice. She hadn't called me Mommy in ages.

"I'm fine," she mumbled. "But it's hard to sleep—it's so hot in here. Can you tell us a childhood story?"

"Of course," I said, already racking my brain. The girls loved to hear about my childhood, or at least the version of it that I shared—they didn't need to find out how, say, I slept in the same bed with Paul for years longer than it was socially acceptable because I was afraid he might up and die on me, just like our mother had.

"Not the one about Uncle Paul stealing your candy," said Isa, who Charlotte must have woken. She was referring to the time he'd pilfered every remaining piece of candy from my plastic Halloween pumpkin, scarfed it all down, then promptly Pollocked our living room walls with regurgitated chocolate. We were five then, so I barely remembered the actual event; it was really my mother's belly-laughing recollection of it a few years later that I'd recounted to the girls.

"Or the one about the time Grandpa made you and Uncle Paul wear the same shirt," said Charlotte.

"You're lucky I haven't used that one on you two yet." I smiled to myself, thinking of how my father had made Paul and me squeeze side by side into an oversized T-shirt—albeit for all of three minutes—as punishment for slapping each other during a particularly heated argument. Paul and I rarely fought, but when we did, it had been epic. "Your grandfather is something else," I said. "Was," I quickly corrected myself.

A sob was bubbling up from deep within, and I did my best to swallow it. It wasn't as though my father would have been able to airlift us off the island. But if I'd been able to talk to him, I might actually believe this was all going to work out—which was pretty much the exact opposite of how I was currently feeling. "You guys have already heard all my good stories," I said.

"What about one about Grandma?" said Isa.

A story about my mother: this was a tall order. Little details remained, like the way her smile felt like the sun on my skin. But many of my memories were tinged with sadness from the years she spent in treatment, and worse, the ones that followed.

I was about to admit the well was dry when something came rushing back to me. "Actually . . . I do remember something I haven't told you before," I said.

"Is it sad?" asked Charlotte.

"I don't mind," said Isa. "Some of my favorite stories are a little bit sad."

All stories were a little bit sad if you stayed with them long enough. But eventually my girls would learn that for themselves. "Depends on how you look at it," I said. "You know your Grandma Charlotte had cancer, right?"

They nodded.

"Not the same kind as me. And unlike me, she never went into remission," I said, making a mental note to finally tell them about my test results if we ever got through this storm. "Anyway, Grandma's treatment made her hair fall out."

"Was it scary?" whispered Charlotte.

I could still remember opening the bathroom door and finding her in front of the mirror, examining a bald patch. I startled at the sight of her scalp, but her smile in the reflection calmed me just as fast.

"Kind of, because I wasn't used to seeing her like that," I admitted. "But she wanted to make it less scary for me, so she put on a hat and asked Grandpa to watch me and Uncle Paul while she went to the store. Grandpa took us to the park, and when we got home our car was in the driveway, so we knew Grandma was back. But when we went into the kitchen, there was a woman with a bright red clown wig standing over the sink. Your Uncle Paul took one look at her and began to scream bloody murder. Which scared the pee out of me—so I ran and got a big umbrella and ran back to the kitchen. I was ready to attack when I saw that Grandpa and the clown were both bent over laughing so hard they could barely breathe. It wasn't long before Uncle Paul and I were cracking up, too."

"But why did Grandma do that?" asked Charlotte.

I smiled, thinking of what Paul had said about using humor to digest hard things. "She didn't want us to be afraid of what was happening to her, and she knew that making everyone laugh was a good way to change the way we felt about it. Now," I said, reaching out to run a hand over their heads, "close your eyes and try to sleep, okay? We'll need to get up soon enough." In just a few hours, Charlotte would have to test her blood sugar and take the long-acting insulin she injected each morning and eat some of our quickly dwindling food supply. After that . . . well, I had no idea what came after that. But whatever it was, I would need to channel my mother and find a way to keep my children from being as petrified as I secretly was.

I waited until their lids had grown heavy and their breathing had slowed to check my phone. The cellular network was down, so the text I'd tried to send Paul still had an exclamation mark next to it, indicating that it was unsent. I squeezed my eyes shut and sent him another kind of message.

Help.

~

The sun was still shrouded by clouds a few hours later, but daybreak was just bright enough that we could get around the house without flashlights. After we'd thrown together a simple breakfast of bread, cheese, and instant coffee, Shiloh pulled me into the hallway. "I think we should move inland," he said. His calm tone belied the fear in his eyes.

"I know we need to find a fridge, or at least some way to cool Charlotte's supplies—but it doesn't look safe outside," I said. We'd cracked the shutters a few times to see how the yards were faring. Debris was strewn across the front lawn, and Milagros' patio was a pond.

"I don't think it's safe here, either," he said, gesturing toward the ceiling. Water had started to seep through a few weak spots in the roof, and the buckets we'd placed beneath the leaks were filling fast. "If this place floods—and I think it might—then it may be too late for us to get out of here safely."

Sure, but evacuating was so . . . terrifyingly real. I must have been secretly hoping I'd click my heels three times and discover this entire thing was nothing but a very bad dream.

"Where do we go, though?" I said, glancing over my shoulder. We'd done our best to reassure the girls, but there was only so much we could do; now they were pacing like a couple of caged panthers.

"There's a school a mile from here that operates as a shelter during natural disasters," said Hector, who'd just come out of the bathroom. He mopped his brow with a handkerchief. "I hope you don't mind, but I overheard you just now and I have to agree. I don't think it's safe for us to stay here."

"You think this qualifies as a natural disaster?" I said, but no sooner had I said this than the house shook violently.

Isa squealed, while Charlotte threw an afghan over her head. Shiloh glanced in the direction of the yard, then looked back at me with alarm. "I'm thinking the tree that just toppled says yes."

"*Dios mío!*" cried Milagros from the dining room. "What's happening out there?"

Hector was already running to her. "A tree fell, *amor*. But not on the house, *gracias a Dios*."

"Are you okay with leaving?" Shiloh asked me. His forehead was beaded with perspiration.

"No," I said. "But I'm not okay with staying, either. We should go see what Milagros thinks."

He nodded. "I think we should. It'll be tight, but the six of us can squeeze into the Jeep—that seems safer than trying to take Hector's sedan. We should get out of here as fast as we can."

Milagros, however, wasn't nearly as eager to leave. After we'd told her our plans, she gazed at the front door sadly. "I don't want to leave *mis perros*," she said, referring to her gaggle of strays. "They were already abandoned during Maria. I can't do that to them again."

When I took her hand, her skin was paper soft beneath my fingers. "Milagros," I began, but then I had to compose myself, because I'd just started to think about how her dogs weren't the only ones who'd lived through this before. What if she wasn't strong enough to survive it a second time? But the thought was as galvanizing as it was terrible. Shiloh was right—we had to get out of there while we still could. "The waves are only getting higher, and the next tree that falls might not miss your house," I continued. "I know it will be terrible to leave the dogs, and I promise I'll personally come back and feed them myself the minute it's safe. But for now, we have to go."

"I believe you, *mija*. And so we go." Her grip was weak as she squeezed my fingers. "Hector, I need your help putting together a bag."

Hector wrapped his arms around her, and she instantly seemed calmer. "I'll get everything, Milly. Don't worry."

"Libby, I'll get a change of clothes for us and start putting together some food," said Shiloh. "Can you make sure Charlotte's kit is packed?"

"On it," I told him.

I found a cooler in Milagros' cupboard, but when I went to get ice packs, I realized they, like the rest of the contents of the freezer, were no longer frozen. Equally alarming, the fridge's temperature was rising fast. As much as I wanted to believe that the cooler would serve its eponymous duty, all signs pointed to it morphing into an Easy-Bake oven before the day was over.

I stashed the kit with Charlotte's insulin, test strips, and meter inside, then said a prayer as I zipped it closed. Through the kitchen door I watched Charlotte, who was sitting beside Milagros at the dining room table, smiling softly about something Milagros had just said to her. At any other time I would have celebrated their burgeoning relationship. Now, however, my heart was pounding and adrenaline zipped through my veins.

Stay calm so everyone else can, too, I commanded myself. *Soon you'll be at the shelter, and surely it will have a generator and refrigerator.*

It had to.

TWENTY

Shortly after we nearly crashed into the ocean, Shiloh remarked to me that life is a near-death experience. While I'd had plenty of opportunities to test his theory over the years, it felt particularly apt as the six of us piled into the Jeep. The rain was coming down so hard that the wipers couldn't keep up, and the roads were flooded and strewn with debris and fallen trees, causing us to reroute again and again. I'd begun to wonder if we'd ever make it when we finally pulled up in front of the elementary school that was doubling as a storm shelter. All around us people were clambering out of cars and running through the rain with duffel bags or stuffed trash bags in hand.

"I'm going to drop you guys off under the awning, then go park," said Shiloh.

"Are you sure?" I said, eyeing a car that had been abandoned next to the school's entrance.

He nodded. "The parking lot's all of two hundred feet away."

"I know, but the lot looks completely full," I said.

"Libby," said Shiloh, swiveling toward the backseat, where I was squeezed between Hector and the girls. "I don't want all of you out in the storm, and I don't want to leave the car somewhere where it's going to block other people from getting into the building. I'll be fine."

I nodded numbly, watching Hector help Milagros out of the Jeep. I knew she was just as tired as the rest of us, but it still pained me to see that she looked so much older than she had when we'd arrived.

"Hey," said Shiloh, reaching for me just before I was about to climb out after Isa and Charlotte. He barely managed to smile. "Where's my Libby? It's going to be okay."

Did he really not know that his Libby had been missing for weeks? Maybe even months, though I couldn't put my finger on the point at which I'd lost my way. Now this fatalistic imposter was trying, and failing, not to imagine her husband flattened beneath a tree or fried by lightning.

"I'm here," I said weakly, waving for the girls to follow Milagros and Hector into the school. "And I'm sorry about our fight. I didn't mean to give you a hard time."

"There was no fight, Libby," he said, looking at me quizzically. "That was kind of the problem, wasn't it?"

When he said it like that, I was forced to admit most of the fighting had happened in my head. "Still, it was a bad way to end the night. I don't want . . ." I didn't want that to be how we left things if he didn't make it back. "I want to make sure we're okay."

"Of course we are. You're right that we should discuss that. But you don't need to apologize, all right? Go take care of the girls. I'll be in as soon as I can."

"Okay," I conceded. "Please be super careful."

"I wouldn't be allowed to fly millionaires three thousand miles above the earth if I weren't careful," he said.

He was attempting to make me feel better, and I guess he did, a little. But the minute I pushed the school's double doors open, I was reminded of what we were up against. If the house had been hot, the school was a sauna, and the air was ripe with the smell of sweat and mildew. By the look of it, there were already several hundred people packed into the building.

I glanced around, expecting to see Milagros and the girls waiting for me just beyond the entrance, but instead I was greeted by unfamiliar faces every bit as weary and spent-looking as I must have been. Though living in New York for so long had given me a ninja-like ability to weave through crowds, navigating the halls felt like swimming through sludge, and by the time I managed to get into the gymnasium I'd grown frantic—where *were* they? Had something happened to Charlotte or Milagros? As I was scanning the crowd, I saw a woman wearing a bright yellow vest holding a clipboard in the middle of the basketball court. I was desperate to find my family, but as the cooler banging against my hip reminded me, I was just as desperate to find a power source. I made a beeline for her.

"Excuse me," I said when I reached her.

"*¿Sí?*" she said, looking up from her clipboard.

"*¿Hablas inglés?*" I asked.

"*Claro.* How can I help you?"

"Do you have a generator here? A fridge? My daughter is a type one diabetic and I have to refrigerate her insulin, or it'll stop working," I explained breathlessly, motioning to my cooler.

The woman had a kind face, but when I asked her this she looked at me like I'd just inquired about catching the next iceberg out of town. "The generator broke during Maria, and they're expensive to fix and run," she said.

"I don't understand," I said, because I didn't. How could an emergency shelter possibly be without a generator? "Where can I find a place with a fridge? What about a hospital?" I said, glancing around with the wild eyes of a trapped animal.

"In this storm? *Lo siento*, but no one has power right now. And there's no hospital in Vieques," she said. "Not anymore."

I couldn't respond right away. In fact, it was all I could do not to keel over and empty the scant contents of my stomach. Charlotte was going to die—and all because I'd been so desperate to fix everything that I'd neglected to do my due diligence and make sure there was still a hospital available for my sick child. Not only had I not turned out to be the mother my own was, I'd somehow managed to become the exact opposite of her. Because I knew as sure as I knew the sun would rise again the next morning, whether we were alive to see it or not, she never—ever—would have made this mistake.

"How can that be?" I finally gasped. "There was a hospital the last time I was here."

"It's been closed since Maria. FEMA was supposed to do something about it, but . . ." She shook her head with disgust. "There are a few health clinics you can try, but I don't know if they'll be open right now. If I were you, I wouldn't go out in this weather."

I thanked her, then pushed back through the crowd to find my family.

After nearly ten frenetic minutes, I finally spotted them in a kindergarten classroom at the far end of a hall. The girls were sitting on the floor beneath a chalkboard, fanning themselves with construction paper, and Hector was cross-legged on a colorful braided rug; Milagros was seated on a cot beside him. I ran to them, then knelt down and hugged the girls so hard that Charlotte sputtered a little.

"Weird, Mom," she said. "Are you okay?"

The opposite, in fact, and seeing her only reminded me of my own stupidity and impotence. "I thought you guys would be waiting for me near the door," I said.

"Sorry, Libby. I ran into someone I knew," said Hector, nodding in the direction of an older man on the other side of the room. "He told us to come over here while there was still room. The school's almost full."

"It's okay," I said, because it wasn't his fault our cell phones didn't work, and it's not like he could have left Milagros or the girls to wait for me. "Thank you for finding a space for us." I turned to Charlotte. "Do you need to check your blood sugar? I have your kit here."

"It's not time yet," she said, flashing her phone at me.

"You should leave that off," I said. "I'll watch the time for you."

"Too late. My battery's at two percent—it'll be dead in another minute." Her eyes scanned the room. "When are we getting out of here, anyway?"

"Soon," I said, more a prayer than a promise. "Have either of you seen Shiloh?" I asked Milagros and Hector.

"Not yet, *mija*," she said.

Isa looked up from the picture book she'd grabbed off a shelf. "Is Papi okay?"

"Fine," I fibbed, because if they were somehow managing to stay calm amid this chaos, I wasn't about to ruin that. "He's just parking the Jeep." That part was true, at least. The question was, what was taking him so long?

I shot Isa a tight smile, then turned to examine Charlotte. She was sweating, but so was everyone, and she didn't look clammy. I began running through a quick mental inventory of the food we'd brought: the last of the protein bars, a couple of unripe pears, some cheese sticks, which we'd need to eat soon, before they spoiled. At any rate, we'd be lucky if it lasted through the next day. And while the emergency coordinator *was* handing out packets of crackers, they were pure, simple carbs—guaranteed to send her blood sugar soaring. I wished I could turn my mind off, or at least put it in low-power mode. Because the more I thought this through, the worse it became.

"Libby?" said Milagros. "You okay?"

For someone with poor eyesight, the woman didn't miss a thing.

"Just really tired," I said. "How are *you*, though?"

Unlike me, she didn't try to sugarcoat it. "I don't like it here," she said, jutting her chin out. "I want to go home, to my comfy bed and my own bathroom. My dogs are probably waiting for me right now and thinking I'm dead."

I winced, because she'd said the only *D* word worse than *divorce*.

But then my eyes darted to the door, where a man about Shiloh's height wearing a black T-shirt, as he'd been, had just arrived. I'd already risen to my feet when I realized it wasn't him.

"He'll be here soon," said Milagros, reading my mind again. "He's fine, and so are we. It's going to be okay, *mija*."

I didn't have it in me to tell her she was wrong.

TWENTY-ONE

The minutes passed at molasses speed. More people streamed in and out of the classroom, but each time I realized Shiloh wasn't among them the lump in my throat grew larger. All of our marital troubles suddenly seemed so insignificant in light of the storm. If only it hadn't taken a matter of life and death to realize that.

"How about some cheese?" I said to the girls. I could tell they were getting squirrelly; Charlotte was pacing back and forth in the narrow space between where we and another family were seated, while Isa kept opening the books she'd taken from a shelf, only to discard them seconds later.

"Ugh," said Charlotte, like I'd just offered her snails.

"Please don't wait too long to eat," I said.

"I *know*," she said in the same annoyed tone.

Did she, though?

"I'll take your cheese," said Isa, holding out her hand.

"Um, no you won't," I said, but before I could launch into a lecture about how I was rationing food for everyone's benefit, I'd just realized that Milagros was starting to look a little peaked.

"You doing okay?" I whispered, crouching in front of her. She was leaning on Hector, fanning herself with a piece of construction paper. "Do you want some food? Water? Anything?"

"Eh," she said softly. "I'm just warm. Don't worry about me, *mija*."

It wasn't possible for me not to worry about her, but I was juggling enough catastrophes that she wasn't the only one on my mind. I turned to Hector. "Can I steal you for a second?" I said in the calmest voice I could muster. Though the thunder had let up, the wind was still howling, and I couldn't help but think of footage I'd seen of weather forecasters clinging to lampposts in the middle of a hurricane. What if Shiloh had literally been blown away trying to get through the parking lot?

"Of course," said Hector, already on his feet and heading for the door. "What is it?" he said once we were in the hallway. The underarms of his linen shirt were dark with sweat, and the bags under his eyes seemed to have doubled in size since we'd left Milagros'.

"I didn't want to worry everyone, but I'm concerned that Shiloh isn't back yet," I said quietly.

"I am, too," he said, glancing around. The hallway was filled with people who looked wary and exhausted. I blinked back tears as it occurred to me how many of them were probably thinking they'd gone through this already.

"Do you think they closed the shelter and he's stuck outside?" I asked.

"I think it's unlikely that they'd turn anyone away. But how about I go check?"

I exhaled. "That would be really great. Thank you."

"Don't thank me," he said kindly. "Thank *you*. Milly wouldn't have come to the shelter if you hadn't been here to convince her."

Maybe not, but now that I knew there wasn't a generator here, I was starting to wonder if it had been a mistake to come. Heat killed all kinds of people, but especially the elderly—and the shelter was even hotter than Milagros' house.

Hector headed for the entrance, so I went back to Milagros and the girls. When I sat down, Isa glared at me. "*Where* is Papi?" she demanded.

"He's coming," I said, forcing my lips into a smile. "Hector just went to go get him, in fact."

"He's a good one," said Milagros, who had a faraway look in her eyes. I couldn't quite tell if it was love or exhaustion.

"He is," I said, sitting in front of her. "He'll be right back."

"Hector or Papi?" called Charlotte.

It was then that I realized she'd just perched on a low stool and was trying to peer through the metal shutters. They were keeping most of the rain out, but the floor beneath the windows was wet from what was leaking through.

"Charlotte, get away from there," I said. "That's not safe."

"A little water's not going to kill me, Mom," she said, wiping the mist from her forehead.

"No, but—"

"Libby."

When I spun around, Shiloh was standing in the doorway. He was drenched and splattered with mud—but he wasn't missing limbs and hadn't been charred by lightning, and none of the other terrible things that I'd imagined had happened to him.

"Oh, thank God," I choked, running to him.

He caught me in his arms and pulled me tight. "I'm sorry I scared you," he whispered. "Hector told me you were worried. I was helping a family whose car had gotten stuck in the mud."

Of *course* he had. "Don't apologize—that was so good of you. And you're here now. That's all that matters." I looked past him at Hector. "Thank you so much for finding him."

Hector shrugged sheepishly. In spite of his polished appearance, I realized that he reminded me of Shiloh. No wonder I'd been jealous of Milagros. "I didn't do much. He was already close to the door when I went to look," he said.

"All the same, thank you. I'm really glad you're here," I said, and he smiled shyly.

"Well, I kind of have good news," said Shiloh, looking back and forth between the five of us. "My cell's still down and I can't check the weather, but I spoke with a guy who just came from the beach. He said the waves are lower now, and the wind is letting up."

My eyes widened. "So it's the eye of the hurricane?"

He cocked his head and gave me a funny smile. "I said good news—not *bad*, cutie. The guy I chatted with has lived here for seventy years, and he said that in his experience, that means it's passing. I can't say for certain, but I'm willing to bet this is just a tropical storm and it's blowing over."

"How soon until we know for sure?" I asked.

"Next couple hours, most likely. If for some reason it's been upgraded to a hurricane and we don't know, the eye still wouldn't last more than two hours." His eyes flitted to Charlotte before meeting me again. "Want to go talk?"

"Yes," I said, already starting for the door.

In the few seconds it took to get out of the classroom and into the hall, his face had shifted from calm to deeply concerned. "What is it?" I said.

He sighed deeply. "Even if the storm does pass—and I do think it will—we're not out of the woods yet. I'm worried about Charlotte."

As much as I wished he'd just told me she was going to be fine, I was relieved to hear I wasn't alone in my concern. "Her insulin seems okay so far, but there's no way to know if her test strips will hold up," I said. "Remember when I left the extras in the car too long last August, right after she was diagnosed?" They'd baked in our ancient SUV for the entire weekend. After we'd finally retrieved them, her meter couldn't read the strip at all. We thought we'd learned everything there was to know about diabetes then, but no one had mentioned that the strips disintegrated in heat, too; it had taken three more tries and a distraught Google search for us to figure out that was the problem.

"Yeah," he said, shaking his head. "There's no way the electricity is coming back anytime soon, either."

I grimaced. "Did you know there's no hospital here? And the emergency coordinator said we shouldn't count on the clinics being able to help."

He looked so stricken I almost wished I hadn't said it. "I should have checked before we came."

"No, I should have." After all, *I* was the girls' mother. Protecting my children wasn't just my job; it was literally my purpose in life. "This whole stupid trip was my idea."

"Hey," he said, reaching for my arm. "It's not a stupid trip at all. I know it wasn't what you had planned—or what any of us had planned—but at least we have each other, right?"

We really did, and though I was still convinced I was on my way to winning a Darwin Award, hearing him say that eased my shame a little. "We do," I agreed. "But how soon do you think we can get off the island?"

"Well, the ferries aren't going to be running until the skies clear, and that's assuming they aren't damaged. Same with planes. We're stuck here for a while."

"Then I'd better start figuring out a way to keep Charlotte's supplies cold," I said.

"Absolutely," he said. He smiled softly. "Team?"

Tears pricked my eyelids as I smiled back. "Team."

After checking on Milagros and the girls, we spent the next half hour circling the school to see if anyone had a cooler that was actually cool. Nearly everyone we encountered was eager to help—but couldn't. Like ours, their ice packs had thawed, and their coolers were warm; no one had the faintest idea where we could find a functioning generator.

"Crap," Shiloh said to me as we made our way back to the classroom.

The relief I'd felt had already gone up in flames. "We're going to have to find a plan C," I said.

"Maybe I can find a plane and fly us back to the mainland," he said, stepping around a woman lying listless on the floor beside her children.

"You know how crazy that sounds, right?"

"Yeah," he admitted. He paused just inside the doorway. "But Libby?"

"What is it?"

"Crazy or not, we're going to have to do something."

"I know," I whispered. "But what?"

"I have no idea," he whispered back. "But between the two of us, we'll figure it out."

"Okay," I agreed, because hadn't we tackled myriad other problems—from the mundane to the truly life-threatening—side by side for thirteen years?

Which is why it was so strange that I couldn't seem to believe we were ever going to find our way out of this one.

TWENTY-TWO

The afternoon stretched endlessly before us. The emergency coordinator passed out cheese sandwiches, which provided all of five minutes of distraction; Hector found a set of dominos in the classroom and managed to engage the girls for another ten. But they'd since abandoned him, as well as the rug where we'd been stationed, and were sprawled out on the tile floor, which they claimed was the coolest place in the school. I didn't even bother warning them about germs, because bacteria and viruses had nothing on the heat. Although—or maybe because—the wind had begun to die down and the rain had slowed to a steady patter, the school felt even more stifling than it had before. I'd sweated through my T-shirt while we were searching for ice packs, and Shiloh's clothes, damp from the rain, had yet to dry. But I was most worried about Milagros, who had given up mopping her forehead with one of Hector's handkerchiefs and was murmuring to herself on the ground.

"How are you holding up?" I said, squatting beside her.

She tried to smile, but it came out like a grimace. "I've had worse days, but not many," she said.

My stomach sank. "The heat?"

"Eh, I'm used to that. Maybe it's having to sit in the same place too long. That's my secret to living so long—I don't stop moving. Except now," she said, motioning toward her legs, "I'm stuck."

"Do you want me to walk you to the bathroom?" I asked. I would have attempted circus tricks if it would have made her feel better. Charlotte's blood sugar had remained steady, and her test strips and insulin were still working. But I wasn't about to celebrate with Milagros looking so worn out.

She shook her head. "I don't have to go."

She hadn't used the bathroom once since we'd arrived, which made me wonder if she was dehydrated. "Have some water," I said, pressing a water bottle into her hand.

"*Gracias,*" she said, but after struggling with the lid for a moment she passed it back to me. "Do you mind, *mija?*"

"Of course not," I said, trying, and failing, not to worry about her weak grip. I opened it and passed it back to her. "Anything else I can do for you? If you need something, Milagros, just say the word."

"*Gracias,*" she said again. My throat tightened as she touched my arm. It wasn't as though she replaced either of my parents, but her hand on my skin gave me the same feeling of security and warmth that I'd always had when I was with my father. "What I need," she added softly, "is to leave."

"Shiloh? Hector?" I said, turning to them. "What do you think? Is it time?"

They looked at each other, then began speaking at the same time. "Not yet," said Shiloh as Hector said, "Soon."

"*Escucha,*" said Hector—listen. Then he said nothing, and then the family next to us was quiet, too, and within a few seconds the whole room was nearly silent. Which was when I realized I could hear twittering from beyond the windows. "The birds wouldn't be singing if this was a hurricane," he explained after a moment. "The storm has passed."

I looked at Shiloh, almost afraid to cheer for fear it was a false alarm. "Maybe so," he conceded. "But it's probably a mess out there. There's no saying if we can get back safely."

"If we stay until it's dark, then we're here until the morning or longer," said Hector, nodding pointedly at Milagros. "Milly wants to leave. And to be frank, I do, too. With all these people packed in here and the heat only rising, this doesn't feel any safer to me."

Shiloh looked at me and I nodded. "Then we go," he said.

That was when I realized Isa was peering up at me from the tile with alarm.

"Mommy, are we going to *die* if we go out there?"

I swallowed hard. "Of course not, sweetheart."

"But you don't know that," she insisted.

"No," I admitted, my eyes flitting to Charlotte. "But what I do know is that it's time for us to try."

At least outside we could begin to look for a clinic, a pharmacy—something or someone who might be able to help us keep Charlotte's medication cool or replace it if need be.

Leaving the shelter was no easy feat, since so many people were just as eager to head home. But the possibility that help awaited elsewhere was enough to keep my spirits afloat as we slogged through the crowd and parking lot. Once we were making our way down the road, how-ever, that hope nose-dived. The corner stores, grocers, and pharmacies we passed were shuttered; many had plywood nailed over their doors. Even pulling up to Milagros' house and seeing that it was relatively undamaged, at least from the outside, wasn't enough to lift my mood. Yes, a roof was important—but not as important as insulin.

"*Gracias a Dios!*" exclaimed Hector, climbing out of the Jeep. He opened the passenger door and embraced Milagros. "*Amor*, it's fine. It's all fine."

Milagros let him help her out of her seat, then put a hand on her heart as she stood on the gravel driveway. "*Ay bendito.*"

Camille Pagán

"What will we eat?" I whispered to Shiloh as we surveyed the house. We had water—we'd filled several large pots before heading to the shelter, knowing that the pressure would slowly dwindle and eventually disappear until the electricity returned. But I only had three more protein bars, which would hardly be enough to get Charlotte through the day, and whatever had been left in the fridge would no longer be edible.

"We have some canned goods and some dry rice, and if we can figure out how to cook the rice, that should be balanced enough to make sure her blood sugar doesn't tank," he said, glancing over his shoulder at Charlotte, who was in the kitchen with Isa and Milagros.

"We still need to figure out how to get out of here," I said.

He put his hands on his head. "I've been thinking that same thing myself."

"Do you think the ferry's running yet?"

"Unlikely. But the sky's clear, so maybe we can get on the first flight out."

"Assuming there are flights heading out," I said.

"Right. Do you think Charlotte's medicine will be okay for another day or so?" he asked.

"I don't know, and I'm super nervous about that," I admitted. "The pharmacies aren't open, so it's not like we can get more. And even if we did, who's to say it would be in better shape than what we have here?"

"The pharmacies might actually have functioning generators, though. I'll go for a drive, see if anything is open or if I can find out anything more about flying out of here."

I didn't even tell him to be careful. His leaving was a risk I was willing to take if it meant keeping Charlotte healthy. "Okay. Thank you," I said quietly.

"Hey." His forehead was etched with all the worry he'd been working hard to keep out of his voice. "We're *going* to get through this."

I squeezed my eyes shut and asked myself: What would Charlotte Ross do? Then I opened my eyes again, and though I couldn't quite force my lips into a smile, I made sure my tone matched Shiloh's. "I know we are," I said.

~

After Shiloh headed out, Milagros and I sat on the front porch, which was marginally cooler than the house, while Hector mopped the floor in the places the roof had leaked. It wasn't time to check Charlotte's blood sugar, but I'd been watching her like a hawk, and had asked the girls to come out front with us so I could continue to keep an eye on her.

We'd just sat down when a gaggle of strays appeared next to the porch, wagging their tails and yipping for Milagros' attention.

"My babies! *¿Mida, cuántos son?*" Milagros asked me as she tossed the cold cuts, which she'd retrieved from the fridge and were no longer cold, onto the soggy lawn.

I counted them silently. "Six."

"*Ay*, there should be seven! I hope . . ." Her voice trailed off as she glanced around, presumably to take in what she could.

"You looking for a little guy?" I asked. A small, fawn-colored dog was peering around a bush with one eye; the other was closed, presumably for good. "Tan, kind of scrappy-looking, half-blind?"

"Pedro! *Mi vida*!" Milagros exclaimed, smiling genuinely for the first time since the storm had arrived. She was right—she *had* needed to come home. "Pedro can't see so well, just like Old Milly. *Pedro!*" she hollered, extending her hand.

The dog came trotting up to her, his tail swinging like a metronome.

"Can we pet him?" said Charlotte, approaching the porch.

"Careful!" I warned as Pedro trotted toward her. "He doesn't know you and might bite."

"Pedro wouldn't hurt a mosquito!" Milagros protested.

"Right, but he probably hasn't been vaccinated," I said, glancing at his matted fur.

157

"He has," she said, patting his head. "I had a vet come to my place last winter to take care of them. Couldn't get Coco or Bene to cooperate, so maybe don't pet the little black one or the brown one with spots," she said to the girls, who were both at the foot of the stairs.

"As you may have gathered, I'm not really a dog person," I told Milagros, grimacing as Charlotte bent before Pedro and put her hand out. He sniffed it, then stuck his head under it to get her to pet him, making her giggle.

"Everyone's a dog person," said Milagros. Now a mangy-looking brown Lab had joined us on the porch and was rubbing against her legs. Its backside was entirely too close to my face. "You just haven't met the right dog yet."

"Maybe not," I said, because at least Charlotte and Isa, who was now running her hand down Pedro's filthy back, were starting to shake the stressed-out vibe they'd had since the storm hit.

"Pet him, Mom!" demanded Isa, looking up at me.

"Do I have to?" I said, and for some reason, this got a laugh out of them. I sighed and rose from my chair. "Fine." After I was down the stairs, I knelt in front of Pedro. "Hey there, fleabag," I muttered under my breath.

Pedro cocked his head and eyed me. Then he lunged.

I was about to scream—my cheek was wet, so surely I was oozing blood—when I realized that I hadn't felt the sting of his teeth. I pulled my head back and examined him. "Did you just . . . lick me?"

He wagged his tail in response.

"Naughty dog," I said, but I couldn't help but smile.

The girls were laughing. "See? You're so paranoid, Mom," said Isa.

I was tempted to remind her that I wasn't the one who'd sworn off the ocean because of a freak jellyfish incident. "It's all fun and games until you get rabies," I said, but then I remembered, yet again, that there was no hospital to go to if Pedro changed his mind and decided to have my face for dinner.

"Pedro doesn't have rabies," said Charlotte, scratching the mutt's ears. She looked up at me with bright eyes. "Mom, can we get a dog when we get home?"

"Yes," I said without hesitation, even though I'd said no each of the four thousand and three times she and Isa had asked me in the past. If all went well, I'd live to regret my impulsivity. But as I resisted the urge to check my phone, which was nearly out of batteries, to see how long Shiloh had been gone, I would have promised them a baby llama if it meant we'd make it off the island without another catastrophe.

TWENTY-THREE

The sun was just starting to set when Shiloh returned. I could tell from his posture that the news wasn't good.

"Ferry's down," he said, leaping over a puddle in the driveway to come to where I'd been waiting on the porch. Hector was inside, attempting to cobble together dinner, while the girls were on the patio, clearing debris under Milagros' supervision. "The dock was damaged, and no one seems to know what's going on. There's no one at the airport, either."

"No one?" I said, incredulous.

He shook his head. "Not a single person."

"Pharmacies? Health clinics?"

He met my eyes but didn't respond.

"Crap," I said.

"I know. And the gas stations are closed, too."

I was staring at him, but for a few seconds it wasn't him I was seeing at all. Instead, Charlotte was in my arms, just as she'd been a few days ago at the hotel in San Juan. Only this time my attempts to save her weren't working. "What are we going to do?" I said, my voice cracking.

He looked away for a moment. "I'm not sure," he said.

This was not what I had been hoping to hear. After all, the man had once calmly landed an engine-damaged plane like it was an everyday event!

But then I realized that however harrowing that had been, our current situation was far more complicated. And if I was being honest with myself—and admittedly, I was mostly trying not to be—I was mostly upset because I was expecting Shiloh to play the role my father had always played. He'd been like a magician, always distracting then amazing us without ever showing us how very hard he worked to pull it all off.

He pushed at the gravel with the tip of his shoe. "I know this is scary," he said quietly. "But something you taught me, Libby, is that when you believe the best, you're a lot more likely to do what it takes to make the best happen."

The evening was surprisingly beautiful, considering the sky had been black just hours earlier, and I squinted at him in the low, golden light. Even if I knew where to find this shiny version of me he was referring to, her wishful thinking would not have done a darn thing to fix our situation.

"There's got to be something we haven't thought of yet," he added.

Such as attempting to swim to the mainland? Or perhaps we should make a giant sign on the beach—*Save Our Stupidity!*—and pray someone would fly over and rescue us.

Then it hit me.

"The waves are still pretty low, right?" I said, shielding my eyes as I glanced past him at the strip of ocean visible over the fence.

He nodded.

"You think it'll stay that way until tomorrow?"

"Maybe . . . why?"

"Someone on this island has to have a boat that we can borrow. Let's go ask Milagros and Hector."

He put his arm around my shoulders. "I like the way you think."

"I'm glad," I said, because at least things between us were starting to feel normal again. Maybe they'd even continue on that path, and we'd never have to discuss the secret phone call he'd gotten.

As we opened the gate, I saw that the girls were on the patio on either side of Milagros, under a tree whose branches had once been host to at least half a dozen orchids. Now only one bright yellow blossom with fuchsia streaks in its center remained. But the girls were talking animatedly as Milagros listened on. I'd just started to smile about the three of them getting along so well when I realized the girls were actually arguing over Milagros' head.

"*I* get to name the dog," Isa was saying.

"No, I do," insisted Charlotte. "Mom told *me* we could get one. So I get dibs."

"Do not!"

Before I could interject, Milagros clapped her hands together. "*Niñas*! Let me tell you about the first time I got a dog. It was a tiny little puppy named Lola, and I kept her in a dresser drawer . . ."

"Wait," I whispered, holding an arm out to Shiloh, who'd just taken a step toward them.

We stood at the gate, listening to Milagros tell them a story about her first dog, who apparently had a thing about doing its business in her parents' bed. By the time she was done, the girls were rolling with laughter.

"We have to name our dog Lola!" said Isa.

"Just so we can watch it poop in Mom and Papi's bed!" said Charlotte, still cackling. "Milagros, we'll send you pictures. Do you know how to text?"

"Hi, you guys," I announced. "For the record, no dogs will be pooping in my bed."

"*Bienvenidos!*" called Milagros, but I noticed that she didn't hop up like she usually did. "Hector is just finishing dinner for us."

Just then, Hector emerged from the house, a large pot in one hand, a flashlight in the other. "It's going to be dark soon," he explained, setting the flashlight on the tile. "I'll be back in a moment with everything else."

I looked at Charlotte. "Hey, sweetheart, it's time to test your blood sugar, okay? The kit is inside." We'd moved our stuff back into the guesthouse after confirming that it hadn't been damaged. In fact, thanks to Hector's repairs, the roof hadn't leaked.

"I'll go get it. Isa, come with?" She hesitated. "It's dark in there."

Isa looked at her like she was going to say no. But then she grabbed the flashlight and sighed. "Fine."

At least they were finally getting along. "Just come back with your meter so I can see the numbers," I said.

Hector returned with plates, glasses, and a bottle of rum, which he poured into each glass and handed to us.

"*Salud,*" said Milagros. "To being home."

To going home, I thought to myself a bit guiltily as I lifted my glass. "*Salud.*"

"Hector, Milagros, Libby and I were just talking," said Shiloh. He leaned forward and put his elbows on his knees, then continued. "If the power stays off—and I see no sign that it's going to come back anytime soon—it's not safe for us to be here."

"*Claro,*" said Milagros. "As much as I wish you could stay, the four of you should leave as soon as you can."

"Oh no, Milagros," I said quickly. "We're not leaving you here without electricity and all the clinics closed."

"Eh, this is my home. I have Hector, and who needs electricity? I didn't have a television until I was twenty years old, *mija,* and didn't I make it through Maria?"

Sure—but I could still remember the days, then weeks, following the storm as Shiloh and I frantically tried to get hold of her, to no avail. Back then I'd been a heck of a lot more optimistic than I was now, and yet it had still been torture to wait—and wait—to hear if she had survived. I was not about to leave Milagros here and twiddle my thumbs until the electricity was turned back on.

Shiloh, who seemed to be thinking the same thing, shook his head. "I don't know, Milagros, that doesn't sound safe to me. There's no saying how long this could go on. But yes, we do need to leave—Libby and I are really worried about Charlotte's diabetes supplies. They'll go bad if they stay warm too long, and if she's without insulin . . ."

She could die.

Shiloh, who couldn't make himself finish the rest, turned to Hector. "Do you know anyone who has a boat? Libby and I were thinking that might be the best way off the island. Maybe even the only way," he added. "I know we'll need to wait until tomorrow, since it's late, but . . ."

Hector reached for Milagros' hand and gave her a tight smile. I was wondering why when he said, "I know someone with a boat, but I don't know if I'll be allowed to borrow it."

Shiloh sat up straight. "You think he'd let us if he knew about Charlotte?"

Hector grunted a laugh. "*She's* Flor—my ex-wife. And she's mad as a hornet's nest about me and Milagros." He sighed heavily. "*Mira*, even if she says yes, that crossing can be rough—and after a storm there's no telling how the water will be. It could be dangerous."

I could feel adrenaline coursing through my veins as I pulled my phone out of my pocket—as if it would miraculously turn on and I could call for help, and we wouldn't have to rely on the mercy of Hector's ex to get us out of here.

The black screen was a potent reminder that we really had exhausted all of our avenues. "That boat is our only hope," I said to Hector.

He nodded with what seemed to be a mix of resolve and resignation. "Then first thing tomorrow, we go see Flor," he said.

TWENTY-FOUR

The four of us went to bed soon after the sun went down. Except my exhaustion was no match for my anxiety-addled brain; I tossed and turned, but sleep was all but impossible. And every time I opened my eyes, Shiloh, barely visible in the pale moonlight, was either sitting up in bed or staring at the ceiling beside me.

"You okay?" I whispered at one point.

"I will be once we get out of here," he whispered back. "I'm sorry this vacation has turned out to be such a disaster."

I reached for his hand beneath the covers. He squeezed my fingers before I could squeeze his. "You have nothing to apologize for," I said. "One day we'll look back on this and laugh."

"You think?"

"No," I admitted, and that made him laugh. "But hopefully it'll be over soon and nothing like this will happen again for a while." And by a while, I meant ever. Hadn't the past year been enough difficulty for a lifetime?

Of course, I knew all too well that it didn't work that way. Besides, hadn't I already sworn I wasn't going to indulge in my first-world problems? I finally fell asleep thinking about all the people who had it far worse than we did.

I couldn't say what time it was when we finally stumbled out of bed, but the sun had just begun to peek from behind the clouds. It wasn't storming, so after checking on the girls, who'd woken up shortly after us, Shiloh and I headed to the beach to see how the water looked.

Though the sandy stretch in front of the guesthouse was strewn with palm fronds and debris that had washed up during the storm, the waves were no choppier than they'd been the night before. "What do you think?" I asked Shiloh.

He put his arm around my waist. "I think it looks like we might just get out of here today."

It was exactly what I needed to hear. The cooler had long since become a hot box, and though we'd been keeping Charlotte's supplies shaded, that was barely making a difference; it was easily ninety degrees with, oh, 200 percent humidity. I knew we had a day, if that, before her insulin stopped working. But if we could get out of here, none of that would matter.

Just as I was about to say this to Shiloh, Charlotte and Isa came tearing through the gate toward us.

"What is it?" I yelled.

Like Isa, Charlotte was panting when she reached me. But unlike Isa, Charlotte almost never got winded. "Are you okay?" I said. "Is it your blood sugar? Your test strips?"

"*Mom*," she said sharply. "It's not me. It's Milagros."

The sand beneath me seemed to sway. "No. What happened?"

"She fell." Isa was tugging on my shirt the way she used to when she was little. "Come on."

I was still dizzy, but she didn't have to ask twice; I was already running toward the guesthouse like a serial killer was behind me.

I saw Hector first. As I approached, I realized he was cradling Milagros' head. She was on her back on the tile, arms and legs akimbo, moaning quietly.

"Milagros!" I cried, kneeling beside her. "What happened?!"

Shiloh, who'd just sat next to me, took her wrist in his hands to feel for her pulse. We'd both been trained in CPR, but unlike me, Shiloh never forgot the steps. "Milly, can you hear me?"

"*Sí,*" she murmured.

"Can you breathe?"

She managed to nod.

"Is either one of your arms or legs painful or numb?"

"My chest hurts," she murmured.

For a split second I'd been relieved—because not only could she speak, one side of her face wasn't drooping, so maybe she hadn't had a stroke; that was how my father had died. Just as quickly, I realized chest pain was a sign of a heart attack.

Which could be every bit as deadly.

Either way, she needed a doctor. A hospital. Immediate medical attention. Basically, everything we didn't have.

"She was fine when we got up," said Hector, still stroking her head. "Then I went to get dressed, and I heard Isa and Charlotte yelling. When I got out here, she was on the ground."

"Tell me more, Milagros," I said, placing my hand on her forehead. Her skin was cool and clammy. "Does anything else hurt?" I asked.

"My arm." She paused. "It's a little hard to breathe."

Cognizant that Isa and Charlotte were right behind us and watching this all, I turned to Shiloh and Hector and whispered, "I think she had a heart attack. We have to do something."

Shiloh looked at Hector. "Your ex. We need to get to her—immediately."

Hector nodded numbly.

Shiloh put his hand on Hector's shoulder. "As fast as you can, pack an overnight bag for Milly and for yourself." He turned to Charlotte and Isa. "Go pack your backpacks—quickly. Charlotte, you know what to bring, right?"

"Insulin kit, protein bar, notebook," she said, watching us with big eyes.

"I'll help," said Isa.

"Thank you," I said. "Don't worry about anything else, okay? We'll get the rest later."

"Go!" he said. "We leave in three minutes."

Whereas Shiloh was cool and collected, my hands were trembling, and tiny stars were glittering at the top of my vision. *Don't freak out,* I ordered myself. *Do* not *freak out.* I knew I was halfway to a panic attack, because I'd had one once before—in Vieques, as it happened, right after Shiloh and I had narrowly avoided a plane crash.

But as Shiloh and I hoisted Milagros into a sitting position, I couldn't help but wonder if we'd be so lucky this time.

As we put her arms around our necks and helped her stand, Milagros was barely heavier than my own children. While that in and of itself wasn't alarming, it struck me then just how frail and vulnerable she was, and how very little I could do about that.

"We're going to go to the Jeep, okay?" Shiloh said. "And then we're going to borrow Hector's ex's boat, so we can get you to the mainland and to a hospital."

This perked her up a bit. "That *pollita* won't let Hector use it," she muttered.

"I bet she will, Milagros," I said, meeting Shiloh's eyes over her head. His were as wide as my own must have been. "This is an emergency."

"I'm sorry," Milagros said weakly as we lifted her into the front seat of the Jeep.

"Don't apologize, *amor. Está bien,*" said Hector, who'd appeared with a duffel bag in tow. While I could tell he was shaken, he was clearly trying to put on a brave face for her. I hadn't doubted his love for Milagros before, but now I saw, in a way that I hadn't earlier, that she was as much his second chance as he was hers—not unlike Shiloh and I had been to each other, I realized with a strange mix of nostalgia and sadness.

"Try to rest, Milagros," I told her.

The girls had returned with their backpacks, and the three of us squished into the backseat beside Hector. As we began to move, Milagros let her eyes fall closed, which sent a fresh wave of freak-out surging through me. Was it safe to let someone sleep after they'd suffered a heart attack—or did that up the odds they'd never wake up again? Was there something else we were supposed to be doing? How had mankind managed to survive before Google?

How would we ever get Milagros to the hospital in time?

Shiloh was navigating the Jeep past potholes and puddles with the same focus and determination that he had when he'd taken me flying. I realized then that I didn't need him to be my father; I needed him to be exactly who he was. The question was, did he still feel that way about me, especially given that I'd turned into a shadow of my old self?

Beside me, the girls kept glancing at Milagros nervously. Hoping to distract them—heck, hoping to distract all of us—I turned to Hector. "I never had a chance to ask you. How did you and Milagros meet?"

He put a hand gently on her shoulder. "Well, it's a small island, so most people meet sooner than later," he said after a moment. "But Milagros was my high school English teacher and was the first woman I ever loved."

"It's not what you think," Milagros murmured.

"No one thinks anything, Milly," said Hector affectionately. "To make a short story long, I never said anything at the time, but Milly must have known that I only had eyes for her. Then I left the island after high school and went to work in shipping in Miami. I was in Florida for many years, then in New York for a while before I moved to San Juan in my early forties. Flor—that's my ex-wife—is from Vieques, too, and she wanted to move back here when I retired. So, a little over a year ago, we bought a house right near the marina. Maybe six months ago or so, I was at the bar one evening, and I saw Milagros walking down the street with a friend. That day I went home and told Flor it was over between us. Man, was she angry. I thought she was going to turn me into shark food."

"Really?" said Isa, whose face had brightened.

"Maybe," he said, chuckling. "She's probably relieved it's over—we hadn't really loved each other for a long time, if we ever had—but no one likes to be left. *Pero* life is short and opportunities for real love don't come around too often." He leaned forward and kissed Milagros' cheek gently, and though she didn't open her eyes, she leaned toward him slightly. "I wasn't going to waste this one."

"Awww," said Charlotte.

"For the record, I couldn't date my teacher," said Isa. "Even if I was old."

"Rude," spat Charlotte.

"It's okay. I hope you don't, Isa," said Milagros with a wan smile.

Hector leaned over the armrest and pointed right. "Okay, turn here. It's just up the hill. See that?"

The house was behind a large wrought-iron gate. Hector gave Shiloh the code, and the gate opened, which was when I realized that the house was more like a manor. A sprawling stucco building that had been painted sky blue, it had a Spanish-tiled roof and a clear view of the ocean. Aside from a few leaves and branches in the driveway and a large puddle in the middle of the grass, it appeared to have been untouched by the storm.

"That's a palace," said Isa.

Charlotte rolled her window down and stuck her face outside. "Why can't we have a house like *that?*"

"Shipping can be a brisk business," said Hector. "Milagros, ¿estás bien?"

Her bright pink housedress only accentuated her pallor, and my heart began to beat faster. I'd been hoping she would regain some of her strength on the ride over, but when she simply nodded in agreement, she looked as weak as she had at the house.

"I'll be right back, okay?" said Hector, hopping out of the Jeep.

We watched him through the windows as a tall, thin woman wearing a flowing fuchsia caftan greeted him. Her blonde hair seemed to have just been blown out, and her face was expertly made up. She was significantly younger than Hector, and I wondered if maybe she was his daughter.

Then she looked Hector up and down . . . and promptly slammed the door in his face.

"I'm going out there," I said.

"Are you sure?" said Shiloh. "We might need to let them work it out."

"We don't have time for them to work it out," I said in a low voice.

He glanced at Milagros. "Fair enough."

I'd just opened my door when I paused and turned to Charlotte. "Hey, how are you feeling?"

Her eyebrow was twitching, just like Paul's did when he was lying. "I'm fine, Mom."

"The truth, Charlotte," I said. I'd been trying to be firm, but mostly I sounded afraid.

She glanced at Isa, who gave her a fierce look; for all their fighting, Isa was more protective of her sister than I gave her credit for. "I kind of have a headache," she admitted. "I'm thirsty, too."

I grabbed my water bottle from my bag and handed it to Charlotte, who immediately drained it.

"You just took your insulin before we left, right?" I asked.

She nodded. "Just before I had the last of the rice and beans and a little papaya."

I swallowed the boulder-sized lump in my throat. If this wasn't about her not eating, then her insulin had started to break down; there was no other way to explain it.

"Please test your sugar," I told her. "I'll be right back, and then we'll figure out a corrective dose of insulin, okay?"

She nodded meekly.

"I'm coming with you," said Shiloh.

"Good," I said. Given that Flor still hadn't opened the door for Hector, it was possible I'd need him. "Come get us if anything happens to Charlotte or Milagros. Got it?" I said to Isa, who nodded.

When I reached the house, I screamed Flor's name so loud that Hector and Shiloh startled. When she didn't appear, I yelled again. "Flor! Open up. *Right now!*"

I was about to do it a third time when the door was flung open. "Who are *you?*" she asked, eyeing me.

"I'm Libby, and one of my daughters is a type one diabetic. And Milagros—"

She held up a perfectly manicured hand. "I don't need to hear about my ex-husband's mistress."

"Maybe not, but I'm guessing you don't want to hear she died because you didn't help," I growled. Flor closed her mouth as fast as she'd just opened it, so I took this as my sign to carry on. "We're pretty sure she had a heart attack and we need to use your boat." Now I waited for her response, but she said nothing.

Well, I wasn't too proud to beg. "Listen," I said, staring into Flor's bright green eyes. "This is literally a matter of life or death. Not just Milagros. My daughter needs new insulin. Immediately, or she. Will. *Die*. Please, Flor," I pleaded. "She's *twelve*."

Flor's gaze flitted from me to Shiloh to the car.

She was softening; I could feel it. But I was almost afraid to look at her too closely for fear she'd change her mind.

Then she sighed deeply and turned to Hector. "The boat only takes six and Mami is wilting in the heat," she said to Hector. "And Papi needs dialysis in the next day or two. They'll have to go with you."

"What are Chaco and Maria doing here?" asked Hector, peering behind her into the house.

"Not that it's your business, since this is my house now," she said pointedly, "but they live with me. Can you take care of them if I send them with you?"

I held my breath waiting for him to respond. After a moment, he sighed and said, "*Sí.*"

"Hector, wait," I said. "You, Milagros, me, Shiloh, and the girls makes six. Two of us will have to stay behind."

Flor was staring at the sky now; she seemed to be working something out in her head. After a moment, she looked at me again. "How old is your other daughter?"

"Also twelve," I said. "They're twins."

"Then they wouldn't weigh down the boat too much." She turned back to Hector. "I have one extra lifejacket. One of the girls can use it. But my parents go, or none of you go. Okay?"

My knees were weak. Charlotte and Milagros were actually going to get off the island.

Hector, too, seemed overcome with relief. "*Gracias*, Flor. So, the girls, Chaco and Maria, Milagros, me . . . can either of you drive a boat?" he asked me and Shiloh. "It's best if we have an extra driver." His eyes shifted to the Jeep. Through the glass, I could see that Milagros' eyes were still closed. "Just in case."

I shook my head—I could barely manage a kayak—but Shiloh, who'd grown up on the water, nodded.

"*Lo siento*, Libby," said Hector. I was about to ask him why he was apologizing to me when he added, "Could you stay?"

Before I could respond, Shiloh said, "No way. Libby, you need to be with Charlotte."

No—I *wanted* to be with her, and everyone else. But what Charlotte and Milagros *needed* was immediate medical attention, and I wasn't going to stand in the way of that. "There's no time to talk about this," I said. "You guys have to leave immediately."

"It's not safe for you to be here by yourself, Libby," said Shiloh in a low voice. Like my own, his T-shirt was drenched in sweat. "Who knows what could happen? There could be a rebound storm, and what are you going to eat?"

"There's a little bit of food left at Milagros', but forget whether or not it's safe for me." I felt more clearheaded than I had in days. Maybe even months. "All I want to know is whether you think it's safe to take the boat to Fajardo. You heard Hector earlier—that passageway can be dangerous. Especially after a storm. And you yourself said it could be choppy."

As we both turned toward the ocean, which was visible over the edge of Flor's property, I couldn't help but think of the dream I'd had of Charlotte, helplessly drifting away from me. The sky was clear and cloudless, but the waves hitting the beach were high and frothy. My heart galloped in my chest. What if the waves knocked the boat over? What if Milagros died on the way or . . .

I stopped myself. I could think of three hundred horrible things that could happen, which was alarming enough. But at least those were all vague possibilities. The horrible thing that would happen if they didn't risk going was a near certainty.

"They'll only be higher if we wait until evening," he said, reading my thoughts.

"Then it's settled." I looked at Shiloh. "Go on without me."

TWENTY-FIVE

I've done a lot of hard things in my life, but not a single one of them compared to keeping a straight face while saying goodbye to my family.

"You're sure about this?" said Shiloh. He was standing in front of Flor's white speedboat, which, however gleaming and glamorous, looked like it could be swallowed by the first large wave that it encountered—not that I was imagining any such thing.

"It's our only option," I said in my firmest, most I'm-the-mom-here voice. In reality, I was so terrified that in addition to my hands, my torso was actually trembling.

If they died, life would no longer be worth living. And yet I would have to go on, knowing that I was the reason why that had happened.

"Libby . . ." He almost looked like he was going to cry. "I wish we'd had a chance to talk first."

"I know." Did I ever. Why hadn't I just told him how hurt I had been, but how very much I wanted us to be like we used to be? What if I never had that chance? "And we will. But right now, you really need to go." I glanced at the girls, who were just about to step into the boat. "Hey, you two. Come give me one more hug before you go."

For once, they didn't complain; instead, they threw their arms around me and buried their faces against my chest. I pulled them close, inhaling the scent of their strawberry shampoo and blinking to clear the tears from my eyes before they could see that I didn't want to send them.

"You still feeling okay?" I asked Charlotte. As I'd feared, her meter had indicated that her insulin was becoming less effective. She'd taken a corrective dose to get her blood sugar back down, and it seemed to be working. But given that it was already less effective, I knew we had mere hours before it stopped altogether.

She nodded earnestly, all of her usual bravado long gone.

"You're going to be fine," I said. "But if anything changes, you tell Papi or Hector right away."

"Or me," said Isa, gnawing on a cuticle.

"Or Isa, who will tell Papi," I said, kissing Isa's head. To her, I whispered, "Thank you, sweetheart. You've been so brave, and so good to your sister. I really appreciate it."

"Thanks, Mom," she said, pulling her hand out of her mouth to hug me again.

"Okay, you guys," I said. "It's time to get moving."

Shiloh put his hand on my lower back. "Cutie, be so careful, okay?"

"Me?" I pretended to scoff. But as our eyes met, my bluster evaporated. "I'm going to miss you."

His face got all funny when I said that. "You'll see me no later than tomorrow morning," he said. "Maybe even tonight, depending on how this goes." He glanced back at Milagros, who was already on the boat. "Wish us luck."

"Good luck," I said. I'd already hugged Milagros goodbye—gently, of course—but I called to her again. "Milly, let Hector and Shiloh take good care of you, okay?"

"*Sí, mija,*" she called back. She looked less sickly than she had in the Jeep, but I knew better than to take that as a sign that she'd be fine. "Just watch my dogs for me."

"You know I will."

She smiled and waved weakly.

I waved back, then looked at Shiloh. "I love you so much."

"I love you even more," he said, leaning in to kiss me.

I let his lips rest on mine and his arms stay wrapped around me, even though they needed to get out of there, oh, say, yesterday. Because even though I was not about to admit this out loud, I couldn't help but wonder what would happen if it was the last time we had this chance.

As they pulled away from Flor's dock, I waved until I could wave no longer. Then I stood and watched the boat grow smaller and smaller in the distance until it was finally swallowed by the horizon. And I prayed that my myriad fears were not premonitions, which my mind was intent on convincing me they were, but rather just a string of terrible possibilities that would never come to pass.

~

When I got back to the guesthouse, I looked around for a minute or two, unsure of what to do next. Then I remembered what my father had often told Paul and me: when you didn't know what to think or say, it probably meant there was still work to be done.

So I packed up all the things that Shiloh and the girls had not taken with them. Then I cleaned every inch of the place, and the patio, too. After that was finished, I went to Milagros' and scrubbed her sinks and mopped her floors. I was about to start dusting when I heard a scratching noise.

I froze.

The scratching grew louder and more insistent.

Adrenaline blossomed in my chest with all the warmth of rum but none of the pleasure. Was someone trying to jimmy the lock? It struck me then how very alone I was—I had no one on the island to call, let alone a way to call them, nor a way to defend myself. No wonder Shiloh was worried about me. I might as well have walked down the middle of the road with a target taped to my back.

I looked around Milagros' kitchen before slowly crouching down. Then I crawled to the cupboard and retrieved a frying pan. Still low to the ground, I crouched in the corner and listened. The scratching had stopped.

Suddenly a sharp yell rang through the air.

Except it wasn't yelling at all. It was a bark.

"Crap," I muttered. I'd promised Milagros I'd care for her dogs, and what did I do instead? Molly Maid-ed the entire place while the dogs were probably out there gnawing on each other for sustenance.

When I unlocked the dead bolt and peered outside, Pedro was peering up at me with his one eye, as if to say, "Are you done freaking out and ready to feed me?"

I examined him for a moment, then opened the door. Pedro stuck his head through the doorway and glanced around—looking for Milagros, no doubt. Then he trotted inside.

"Make yourself at home, Cujo," I muttered, following behind him. "Sorry to disappoint you, but the woman you're looking for is approaching Fajardo right now." But as soon as I said this, I felt tears pricking my eyes. *Was* she? Or were they all stranded in the Atlantic—or worse, sinking toward the bottom of it?

"Of course they're about to dock," I said, as though Pedro was the one who'd put this thought inside my head. "How horrible to even put that kind of energy out into the universe."

It occurred to me that I was talking to a one-eyed dog. It was better than a volleyball with a face painted on it—but still.

I'd ended up back in the kitchen, though I hadn't remembered walking there, and Pedro plopped down right in front of my feet and cocked his head, like he was listening. Maybe that's why I added, "I'm not really used to being alone, if you must know. You're welcome to stick around if you want to."

He whimpered a little.

"You're hungry, right?" I said, and he barked. In spite of everything, I laughed. "I'll take that as a yes. We're low on food over here, but I think Milagros has some dog food, and lucky for you, I have a key so I can feed you. Come on," I said, like he was one of my kids.

I found the food in a far cupboard and put it in a bowl, but when I set the bowl in front of him, he plopped down on his hindquarters.

"She doesn't let you eat inside, does she? And you're not some dumb puppy, either. You've been around the block a few times." I eyed him. He had a white little dog beard and—well, maybe this is a strange way to describe a dog, but he had an aura of *knowing* about him. "If I had to guess, you're probably forty-seven in dog years. Midlife isn't for the faint of heart, am I right?" I said.

He looked down at his paws, then back up at me.

"All right," I said, picking up the bowl. "Let's go outside. When you're done, I'll feed your friends."

I let us both out the back door and set the bowl in front of him on the patio. I'd say he ate the whole thing, but really, he inhaled it; the bowl was empty before I heard a single crunch. He glanced at me and licked his lips, or whatever it is dogs have over their fangs. Then he darted under a hole in the fence that I hadn't noticed before.

"Hey! Dine and dash isn't allowed around here!" I called after him, but he was already gone.

He was just a dog—I knew that—but I felt horribly alone after he left. I went to see if the other dogs were out front, but even after I waited on the porch and called for them, they didn't appear. After some internal debate I left a couple bowls of food on the front porch, though I had a feeling that the iguanas would make a meal of it, and went back to Milagros' to finish wiping down the shutters.

Ten minutes later I was done, so I returned to the guesthouse. Without a fan running or air-conditioning, the air was oppressively hot, and though I had no way to tell time, the position of the sun suggested to me that there were hours to go before it set. Attempting to relax was out of the question; when I sat on the patio to try to read one of the novels stocked in the guesthouse the words blurred, and I found myself imagining Charlotte's meter with a deadly number across the screen, and Milagros clutching her heart and keeling over. After ten or so minutes of this—or who knows, maybe it was an hour—I finally gave up and went back inside to arm myself so I could go for a walk.

I chose a fork with sharp-looking tines, stuck it in my pocket, locked the door, and then headed out.

Milagros didn't live in a neighborhood, not in a traditional sense; instead, the homes along her stretch of the southern coast were on large lots, each set back several hundred feet from the main road. It was eerie seeing so few cars out, and though I didn't wander onto anyone's property, I couldn't hear a single person, either. I supposed I'd been looking to see if anyone needed help—or maybe I was just hoping to see another human being.

No such luck. But I probably would have kept walking if I hadn't started getting woozy. I'd never been the kind of person who had to be reminded to eat, but then again, I'd never had to send my family across the ocean without me, and so I hadn't had a single morsel of food since the night before. I turned and began to walk back, hoping I wouldn't pass out before I got home.

I was nearly at Milagros' when Pedro came shooting out of the bushes. His little legs were going so fast I thought for sure he was going to charge me. But when he reached me, he immediately began running circles around my feet.

"No more running away and then surprising me!" I scolded as he continued to spin. "I almost peed myself."

He cocked his head.

"Okay," I admitted. "Maybe I did already. But you try giving birth to two children at once and see how your bladder holds up."

Pedro circled me for a moment, then started for the house.

"Right," I said, following him. "Let's go hold down the fort."

~

As the sun began to set, I was forced to admit that Shiloh would not be making it back to Vieques that night. I wasn't worried about being on my own, though; I just feared his absence meant something terrible had happened to Milagros, or Charlotte, or maybe all seven of them. Worse, I would have no way of finding out for at least the next eight to twelve hours.

Why wasn't the electricity back on yet so I could charge my phone and call them? Was there some magic carpet I hadn't thought of that would get me out of here? Maybe Flor had another boat, or a rich friend who could lend me one, as well as a captain with a jaunty cap—or maybe just someone who knew how to navigate a boat through choppy water.

I let myself continue down this pointless path for a few minutes. Then it occurred to me that it was probably cocktail hour. I wasn't feeling particularly festive without Milagros there, but I knew she'd have wanted me to keep up her tradition, and anyway, I had nothing else to do. So I let myself back into her house to get some rum. I was prepared to down the stuff straight, but I located an unopened container of guava juice in her cupboard and decided to see if it made a decent mixer.

Spoiler alert: indeed, it did. An hour later I'd finished two tumblers of island elixir, and the guesthouse had started rotating faster than the earth. It was not unpleasant, in that at least I couldn't focus long enough to obsess about the terrible string of possibilities that my mind was insistent upon bringing to the surface. Maybe that's why I decided a third drink was in order.

"I appreciate you not judging me," I said to Pedro. Though his furry friends still hadn't shown up to have their food, I'd been pleasantly surprised when Pedro decided to stick around the guesthouse. Now he was on the table—I wasn't sure how he'd gotten there, exactly, but sanitation had quickly made its way down my list of priorities, and I had convinced myself his perch made him more effective as a watchdog.

"I'm not sure if anyone's ever told you this before, but you're a pretty good listener," I said, and I may or may not have been slurring. It was nearly dark, and I'd had to position a flashlight to shine on my makeshift cocktail station—so I couldn't be faulted for missing the glass once or thrice. I added a splash of guava juice, mixed it with my finger, then lifted my tumbler to the dog. "Here's to us."

But as I put the concoction to my lips, I was forced to admit that no amount of alcohol was going to make me forget how much I longed for my family. I abandoned the glass on the counter, walked to the sunroom, and before I could chastise myself for being dramatic, threw myself down on the pullout sofa. The cushions still smelled like the girls' strawberry shampoo, so I buried my face in them for a moment and inhaled deeply. When I finally came back up for air, I was crying like a baby. Or, you know. A woman who had no idea whether the people she loved most were alive.

I was crying so hard that I didn't see Pedro hop off the table and trot over to the sofa, but he whimpered to let me know he was waiting just below my knee. I stopped midsob and looked down at him. Then I put my hand on his back, wondering how he'd react.

He closed his eye contentedly, but feeling his mangy fur beneath my fingers only made me cry harder, and he opened his eye again and jumped up on the sofa beside me.

"Well hey there, buddy," I said, but he was regarding me rather skeptically. "You're right," I conceded. "You're a tough little guy. I feel like you can handle the truth."

He stared at me and waited.

I wiped my face on my T-shirt. "The truth is, I am so freaking tired, Pedro. I've been trying to keep it together for . . ." I was about to say *weeks now* when I realized what a vast understatement that was. My chest shuddered as I tried to take a deep breath. "Since my dad died,"

I admitted after a moment. "I know he lived longer than lots of people get to live, but it doesn't seem right that the only parent I had for most of my life is gone."

My father was seventy-four years young, as he liked to call himself, and had been staying with us in New York for the twins' birthday. Except he never did get to see them blow out their candles; the night before they turned twelve he bundled up and went out for a walk after dinner, and around the time he should have returned, a stranger called me and said she'd found him unconscious in the middle of a snowy sidewalk. We thought maybe he'd slipped on ice, but it turned out that he'd had a massive stroke.

Later I would tell people that at least he was with Paul and me in New York when it happened, which gave us a chance to say goodbye to him.

That was true. But to be clear, it was awful. When we could finally see him at the hospital, he was barely conscious, and half his face was just hanging there, like it had forgotten what his bone structure was for. The worst part was that he'd always said he wanted to go out with a bang when he was a hundred or while he watched the Tigers win the World Series—whichever came first (though he was the first to admit that the former was far more likely, as his beloved baseball team had been disappointing him for as long as he'd been a fan).

Come to find out he'd end up exiting this world the same way my mother had: tethered to a hospital bed, forming a final memory that involved leaving behind everyone who loved him most and being unable to do a damn thing about it.

But just before he slipped out of consciousness for good, his eyes met mine and he tried to speak. I couldn't understand the first part of what he'd been trying to say. But his last words—there was no mistaking those. They weren't *Goodbye*, or *Get Paul*, or even *Charlotte*, which was my mother's name.

They were *Libby Lou*.

It was the name he'd been calling me since I was old enough to respond to it, and it was synonymous with *I love you.*

And he had.

How could I live without that?

I didn't even bother wiping my tears away as I looked at Pedro again, because in spite of all my worries and heartache, it felt good to let myself go—to admit the truth, even to a dog.

"You know what *really* sucks?"

He tilted his head as if to say, *Go on.* So, naturally, I did.

"After Charlotte was diagnosed with diabetes, I thought, 'Okay, we've used up our bad luck for a good long time.' But only an idiot would think it works that way, because six months later my dad died. And guess what, Pedro? Dunderhead that I am, once again I thought: 'We're finally in the clear!' But it turns out that this existence is just a bottomless well of bad things, because my brother just announced he's getting a divorce, and my husband is being as sneaky as my ex-husband was, and my family might be dead right now because I was so insistent on dragging us here and acting like everything was fine. But as anyone who lives on Vieques can attest, there's no amount of wishful thinking that's going to change that it's not fine at all. Life is just so damn *hard.* No matter how good you have it."

He barked once, but it wasn't a mean bark. It was almost like he was agreeing with me.

"Thanks for listening to me, Pedro," I said, blinking back new tears. But for once they were tears of relief, not sorrow. "Maybe honesty really is the best policy. Or something."

The sun had slipped beneath the horizon, but the moon was high and bright, and its reflection on the water filled the guesthouse, so I flung an arm over my eyes to block the last of the light. And then, before I could think any more terrible thoughts, my brain took mercy on me and shut off.

TWENTY-SIX

The next thing I knew, Pedro was barking his mother-loving head off and someone was banging on the door.

My sleep-crusted eyes sprang open, but it took me a moment to remember why I'd woken up on the sofa. "Coming!" I tried to yell, but the rum and weeping must have taken a toll on my vocal cords, because I sounded like a bullfrog at the height of mating season.

Pedro was still yapping and running back and forth in front of the door. I tried to *shhh* him as I reached for the lock. "Who is it?" I called, because my mental fog was slowly lifting, and it had occurred to me that Shiloh, who I'd been expecting, had a key and would have let himself in.

"It's me, you lunatic. Open up."

"Paul?" As thrilled as I was to hear my brother's voice, I had no idea what he was doing here. Sure, I'd sent him a telepathic cry for help. But where were Shiloh and the girls?

I flung the door open and found him standing there wearing an enormous smile. "The good news is," he announced as he stepped inside, "Charlotte has new insulin and test strips, Milagros is in the hospital, and obviously, in addition to being a stellar pilot, Shiloh is one hell of a boat captain. Everyone is okay."

"Oh, thank God," I said, reaching for the wall to steady myself.

"I go by Paul these days, but you're welcome."

I would have laughed if I hadn't just burst into tears. My family had survived! Milagros was fine! I was wrong, wrong, wrong, just like I'd been about my diagnosis!

"Libby?" said Paul, examining me. "You do realize I just gave you *great* news . . . right?"

Instead of responding, I threw my arms around him. I was hugging far tighter and longer than he normally allowed, but I must have looked particularly rough because he patted my back and said, "It's okay, Libby. I'm not sure why you're crying, and I'm going to assume it's stress, but it's all right."

"Thank you," I whimpered, spreading snot all over his three-hundred-dollar shirt. "Thank you for coming here and telling me that and being you. I love you, Paul."

"I love you, too," he said slowly. "But . . . are you okay?"

"No, but I will be," I said, finally releasing him. I wiped my eyes. Only then did I realize I still had no idea what he was doing in Vieques. Especially since he had a fear of flying that was impervious to cognitive behavioral therapy, hypnosis, and hard liquor. "Where is Shiloh? And *how* did you get here?"

"It's called flying private. Perhaps your spouse has mentioned it to you?" he said with a wry grin.

"Ignoring you. Now, details, please."

He smirked. "As a frequent consumer of media, including but not limited to national and international weather reports, I saw the news about the storm, and when I couldn't get hold of you after calling and texting forty-two times, I knew it was bad. After procuring some perfectly legal sedatives from my doctor, I got on a commercial flight to Florida last night. It was super unpleasant, for the record, but this morning I finally spoke to your husband, then flew private from Orlando to Fajardo, and had a helpful man named José jet me to Vieques on a boat, where I flagged down a lovely taxi driver named Luisa at the marina.

In fact, she's outside waiting for us." Now he smiled. "You do know I'd sell the brownstone if it meant keeping you safe."

"Thank you," I said sincerely. "But how did you manage all that this early in the day?"

"It's—" He examined his watch. "Nearly noon, Sleeping Fruity."

"Oh." My cheeks flushed with embarrassment. I'd been asleep all this time, even as my family could have been bobbing in the Atlantic?

"But to your point," he continued, "it wasn't just the news about the storm and Vieques losing power. I . . . well, I sensed you needed me. Was I wrong?"

"No," I sniffed, because I'd started to tear up again. "You were a hundred percent right. Thank you for coming."

"I'd say my pleasure, but I'm still rattled from the landing this morning."

I examined him. He was dressed in a crisp if now slightly booger-covered button-down and a pair of linen pants that looked like they were freshly pressed, and he wasn't even *sweating*.

"Shiloh wanted to come with me," he explained, "but Isa wasn't doing so well."

"Isa?" I said. "You mean Charlotte?"

He shook his head. "Apparently Charlotte was pretty shaky when they landed in Fajardo, and—well, Isa freaked out. I'll let them fill in the rest."

"Oh no," I said. Here I'd been so worried about Charlotte that I hadn't spent nearly enough time thinking about how this was affecting Isa. "Where are they now?"

"At the hotel I'm staying at in Fajardo. I got you a room."

"That was generous of you."

"Don't mention it," he said, arching a brow. "And you do know I mean that literally, right?"

I rolled my eyes. "Noted. So Milagros is fine?"

His smirk disappeared. "She is struggling, Libby. She's in the hospital, and she's not doing super well. That's all I know."

My face fell. "You know that's what they said about Dad, right?"

"Sweetie, they're not the same. Let's focus on something more positive."

I pulled my head back and looked at him like he'd just told me he was planning to break into the Federal Reserve. *He* was telling *me* to be positive? I really must be in bad shape.

Ignoring my expression, he said, "When's the last time you were intimate with a bar of soap?"

"I had a rough couple of days," I said, crossing my arms over my chest.

"Oh, I can smell that," he said, fanning his face.

"I can tell you're trying to change the subject to make me feel better, but I'm serious."

"I know you are, Libs, and that's progress. Let's focus on what we can control for now, yes? Get your stuff and let's get out of here so you can go see Milagros."

"Just like that?" I said, because I'd looked at the dog, who must have surmised that Paul was of no threat and was now doing a little tap-dance routine between me and him. "I can't leave Pedro here."

"*Pedro?*" said Paul, watching as the dog stopped pacing so he could plop down directly on top of my feet. The bruised flesh between my toes was still tender, but I liked the way he felt.

"Yeah," I said, reaching down to pat his head. "He's one of Milagros' mutts, but he's grown on me pretty quickly."

"Like a fungus," remarked Paul.

"Come on, he's adorable," I said. "And a very good listener. In fact, Pedro helped me see that it's time to stop holding it all in."

"So, I should expect more spontaneous sobbing?"

Probably. "No."

"Thanks for the heads-up."

I sighed. "You're welcome. By the way, where's Charlie?" I asked.

"Still on Fire Island." He didn't say more, but his face had always been its own form of shorthand. And his had just revealed that he was deeply hurt.

He didn't want this divorce at all, I realized suddenly.

"We will discuss this later," I said gently. "For now, we need to get to the hospital."

He looked relieved. "Are you really bringing the dog?"

I glanced over at Pedro, who was watching me with his one good eye. "I can't just leave him here, not when there's no one here to feed or take care of him," I said. "He can come back with Hector—that's Milagros' boyfriend—when he returns the boat we borrowed."

"Fine," sighed Paul, "but if he gnaws off my face, you're paying for the plastic surgery."

I threw my arms around him and gave him a huge smooch. "Thank you. He's a good dog—you'll see."

"I didn't take you for a dog person," said Paul, shaking his head with disbelief.

"I'm not," I said.

But an hour later, as I pressed my face to the boat window and watched Vieques disappear in the distance, I was glad I didn't have to say goodbye to one tiny part of the island just yet.

TWENTY-SEVEN

Paul, who had rented an SUV in Fajardo, drove me directly from the marina to the hospital. When we pulled up, he looked at Pedro, who was lounging at my feet, and then back at me. "You can't take him in, you know."

I supposed I knew that in the way one knows the ozone layer is rapidly thinning but can note no difference in the quality of the air they breathe. In reality, I hadn't thought about having to leave him behind, even for a few hours. "Can you please keep an eye on him?" I asked. "I really need to get in there and see Milagros as soon as possible. I promise he'll behave for you." As if to demonstrate this, I patted my lap, and Pedro—who, up until this point had never made any indication he'd been trained to do anything except run wild—jumped up and licked my face. His tongue was probably host to seventeen different diseases, but I still laughed. "See?" I said.

Paul sighed deeply. "Listen, I can't believe I'm offering this, but why don't I see if I can find a place to buy him a leash and some food?"

"Really?" I said. "You would do that for me?"

When he nodded, I leaned over the armrest and kissed his cheek. "You really love me, don't you?"

He pretended to be offended. "Would I have flown over shark-infested waters in two-winged death traps to save you if I didn't? All the same, you owe me."

"That was true long before you offered to dog sit. I'll have Shiloh text you when we're on our way back." I gave Pedro a quick scratch under the chin before hopping out of the SUV. "Wish me—" I stopped myself before I could tell him to wish me luck, because I wasn't the one who needed it. "Wish Milagros the best," I said.

"Already done," he called through the window. "Love you the most!"

I didn't yell back that he was wrong. After all that he'd done for me, maybe that was actually true.

~

I was awash with equal parts anticipation and anxiety as I walked through the hospital's double doors. Milagros was alive; that was no small victory. But when Paul said she was "struggling," what did that mean, exactly?

I was ready to pull my head out of the sand and find out.

I broke into a run as soon as I spotted Shiloh in the lobby. "Where are the girls?" I said breathlessly, throwing my arms around him.

"Hi to you, too," he said, planting a kiss on my lips. "They're at the hotel. I double-checked Charlotte's blood sugar before I left and she's totally fine—I take it Paul told you we swapped out all her supplies yesterday?"

I nodded. "What about Isa? Paul said she wasn't doing well."

"She was freaked out about Charlotte's health, but she's calmed down a lot. Now they're vegging out in front of the TV in a room that's nearly freezer temperature. They claim they never want to be warm again."

"They're *alone*?"

"It's only ten minutes away, and I didn't want to bring them to the hospital," he explained apologetically. "They promised to be good, and there's a doctor on call at the hotel if anything goes wrong."

"That makes me nervous," I admitted, "but I trust you." His arms were still around me, and I pressed my face into his neck. He smelled so good, and he felt so solid and reassuring and *alive*. "Thank you," I added.

"For what?" he said.

"Getting everyone here safely."

"It's no big deal."

"Yes it is," I insisted. "I was so scared."

"You're the one who thought to look for a boat. But Libby," he said, too gently. "Are you all right? Did anything happen after we left?"

I was about to tell him I was fine when it occurred to me that I wasn't, and I was done pretending that I was. "We'll talk after I see Milagros," I said, tugging on his shirt so he'd follow me to the elevator bank. "Which floor?"

"Fourth," he said as I pressed the button that would take us up.

"Have you seen her recently?" I asked.

He nodded. "I've been here for about an hour."

"And?" I said.

He hesitated.

"I can handle it," I said.

He exhaled audibly. "The damage to her heart muscle was pretty extensive, Libs. And the longer you wait after a heart attack, the worse it is. She probably wouldn't have made it if we'd waited any longer."

"Thank you for being honest with me," I said, touching his face; his usual stubble was now a short beard, and with the deep tan that he'd somehow managed to get in the middle of a storm, he looked as handsome as he ever had. "I don't tell you often enough how much I appreciate you."

"Libby, you don't have to," he said, giving me a quizzical look. "I know that."

"I know you know, but—"

There was a ding, and the elevator doors opened before I could finish.

"You ready?" he said.

I had been until he said that. "No," I said, stepping off the elevator. "But I want to see Milagros, so let's go."

Save for the beeping of machines and the sound of someone moaning down the hall, the floor was eerily silent.

Then I saw Hector.

He was bent over making a terrible wheezing sort of cry, and as soon as he lifted his head, I recognized the agony in his eyes.

Because it was the same pain that my father had shown when he told me and Paul that our mother was gone.

"No!" I cried. I started to run, but I'd only taken a few steps when a wailing sound filled the hallway. It took me a moment to realize that it was coming from my mouth.

I didn't even bother trying to stop myself. Shiloh was rushing toward me, but I held out my hand to indicate I didn't want to be held or comforted. I was done pretending things were fine. It was time to face reality.

I steadied myself and took several lurching steps past Hector into Milagros' room. Tears blurred my vision, but I could see that her eyes and mouth were shut. At least she looked peaceful. But it was little comfort, because after all that, I hadn't even had a chance to say good-bye to her.

"Oh Milagros," I said, taking her hand. Her fingers were still warm and her skin felt like crumpled tissue paper beneath my fingers. "Did I even tell you how much I loved you? Or that you saved my life—not just when I had that infection, but at least a dozen other times, just by being there for me?" I said, and now I was sobbing again. "I'm sorry I didn't tell you that I loved you so much. I'm sorry I didn't thank you half as much as I should have."

But just as I bent to kiss her cheek one last time, her fingers tightened around mine and her eyes flew open.

And then I'm sorry to report that I screamed and lurched backward like I'd just seen a ghost.

"Libby," she said hoarsely. *"Estoy aquí. Tu estás aquí. Todo está bien."* I'm here. You are here. Everything is fine.

"Milagros!" I cried. "I thought you were . . ."

"¿Muerta? Not yet, *mija,"* she said, her lips curling into the faintest smile. "Soon enough, but *ya no."*

Now I was crying with happiness. "I'm so relieved! I'm sorry I thought the worst, I just . . ." I just couldn't seem to turn off my worst-case-scenario mode.

Hector appeared in the doorway, with Shiloh just behind him. *"Lo siento,* Libby—I didn't mean to scare you. Milly was asleep," he said apologetically. "I just needed a minute."

Through my tears, I managed a smile. "Yeah, I figured that out. It's okay," I told him, because it was. Milagros was alive. And maybe because of that, I felt that way, too.

"Hector, Shiloh, can Libby and I talk for a second?" said Milagros.

"Claro que sí," said Shiloh, as Hector nodded.

"We'll let you know when we're done," said Milagros, and Hector nodded.

Milagros gestured to the chair beside her bed. I sat in it and reached for her hand again.

"This has all been so scary for you. How are you doing, *mija?"* she asked.

I frowned. "I'm not the one who just had a heart attack."

"Don't worry about me, Libby." The lines around her eyes deepened as she smiled at me. "Eighty-three is a good long life. If the time comes, I'm ready."

"Milagros, please don't say that," I said. "I need you. Now more than ever."

"I'll always be with you, even after this body's long gone," she said, squeezing my arm.

I spoke before I could think. "If that's true, where's my father?" I said. "It's been six months, and I'm still waiting for some sign he's still with me."

She looked at me for a moment. "*Mija*," she finally said, "you just got your family—and me and Hector—out of a disaster. Do you think your father wasn't with you during all that?"

I blinked hard, but the tears streamed down my cheeks anyway. "Yes," I said softly. "You're right."

"Like I said, I'm always right most of the time," she said, winking. But then her face grew serious again. "You're having a hard time. I see now that it's even harder than we talked about earlier. And don't tell me how great your life is—we're *all* entitled to feel pain, no matter how good we think we have it. You've had a whole lot of stuff thrown at you lately, and now this," she said, gesturing toward her hospital bed.

I bit my lip, then said, "Yes—I've really been struggling, and on top of that, I've felt horribly guilty."

"Good girl. Say it. Let it be hard."

Wasn't I already doing that? "What do you mean?"

"Life is filled with difficult things," she said, sighing so deeply that I wondered for a second if she was having a hard time breathing. "Not always—let's say sixty-forty. But that forty percent is tough, terrible, ugly stuff. Don't you think so?"

The trip I'd planned for my family had morphed into something terrifying. Charlotte had suffered multiple health scares, and Milagros had gotten far cozier with death than I ever wanted to witness. And of course, my father—my North Star, my voice of reason, arguably the person who loved me more than anyone else had—was gone. Never had

I known quite so acutely that life was filled with tough, terrible, ugly stuff. "Of course," I said in a choked tone.

"*Bueno*," she said. "You know I like to look for the good in every situation, if only because it makes the days brighter. I don't want you to stop doing that, either. But you know what one of my ex-husbands taught me?"

"I'm almost afraid to ask."

"Repression turns into depression," she said, nodding sagely. "You get that, Libby?"

"Yes," I whispered. Was *that* what had happened to me?

Now she nodded even more emphatically. "You have to tell Shiloh how you're feeling. Tell him everything."

But when I told him I didn't feel alive, his response was to try to kill me in a tiny plane. I'd attempted to let him in, and he'd responded by keeping secrets from me. "I tried that, and it didn't work," I said.

She smiled. "Then try again."

A nurse had just appeared in the doorway. "Visiting hours are almost over. We're going to run some tests, so I'll have to ask you to wrap this up."

My face crumpled as I met Milagros' eyes. "I can't believe we have to say goodbye tomorrow. This wasn't how this trip was supposed to go."

"Even so, how good it was to spend time together," she said, patting my hand. "To see your wonderful daughters and spend time with the four of you, and for you to get to know my Hector. Things worked out just like they were supposed to."

I kissed her cheek. "I meant what I said when I thought you were dead," I said, and she laughed. "I love you. Thank you for all you've done for me."

"No, thank *you*. The doctor said I would have died if I'd stayed on the island. If you hadn't been in Vieques and made me come to Fajardo . . . Well, it's a good thing you were there."

"Yes," I said, smiling at her. "I guess it was."

TWENTY-EIGHT

The girls were lounging on the bed when Shiloh and I returned to the hotel. I didn't even tell them to put their phones down; I just jumped between them, scooped them into my arms, and kissed their faces over and over until they squirmed away from me.

"My babies!" I said. "I can't tell you how hard it was to be away from you. Are you both okay?"

"Mom, we're fine," said Charlotte. "We have food. Electricity. Insulin," she said pointedly. "What else could we possibly want?"

"Well, your mother, for starters," I joked. "But I'm glad to hear that gratitude. How are you feeling? How's your blood sugar? I really think it's time we talk to your endocrinologist about a continuous glucose monitor and an insulin pump. Because I can't help that I'm always going to be concerned about you, but I *can* do something about the way we monitor your health."

She was looking at me like I'd sprouted a horn. "Um, whoa. Papi got me everything I needed from the hospital pharmacy. No biggie."

I almost said nothing. In fact, a day earlier, I probably would have bitten my tongue. But Milagros' comment about repression was fresh in my mind. "Actually, it *was* a big deal," I told her. "I know you didn't choose this, and that living with it is not fun. But you can't keep blowing this off, and I'm not going to pretend it doesn't scare the living daylights out of me anymore. What happened in San Juan was preventable."

"I can't believe you're talking about *that* after what happened on Vieques," she said, glancing away from me. "I mean, *hello*. I didn't ask for the electricity to go out."

"You're right, and there's a lot about that trip that I should have done differently. Still, that's not my point." I could feel Shiloh's eyes on me, but I kept going. "Charlotte, maybe hearing how much your father and I love you and want to keep you healthy isn't that important. But at least think about Isa. Your sister was *terrified* in San Juan, and from what I heard, when you guys got off the boat in Fajardo. This affects her, too. A lot."

"Oh, you finally noticed?" remarked Isa, who was lying on her back on the bed.

"That's fair. I owe you a big apology. Your father and I—but especially me," I clarified, shooting him a look that I hoped conveyed solidarity, "have been paying so much attention to Charlotte's health that you've gotten the short end of the stick. That's not how it should be, and it ends here and now."

"Hmph," she said, but she'd sat up. After a moment she added, "Thanks."

I put my arm around her shoulder. "You're welcome. Listen, you two," I said, glancing back and forth between them, "I know you're just twelve—"

"Practically thirteen," interjected Charlotte.

"Exactly," I agreed, even though they were still six months from their next birthday. "My point is, you're active participants in this family. If you need something from me or Papi, or feel like we're glossing over stuff, or—well, anything—then I want you to tell us."

"Okay . . . ," said Isa.

"Is that a sincere okay, or a 'yeah right' okay?" I asked.

She frowned. "It means that you don't *like* when we tell you things aren't good. You're always telling us to look on the bright side, blah blah blah."

I winced, because it was true. "Also fair," I said. "I *do* like focusing on what's good—that's always been my go-to for dealing with hard stuff. But I'm also starting to see that sometimes I go overboard on it when I'm struggling, and I'm going to stop trying to do that, okay? I can handle whatever it is you need to tell me."

Shiloh arched an eyebrow. "Well put, Libby," he said after a moment.

"Thank you," I said. As soon as we had a moment alone, I intended to ask him about that phone call.

Then I kissed both girls' foreheads again. "I love you both so much," I repeated. "I don't know if I tell you that nearly enough."

"Oh, you do," said Charlotte, but she wasn't scowling anymore.

"Ditto," said Isa. "But Mom?"

"What is it, love?" I asked.

"You're still acting really weird."

I smiled at her. "Get used to it, sweetheart, because this is my new normal."

~

"Well, isn't this nice," said Paul. The five of us—or perhaps I should say six, as Pedro, newly leashed, was at Shiloh's feet—were having dinner on the patio of a nearby restaurant. The tropical storm hadn't hit the mainland as hard as Vieques, but there had been some flooding. Now all signs of the storm were already gone, and the night was still and clear.

"Isn't it?" I smiled at him from across the table. "Just think—if you hadn't come to get me, Pedro and I might still be stranded."

"It's nothing," he said.

Shiloh cleared his throat. "No, it isn't. Paul, I can't thank you enough for going to Vieques to get Libby. And then booking a hotel room for us . . . Well, you really shouldn't have."

Paul smiled to himself. "I help where I can."

"Too bad Toby and Max aren't here," said Charlotte. "They'd love this place."

"I bet they would. Maybe we can join you the next time you head to Puerto Rico for vacation."

"With Charlie?" I said pointedly.

"I was thinking of the three of us." There was an edge in his voice, and Shiloh glanced at me nervously.

"Is there anything you want to discuss?" I said. "Because you can. You don't have to hold it back. The girls know you're talking about getting a divorce."

"We don't want you to," said Charlotte, who was seated beside me.

"Oh honey," I said, reaching for her hand. "Uncle Paul doesn't want to, either. But we're going to support him no matter what, right?"

"Libby," said Paul pointedly. He leaned in toward me over the table, and in a stage whisper said, "I know you've just been through a lot, so I'm going to forgive you, but it's time to stop talking."

"How do you know he doesn't want to?" said Isa, ignoring Shiloh, who was shaking his head at her.

I shrugged. "I'm his twin sister. You two know how that goes."

"Again: not the time or place," said Paul, waving down a server.

Now Shiloh's eyes were darting back and forth between us, and the girls were stealing glances at each other.

"Anytime you're ready," I said as the server appeared beside our table.

After we'd ordered, Paul, who was clearly trying to redirect the conversation, asked if we were ready to leave the island; our flight left the following afternoon.

I reached down and scratched Pedro, who responded by thumping his tail against my leg. "Not even a little bit," I admitted.

"Really, Mom?" said Charlotte. "Because I am. I miss my friends. I want to be somewhere where the electricity isn't going to go out, and I don't have to worry about my insulin getting all wonky."

"I know, sweetheart. We had a few nice moments—like now," I said, looking around the table before glancing at Pedro. I knew I'd told the girls we could get a dog; it was a shame that Pedro wouldn't be the one. "But on the whole, I'll be the first to admit this vacation was kind of a bummer. When my oncologist told me to celebrate, I'm pretty sure getting stranded in a storm wasn't what she had in mind."

"What?" said Charlotte, sitting up suddenly. "An oncologist is a cancer doctor, right?"

"Yep! But it's just a routine thing. I go every couple of years now. The day we went to the bay? That was ten years cancer free for me."

"You didn't *tell* us?" said Isa, pushing away from the table. "Like, did you think we weren't grown up enough to handle it?"

"Not at all! I mean, initially, yes—I didn't bring it up before I got the results back because I didn't want you to worry. Then I found out I had an all clear, and I *meant* to tell you," I said. "But it's kind of been one catastrophe after another, and I just hadn't gotten around to it."

"Ugh, I can't believe this," said Charlotte.

"Right?" said Isa. "She thinks we're babies."

"You guys, don't give your mother a hard time," said Shiloh. "Keep in mind I didn't think telling you in advance was a good idea, either."

"It's okay. They can be honest with me," I told him. "I messed up."

"Sure, but there's a difference between honest and rude," he said.

"Let's just worry about honest for now," I said.

He met my gaze, and I could tell he was trying to figure out what to think. "Okay," he said after a minute. "Let's start with honest."

$\sim$

"So, speaking of honesty . . . ," I said.

Paul and I were standing in the leafy green courtyard between the hotel and the beach, taking Pedro on a quick walk. The sun was just beginning to set, and Shiloh and the girls were squeezing in a quick swim at the pool (because, as Isa had reminded us yet again, there were no jellyfish there).

"Oh boy. I'm afraid to know what you're about to ask me," he said, taking a sip of the cocktail he'd fetched from the bar on the way over. It was the kind of drink that begs to be photographed—pale yellow, with a pink paper umbrella—but after the island elixirs I'd had at Milagros', the smell of alcohol wafting at me made my stomach recoil.

"Now that it's just the two of us, I want to know: Do you actually want to divorce?"

"What I want doesn't matter," he said, looking away. "See also: my husband being in Fire Island without me."

"Is he there with someone?"

Paul's shoulders slumped. "Yeah, this smug-faced prick named Trevor."

I whistled. "Tell me how you really feel."

"He looks like a mole rat who's been injected with high doses of steroids," said Paul indignantly. "Worse, he's seemingly incapable of using words containing more than two syllables, and"—he shuddered—"he's a mouth breather."

"Maybe he has a deviated septum," I suggested.

"Ahem. Whose team are you on, again?"

I threw my arm over his shoulder. "Yours, Paul. Always and forever. Which is why I want you to tell your husband you don't want to split up."

"Why bother? It's not like Charlie said at any point that he wanted to stay together. I mean, do you know what his response was when I suggested we consider separating?"

I unlatched my arm and waited for him to continue.

"'Okay.' That's literally all he said, Libby," said Paul. His eyes were kind of misty, and I was pretty sure it wasn't the alcohol.

"I'm sorry, Paul. I really think you should tell him how you feel, though."

"Like you've been doing?"

My cheeks got warm. "I don't know what you mean."

"Don't you? Because I was going to suggest Imodium for your raging case of verbal diarrhea. I'm guessing it has to do with some sort of breakthrough in Vieques?"

"There was no breakthrough," I said, but his expression was so dubious that I had to laugh. "Okay, I had a minor epiphany or two, compliments of this guy," I said, smiling at Pedro.

"Aha. Well, I'm glad. But epiphany or no, you should know that Charlie and I are moving forward with our divorce. It's not something we can be talked out of."

"Because you cheated?" I said frankly. "I wish you'd told me when you were thinking about it so I could have talked you out of that."

We'd just reached the beach, and he set his drink on one of the small wood tables the hotel had placed beside lounge chairs along the perimeter.

"Libby, don't take this the wrong way, but I tried to. Remember all those nights when I kept you on the phone way too late because I couldn't sleep?"

My eyes smarted as I thought about what I'd said to him. "And I told you to try and be grateful and think about all the good times with Dad."

He nodded. "I know you were trying to help me, and it wasn't the worst advice. But I needed to talk about the bad feelings as well."

"I'm sorry, Paul," I said sadly. "I was feeling dead inside, too, but I didn't want to. It made me feel like I wasn't grateful for all the good things in my life—like I didn't appreciate any of it. I didn't see how damaging it was to try to plow past my emotions. That's what I realized when I was stuck in Vieques by myself. As Milagros told me the other day, repression backfired. Instead of feeling better, I felt worse."

"I know what you mean." He managed a smile. "You and I were having yet another parallel experience without even realizing it."

A wave of sadness came over me when I thought about Toby and Max, and all the family gatherings that would never be the same if Charlie and Paul split up. "Maybe if I had been honest with you, you never would have sought out Andy."

"No," he said, shaking his head. "Libby, as much as I wanted to be able to open up to you, my actions and our divorce—well, that all comes back to me and Charlie. I really needed my partner to be there for me, and he couldn't be, because he was working all the time. Like, he makes my hours look sane. And because he has a couple months off when he's not working, he seems to think that's okay."

I knew Charlie's schedule could be grueling when he was shooting the show. But because he and Paul had always seemed so solid together, I'd never considered that it had the ability to wear away at their marriage.

"I'm sorry," I said. And I was. It was heartbreaking to see him so crestfallen. "Did you say that to Charlie?"

He frowned. "I guess not. At a certain point in marriage, you figure your needs should be met without having to post a billboard outside your bedroom window."

"As much as I want to tell you I understand, that's basically backfired on me. But it's not too late for you to talk, you know," I said. "Do you still love him?"

"Andy? I never loved him," he scoffed.

For such a smart person, my brother could be incredibly dense sometimes. "*Charlie*, you dodo."

"Oh. Yes, obviously. I always will."

"So, do you really want a divorce?"

He hesitated, then said, "Yes and no? I know you want me to focus on the 'no' part of that answer and vow to save my marriage, but I need you to give me the room to work this out. Even if the outcome isn't what you're hoping for."

He was right—I didn't want them to get divorced. But he was also right that I owed it to him to let him figure it out. "Okay," I told him. "I can do that."

"That means more to me than you know," he said with a small smile. Then he narrowed his eyes. "Hey, when you said you were feeling dead inside—"

"More like not alive," I clarified.

"Fair enough. Either way, is that why you haven't wanted to bury Dad?"

I glanced out at the ocean, thinking about what Milagros had said about him being with me, even if I hadn't realized it. "I think so, yeah. I knew it was going to make me feel awful, and I was telling myself that I could somehow avoid that by looking on the bright side. But pretending only made it worse, you know?"

Paul leaned forward and hugged me. "Of course I do, Mad Libs. I was just waiting for you to figure that out."

TWENTY-NINE

"I wish we didn't have to leave today," I said, leaning into the overstuffed pillows lining the back of the bed. Our room was actually a suite with a small living area, where the girls were still asleep, and a balcony overlooking the ocean.

"Me, too, but maybe we can come back over the holidays," said Shiloh from behind the newspaper he'd picked up in the lobby. Pedro was dozing at his feet, looking like there was nowhere in the world he'd rather be. I knew it was irrational to wish we could take him with us—he probably needed ten more shots and a mountain of paperwork just to get on a plane, and anyway, he belonged to Puerto Rico, if not Milagros. Nonetheless, I couldn't help but imagine him wandering around our apartment or playing fetch with the girls in Prospect Park.

"I'd like that," I said. "Well, provided the weather cooperates."

"Definitely. Speaking of which . . ." He peered at me over the edge of the paper.

"I'm waiting."

"The power's back in Vieques! There's a story about it on the first page."

I exhaled. "What a huge relief."

"For sure. And it'll certainly make life easier for Hector," said Shiloh. In the hospital the day before, he'd told us that Flor's parents were ready to return to Vieques, and that he intended to bring them back on her boat as soon as he was able. Pedro would also be making the trip with them. "And Milagros, when she's ready to go home."

"We should get up and ready if we want a chance to say goodbye to her before we leave."

"You want to wake the girls?" he asked, glancing toward the pull-out sofa where they were both snoring lightly.

I smiled at him. "No. Do you?"

"Not even a little bit. Hey, Libs?"

I cocked my head and waited for him to continue.

"I liked what you said to Charlotte yesterday. To both of them. I'm sure it wasn't easy, but Charlotte needs to hear that however unfair it is that she has diabetes, she has to take it seriously."

"Thanks," I said. "I just wish it hadn't taken a couple of life-threatening moments to get to that point."

"I know. But what you said to Isa was important, too—it was probably good for her to know we know she's been on the back burner, and that we're going to try to remedy that."

"We're?"

"We're a team, remember?" He stood from the small table where he'd been sitting and strode over to the bed. Then he leaned in and kissed me. It was the best kind of messy, lingering kiss, and when he pulled away, we were both smiling.

"I love you, you know," he said to me.

"I do," I said. "I love you, too."

"We're going to get through this," he added.

"What's 'this'?" I almost asked him about the phone call, but the girls had started to stir, and it felt like a conversation that was best had when they weren't around. Especially because I intended to bring up our erotic embargo.

He gave me another smile, smaller this time but still reassuring. "This stage of life. It's hard now, but it won't always be."

"Then it'll get hard again," I said, recalling the 'chat' Pedro and I had in the guesthouse.

"Maybe," he said, and he bent to kiss my forehead. "But we'll get through that, too."

I almost told him I sure hoped he was right when I realized that was a reflex and wasn't actually what I believed. "Yes, we will," I said.

He grinned. "Welcome back, Libby."

~

An hour later, Paul dropped us off at the hospital on his way to the airport. After the girls hugged him, Shiloh took them to Milagros' room, so they could say goodbye.

"Lunch when I get back?" I said to Paul.

"How about a funeral date in Detroit?" he said.

I had to laugh. "Fine. Labor Day weekend?"

"Believe it or not, I think Charlie and I are free. I'll text you."

"Charlie?" I said, arching an eyebrow.

"He loved Dad, too. More later."

"Okay, okay," I agreed. "But we will *talk* more soon. Safe travels."

"They'll be safe, provided I take a sedative before jetting off into the sky. Love you."

"Love you more," I called as he sped off.

Once he was gone, I walked Pedro over to the small park next to the hospital. Ten minutes later, Shiloh and the girls reappeared and traded places with me. "How was it?" I asked.

"Kind of sad," said Isa. "She's really sick."

I was tempted to tell them she was getting better, but I didn't actually know that, and anyway, it wasn't what they needed to hear. "She is," I agreed. "It's difficult to see."

"I'm glad we got to see her, though," said Charlotte.

I touched her arm lightly. "I'm so happy to hear you say that. I am, too. She really adores you both."

"Yeah," said Charlotte. "Oh, and before you ask, I just checked my sugars. I'm fine."

I grinned and ruffled her hair. Maybe, just maybe, she had taken what I said to heart. "Thank you," I said.

"Don't mention it," she said with a smile, grabbing the leash from me. "Seriously."

"I will, but nice try," I told her.

"You want me to go with you?" Shiloh asked, giving my arm a quick squeeze.

I shook my head. "Thank you, but I'm good."

Milagros' eyelids were heavy when I walked into the hospital room, and my heart sank. Then she called to me. "*Mija*. I'm a little sleepy today. They've got me on the good drugs."

I laughed. "I'm glad, and I won't stay. I just wanted a chance to see you before we flew back. How are you feeling otherwise?"

"Eh, like someone who just had a wire stuck in her veins," she said. The doctors had put a stent through her artery the previous afternoon. "But otherwise, full of life."

"I'm so glad." I smiled at her, but then my face crumpled, because this was not how I'd planned to see her, let alone leave her. "I'm going to miss you so much."

"Sure, until I call you two days from now. Then you'll say to yourself, 'Why doesn't this old bat leave me alone?'"

"Never," I said, taking her hand. "You mean the world to me."

"And you to me, Libby. I'm so glad you found your way to my island all those years ago."

She looked exhausted, and I knew I needed to let her rest. "I am, too," I said.

"Come give me a hug before you fall to pieces," she said, sticking her arms out.

My throat was tight, and I was about to cry yet again, because she was so small beneath the sheet; so fragile and, well, so mortal. "Goodbye, Milagros," I whispered.

But a tiny voice in me said, *This isn't goodbye.*

And to my surprise, a louder one said, *Even if it is, you can handle it.*

"Goodbye is for quitters," said Milagros, squeezing me hard. *"Hasta pronto, mija."*

I laughed and kissed her cheek. "See you soon."

~

Hector followed Shiloh and me to the park to get Pedro. "Don't worry, Libby," he said as Charlotte scratched behind Pedro's ears and Isa snapped photos of him with her phone. "We'll take care of him."

"I know you will," I said, sniffling. Then I bent down to look Pedro in the eye. "Now, Pedro," I said, "I want you to be extra good for Milagros. She's recovering, so don't bark too loud or go missing, okay? She's going to need someone to help take care of her. Well, she has someone great to do that," I clarified, looking up at Hector with a smile. "But he might need a little help from time to time."

In response, Pedro licked my face. I laughed and wiped the slobber off my cheek before standing and surprising Hector with a hug. "Thank you," I told him. "Milagros is lucky to have you."

"You don't need to thank me," he said, looking bashful. "I'm lucky to have her."

"True, but I still appreciate everything you've done," I said, handing him Pedro's leash. "Will you call us to let us know when she's home safe, or if anything changes? And, you know . . ." I bit my lip, then added, "Tell me if anything happens to Pedro, too?"

He glanced down at Pedro and laughed. "This dog is going to live to be a hundred and two in dog years. But I promise to keep you posted."

"Hector, *gracias por todo*," said Shiloh, extending his hand.

Hector shook it, then looked at us both. "I hope our paths cross again soon."

I could feel the tears rising in me again. "Me, too," I said.

"Libby, we should probably get going," said Shiloh.

"Right." Our flight left in three hours, and it would take forty-five minutes just to get to the airport. I looked at Pedro, then knelt again and put my arms around his neck. "I'm going to miss you, buddy," I whispered as his tail wagged. "Thank you for helping me get through this."

"You okay?" said Shiloh, putting his arm around me as the four of us walked back to the hospital entrance, where our Uber was waiting.

"Not really," I said, glancing over my shoulder to see if I could spot the dog one more time. I'm not sure why I bothered; Hector had already loaded Pedro into the taxi he was taking to the marina. But in the distance I could see a sliver of the ocean, shimmering and silver in the late morning light. So much had changed since the last time I'd been to Puerto Rico. The ocean was unaltered, though, and there was something comforting about that. I couldn't see it, but I knew Vieques was out there in the distance, constantly shifting even as it remained the same. I let my gaze linger for a moment before looking at Shiloh. "But it's time to go."

THIRTY

When we arrived at the apartment, I set my bags in the hall and walked from room to room. The kitchen, which I'd long said was too small for more than one person, was clean and lovely and well lit. The rug in the living room was wearing thin and stained from—well, from children—but looking at it made me remember the time Shiloh and I simultaneously decided there were no other contenders at the carpet store where we'd purchased it, right after we'd first moved in together. And our bedroom! How had I ever complained about it being cramped or loud? It was our own space in a solid brick building with a roof.

It was so very good to feel grateful without having to remind myself to do so.

As soon as the girls threw their things in their room, they asked if they could go over to Cecelia's.

"Libs? What do you think? I don't mind if you don't," said Shiloh, who was pulling clothes from his suitcase.

"Go ahead," I told them. "But be back in an hour for dinner. Charlotte—"

"Already checked," she said, holding up the finger she'd pricked to use a test strip.

"You're the best," I told her. "And, Isa?"

Isa paused in the doorway. "Yeah, Mom?"

"Bookstore tomorrow?"

She grinned. "Yeah."

As soon as they were gone I sat on the end of the bed next to Shiloh's suitcase. "Hey," I said, looking up at him. "Can we talk?"

He'd been about to pull out the last of his clothes, but he pushed the bag aside and sat beside me. "Of course."

I took a deep breath. I'd thought about bringing it up on the plane ride back, but the girls had been in the same aisle as us, and besides, I hadn't wanted to give the couple behind us something to talk about. "I want to know what's going on with us."

His face went kind of sideways, but he didn't say anything.

"To be specific, I'm referring to us not having sex," I said. "It's been at least a month, and I just want to know what's going on. Don't just say you're tired or you've been stressed. You know this is what happened with Tom. He was always 'exhausted,' 'overworked,' or 'fried,'" I said, making air quotes around each word. "I'm not implying that you're not attracted to women, but I do want you to know that I've been having major flashbacks to my divorce, and this has been harder on me than I've let on. And then you got that weird call on the beach, and you know that my brother's getting a divorce, and—my mind is just going all over the place. I want you to tell me the truth, so I don't have to keep guessing."

"Crap," he muttered.

"'Crap' as in you're not into me anymore?" I said. I sounded offended, and maybe I was jumping to conclusions. But I was done beating around the bush.

He lifted his head. "I didn't think about the Tom thing."

"Yeah. Well. I have."

He looked away, and I suddenly felt more afraid than I had when I'd been sitting in front of Dr. Malone waiting for her to give me my test results.

"Oh, Libby," he said after a minute. "You really think I don't want to sleep with you?"

I almost said no. I *wanted* to say no. But I lifted my chin and stared him straight in the eye. "Yes," I said. "That is what I think. Because if you wanted to, we would have. I know I've been opaque about a lot of stuff lately, but I've been pretty darn clear about wanting to do the deed with you."

"That call I got on the beach?" he said, putting his head in his hands. After a moment he raised it and looked at me. "That was my doctor."

For all they'd done to keep me—not to mention my husband and daughter—alive, the very word *doctor* hit me with the same kind of panic beachgoers got when they heard someone say *shark*.

"What did your doctor want?" I made myself say.

Shiloh looked at me. Like, *really* looked at me—so raw and vulnerable that I was tempted to burrow under our covers before he could go on.

"I found a lump."

The breath flew out of my lungs. "What kind of lump?"

His face was drawn. "The kind that showed up in my groin. I found it in the shower at the end of June."

That was how he'd discovered he had leukemia in his twenties. "June," I said quietly. "That was two months ago. Why didn't you tell me?" But as soon as I heard myself say this, I knew why. "Were you afraid?"

He looked like he was going to cry. "I'm sorry, Libby. I know you've been having a tough time since Charlotte's diagnosis. Then your dad died and . . ." He took my hands in his. "You were concerned about your own tests, and I didn't want to give you one more thing to worry about. And every time we were going to be intimate, I thought about how I was keeping this thing from you, but . . . then I started thinking about the fact that I might have cancer again, and I couldn't get into it. So when I say it isn't you, I really mean that. It isn't."

"Oh," I said. And then I didn't say anything else for a solid minute, because I was too overwhelmed. Finally, I said, "I'm sorry you were afraid to tell me that. I know that since my dad died, I've been pushing everything hard under the rug and pretending I'm fine with all of it. But I'm trying not to do that anymore. I'm trying to get better with letting myself feel fear and shame and anger instead of just pushing them away."

"I know," he said. "I could tell by the conversation you had with the girls the other day, and when we were seeing Milagros."

I bit my lip. "Then . . . is it cancer?"

"I don't know yet," he admitted. "I'm waiting on test results."

"I'm sorry," I said again as my eyes filled with tears. And I was. So incredibly sorry that my own self-protection had gotten in the way of my family's ability to connect with me. Sorry that he was having to grapple with the possibility of having cancer—again. Sorry about all of it. "Are you okay?"

He looked at me with such tenderness that my heart broke. All that time we were on our trip and he was carrying around this terrible secret. "You don't have to apologize for being a human, Libby," he said. "No matter how you were going to take it, I should have told you. I guess . . ." He sighed. "I just didn't want you to tell me it was going to be fine."

I thought about all the people who told me that I was going to be fine after I was diagnosed with cancer. It turned out they were right, of course—but that wasn't really the point. When someone insists that you're okay and everything is going to be just dandy . . . well, it makes you feel like all of the fear and terror and sadness you're experiencing aren't legitimate. But they are. They're as real as your own two hands, and it's horrible to have to pretend otherwise.

"How can I help?" I said. "Do you want me to go with you to the doctor?"

He shook his head. "I wish I'd taken you, but I went in two days before we left. The doctor did an ultrasound and a needle biopsy. The results are in, but I haven't called yet. I was waiting until we got home. I'll call Monday."

It was Saturday, but naturally I wanted to tell him to find out his doctor's home number and call immediately. I wanted to tell him to break into the diagnostic center if that's what it took to get rid of the uncertainty hanging over us like a slab of concrete dangling from a crane.

"All right," I said. I sounded surprisingly calm for someone who wasn't. It was entirely possible that his leukemia had returned. Or that it was another form of cancer. Maybe he'd have to get chemo and radiation. He would spend months out of work, and depending on the outcome, he might have to retire early. The medical bills might bankrupt us, and we'd have to sell our apartment and make all kinds of choices that would devastate the girls and our plans for the future.

Or maybe not, I thought suddenly. And damned if that thought didn't feel like bumping into a long-lost friend.

"All right?" he said.

"Yes," I said, nodding. "We don't know what we're dealing with, but whatever it is, I'm here for you, and so are Charlotte and Isa and everyone else who loves you."

He didn't respond, but the worry had left his face.

"How intent are you on unpacking right now?" I said.

"On a scale of one to ten? I'm a two," he said, cracking a grin. "How about we just lie here and cuddle for a bit?"

I smiled. "Thought you'd never ask."

THIRTY-ONE

The next morning, Charlotte asked if she could talk to me. "Real quick," she said. "I know you and Isa are going to the bookstore soon."

"Not for another half an hour or so," I told her, gesturing to the newspaper that I was still in the middle of reading. It was a Sunday, and I'd just made the girls their favorite brunch—bagels and bacon. "What is it?"

She pulled up a chair beside me at the dining room table. "I think we should go back and talk to Dr. Ornstein," she said, referring to her pediatric endocrinologist.

"Really?" I said. "What about?"

"Getting an insulin pump and one of those monitor thingies."

My mouth hung open. When Dr. Ornstein had brought up a pump and continuous glucose monitor two appointments ago, Charlotte had recoiled at the idea of having the small device attached to her body via a port. She was worried it would be too easy to rip out when she was playing sports—but her bigger concern was that people would see it and know she had diabetes. Although I wanted to tell her it was nothing to be ashamed of, her doctor had gently reminded me and Shiloh that she would come to that conclusion on her own. *Not* as a result of us constantly hammering home that message. "I see," I said, careful not to sound like I was pushing her. "It's a big commitment, and we'll need to make sure you still fit the requirements."

"I know."

"I asked her to do it," said Isa, coming up from behind us. "I'll even help her if she needs."

I swiveled around to look at her. "Is that so?"

She nodded. "Vieques was scary. I cried the whole boat ride back to Fajardo because Charlotte was so shaky. I thought she was going to die. If she had that continuous thingy, we wouldn't have to worry about her blood sugar tanking all the time."

"Oh, Isa," I said, reaching out to take her hand. "That must have been frightening for both of you. I wish I'd been there for you."

"You would have told me not to freak out," she said.

I winced. "I might have, yes. But listen, I've been doing a lot of thinking, especially since Vieques. I've always been an optimist—you guys probably know that—but since your grandpa died, I've been really struggling."

"You?" said Charlotte, scrunching up her nose. "Yeah, right."

"No, I'm serious," I said. "I'm sorry I wasn't more open about it. I should have told all three of you I was struggling, but instead of saying that, I doubled down on being positive, to the point where it was more harmful than helpful. It was the wrong way to handle my feelings, and it backfired."

"Mommy, it's okay," said Charlotte, putting her hand on my shoulder.

I smiled. She'd been calling me that since we'd gotten back. It probably wouldn't last, but I liked it. "I appreciate that, love. But if you guys feel like I'm being too rah-rah, just know that you can tell me."

The girls glanced at each other. Then they looked back at me.

"Okay," said Isa.

"Deal," said Charlotte.

"Thanks, you two," I said. I looked at Charlotte again. "I'll get in touch with Dr. Ornstein tomorrow to make an appointment, and we'll take it from there. Sound good?"

She nodded. "Thank you."

I smiled at them both. "That's what I'm here for."

~

"How are you feeling about work?" Shiloh asked that evening. We were on our patio, and the neighbor's mosquito zapper was buzzing; someone a few doors down was blasting eighties rock. I missed Puerto Rico, but in a strange way I was content to listen to the sounds of home, too.

I took a sip of my sparkling water before looking at him. "What makes you ask?"

He shrugged. "Nothing. It was just that you hadn't mentioned it once while we were traveling."

Even a week earlier, I would have deflected his remark by saying something about how I'd had bigger things on my mind, or how the whole point of vacation was not to think about work. And for a second I worried about overstating my ambivalence, especially given the "verbal diarrhea" Paul had accused me of having. But then I remembered what Milagros had said about repression and decided that I'd need to give myself the time and space to calibrate—even if that involved occasionally sticking my foot in my mouth.

So I said to Shiloh, "I need to make some changes. I've lost my enthusiasm for the work, and it's not doing me or the foundation any favors. The trouble is, I'm not sure what to do. Every day has been feeling the same, but Rupi's big idea about creating a camp seems impossible."

"Lots of things seem impossible until you do them," said Shiloh. "The real question: Do you want to do it?"

I took a deep breath. "That's the tricky part—I'm not sure."

"Hmm," he said. He took a drink of his soda, then set it on the ground and looked at me. "There's no wrong decision, you know. Anything you choose can be okay if you commit to making the most of it. If you had to decide right now about the camp, what would you do?"

I pressed my lids shut, trying to envision a camp. It took a few seconds before I could see it, but when it surfaced in my mind, it was clear and bright. There was a wood sign over a dirt road. A set of cabins. A lake and a dock and loads of happy kids.

And two of those kids were Charlotte and Isa.

My eyes flew open. "What if it wasn't just for kids who lost a parent to cancer?"

"What do you mean?" said Shiloh.

"Well, what if we had different weeks for different kinds of kids, and at least one of those weeks was for kids with diabetes and their siblings? You know how we didn't send the girls to camp this year because we were worried? We could have nurses on staff, more than usual. A doctor or two, and all the meals could be the kind of food that won't cause problems. We'd set it up so that it was as normal as possible, but with all the help that was necessary in case anything went wrong."

"Huh," he said, looking impressed.

Then it hit me. "That's not at all on point for the foundation's mission," I said quietly.

Shiloh laughed lightly. "Libby, who says you can't change?"

"Our entire branding is centered around children and cancer," I explained. "We can't just abandon that."

"Right . . . but you're steering the ship. What would your mom have thought about branching out?"

I answered without even thinking about it. "She would have told me to go for it."

He grinned. "Exactly."

"But there's a *lot* to consider," I said.

"Sure—it's a huge project. But I can tell by the light in your eyes that you're excited about it. And you have a great team, Libby. You wouldn't have to do it on your own."

I felt a smile form on my lips. I guess I *was* excited. "I'm not sure what Rupi will say," I told him.

"You won't know until you ask her. But she's ambitious and she's already told you she's up for a challenge. I bet she'll be thrilled."

"True. Still, it would be a lot of work, and the summers would be nuts. I wouldn't be able to be there for the girls the way I want to. They need me."

"Libby," he said gently. "The girls do need you—they always will. They're getting older, though. I think it'll be okay for you to put more into your work, provided it's the kind of 'more' you're excited about."

I blinked hard, suddenly overcome by the thought of the two of them, running out of their elementary school and across the playground with their arms flung wide open to me at the end of the day. That was our ritual: They ran, I scooped them up in one big hug, and then we walked home hand in hand. When we got to our apartment, they'd perch at the table while I made them a snack, which they would then devour even as they talked over each other, mouths full, in an attempt to tell me about their days. Which had always been the best part of *my* day.

But things were changing; now they needed me in a different way. And instead of a cheerleader or watchman, they needed someone who would listen to them and be honest with them, even when the truth wasn't pretty or palatable. They needed less hovering and more . . .

Well, more letting go.

"You're right," I told him.

Then I looked up. Above us, only the thinnest sliver of moon hung in the sky. After a few seconds my eyes adjusted, and the stars began to surface. They were fainter than they'd been in Puerto Rico, but I could make out a few of the constellations that Shiloh, who was something of an astronomy buff, had taught me. Though I couldn't find Lyra, I easily located Aquila and Hercules. I'd just spotted Sagittarius, which made me smile—I wasn't really into astrology, but I knew my father was a Sagittarius—when a shooting star shot clear through it.

The star wasn't really a star; it was a meteor flaming out in the atmosphere. Though you could spend a whole evening stargazing without seeing one, they weren't truly rare.

But my father had always said that everything was only ever what you made of it. And I knew what I'd just made of that shooting star.

"Did you see that?" asked Shiloh.

"Sure did," I said, smiling up at the sky. "Call me crazy, but I'm going to take that as a sign that I'm on the right path."

THIRTY-TWO

The following morning, I decided to walk the mile and a half to work instead of taking the F line two stops north as I usually did. I wanted a chance to gather my thoughts about the camp, and to consider whether there were other ways to bring excitement back to my job—and if not, whether it was time to hand over the reins to someone else. Because I knew the camp, however invigorating an idea, wasn't going to be a silver bullet. It would not change the monotony of having to open and answer all those emails. It would not lessen the immense workload that I faced every single day.

But as I admired the brownstones I passed, the flower boxes hanging from their windows, and the fruit stands at the end of the street, I didn't feel overwhelmed at what I was returning to. Because I had more agency than I'd given myself credit for, and maybe finally, the mental space to do something with that agency. I didn't have to do it all on my own. Not anymore.

"Good morning," I announced as I walked into the office.

"Libby, hi!" said Rupi, looking up from her computer. "How was your trip?"

"Oh my gosh, where to even start," I said, making my way toward her desk. "I got stung by a jellyfish, stuck in a mud puddle, then stranded without electricity in Vieques during a tropical storm. My dear friend had a heart attack, and Charlotte's insulin started to break down."

"That sounds . . ." She cringed. "Horrible, actually."

I laughed. "It was the *worst*. But believe me when I say that in the strangest way, it turned out to be what I needed. Hey—do you have a few minutes to talk?"

"Of course!" she said. "Here, or in your office?"

I looked around, and it occurred to me that it was okay if Kareem or Lauren, or anyone else for that matter, overheard our conversation. "Here is great," I told her, pulling up a chair. "So . . . I thought a lot about what you said about the camp."

She leaned forward, eyes wide with excitement. "I'm so glad. What do you think?"

"Well, first of all, I owe you an apology. I've been struggling to maintain excitement at work, and I glossed over that because I thought I had to lead by example."

"That's okay, Libby," said Rupi kindly. "You're our leader, sure. But you're a human, too. I think you forget that sometimes."

"You're right, and I appreciate that more than you know," I said, smiling at her. "With that in mind, I'm open to exploring the possibility of the camp. I think it'll take four to six months to research, and if we decide to go forward, about two to three years to fund it and get it up and running. But here's the catch."

"I'm listening," she said, leaning in even closer.

"I don't want it to just be for kids who've lost a parent to cancer. I want to have some weeks designated for kids who are differently abled or who have medical conditions like diabetes—and I want their siblings to be able to join them. Maybe even their close friends. I haven't figured it all out yet," I said. "But I'm hoping you can help me with that."

Rupi's eyes were saucers. "Whoa. Really?"

I gave her a pained smile. "Terrible idea?"

She erupted into laughter. "How did you go from glossing over things to assuming the worst?"

I had to laugh, too. "I'm still figuring this all out. Bear with me."

"Happy to. And to answer your question, it's not a bad idea at all. In fact, I think it's pretty darn amazing. Is it going to take a ton of work? Absolutely. But that's not a reason not to do it. And we're going to have to get buy-in from the rest of the team, though something tells me that won't be hard to do."

I beamed at her. "I was hoping you would say that. But I have to run one more thing by you." I was right outside the foundation office that morning when I realized that there was a way for me to lighten my workload—and the minute I thought of it, I couldn't believe I hadn't earlier.

"Okay," she said, nodding.

"I'd like to make you codirector, effective immediately. We'll need to bring someone else on board to handle some of your current tasks—and mine," I said. "There are parts of my job that are sapping my joy, and I'm sure you feel the same. I'd like to bring in someone new to help, so that you and I can focus on bigger initiatives. I've been so focused on keeping our overhead low that I didn't realize how short-staffed we are. It's time to grow. Especially if we want to make this camp happen."

Her mouth hung open. "Really? You're going to make me codirector?"

"Absolutely. If you want it, of course," I said, but she was already jumping up to hug me.

"I hope this isn't too unprofessional," she said, still squeezing me.

I hugged her back. "Not in this office, it's not. Congratulations— and thank you."

"For what?"

I smiled. "For keeping me from coasting."

~

Shiloh wasn't due in to work until Tuesday, so he told me he'd handle dinner. But when I got home, the kitchen was empty. He wasn't in the family room or dining room, either. I went to the bedroom to change, figuring I'd text him in a few minutes to find out where he was.

I'd just started to pull my shirt off when I realized he was on the floor beside our bed.

His shoulders were shaking, and for a split second I thought maybe he was laughing.

Then I realized he was weeping. I'd seen him cry plenty of times, but I'd never seen him weep before.

"Sweetie," I said, sitting down beside him.

He startled, then wiped his eyes on his forearm. "I'm sorry," he said in a choked voice.

"Don't be," I said, wrapping my arms around him. I wanted to assure both of us it was nothing, but I knew he was supposed to get his test results back today. I swallowed the lump in my throat. "What's going on?"

His eyes were red and watery as he glanced at me. "I just needed a moment."

"Take all the moments you need," I said.

He looked at me again. Then his face cracked open. "It's a swollen lymph node."

I pulled back to look at him. "That's good news, right? Why are you crying?"

"There was some sort of abnormal cell activity in the node."

I couldn't breathe. Because I knew exactly what caused abnormal cell activity.

Cancer.

That's what.

"Oh honey," I said quietly, wrapping him in my arms. "I'm sorry."

"The doctor said it's not necessarily malignant," he said. His voice was raw. "I have to have the lymph node removed and have a full-body CT scan."

Inhale, Libby. Now exhale. And again. "Okay," I said slowly. "When will that happen?"

"Next month. That's the soonest they can get me in. My doctor said to try not to jump to any conclusions."

"Right," I said, but in my mind, I was jumping all over the darn place. Chemo, radiation, recovery, repeat. He would have to stop flying for at least a year, and depending on the prognosis, might be forced into early retirement. Basically, everything Shiloh and I had spent the last thirteen years creating could come to a grinding halt—and that was if all went well. As Dr. Malone had once explained in more eloquent terms, a second cancer diagnosis was often particularly dire, because it meant those damn cells were determined to colonize.

But then I looked at Shiloh—the fine lines around his eyes, which crinkled when he smiled, the freckle above his lip, his salt-and-pepper curls. "I love you," I told him. "I'm here for you, no matter what happens. We'll get through this."

He buried his face in my hair. "I don't want to die," he said, crying softly. "I don't want to leave you here all by yourself to raise the girls without me. I want us to grow old together, Libby. That's all I've ever wanted. I'm not ready for that to end."

I wasn't, either, and the thought of losing him filled me with sorrow. "Me neither," I admitted. "That would be awful. But we're going to play this as it lays, right? And the one thing I can tell you is that as long as I'm alive, I'll be here for you."

Because hadn't that been the commitment we'd made before God, man, and a whole bunch of random people walking down the beach where we'd gotten married? The good, the bad, the unbearable.

But it *was* bearable when there was another person at your side.

His choking sobs had slowed to a quiet cry, and after a moment, his breath normalized. He gazed at me with bloodshot eyes. "Thank you," he said quietly.

"For what?" I said.

"Listening," he said. After a moment, he added, "For letting me say what I needed to say."

Better late than never, I thought. "I'm only sorry I didn't do it sooner."

I don't know how long we sat like that, wrapped around each other. When I finally looked up, I realized Shiloh was gazing at me. Instead of saying anything more, he put his lips to mine.

He tasted like tears. But after I ran and locked the door, then returned to him and let him tug off my clothes with the same urgency I was using to undress him, and he entered me and I bit my lip, lest I cry out and risk scarring our children for life . . .

Well, he felt just like the man I'd fallen in love with in Puerto Rico thirteen years earlier.

THIRTY-THREE

I could have thought of seventy-three different ways to spend Labor Day weekend, none of which involved burying my father. But I could no longer justify delaying the inevitable, and the cemetery had been able to fit us in that Sunday. And so we were in the Detroit suburbs until the holiday, when we would head back to New York.

"Well? How was the drive?" I asked. It was Saturday night, and Paul, Charlie, and the boys had just joined us at the hotel restaurant where we'd decided to have dinner.

"Better than a stick in the eye?" said Max. He had my coloring, but otherwise looked just like Paul, if Paul were constantly grinning and cracking jokes. Toby, on the other hand, had Charlie's broad shoulders and easygoing personality. Unlike Isa and Charlotte, I couldn't remember ever having heard the boys argue with each other.

Toby laughed. "Barely."

"Us, too," said Isa, rolling her eyes.

"Should we get our own table?" I said jokingly.

"Why don't we?" said Charlie. "The place is empty—it shouldn't be a problem to get a couple of separate booths."

"We're happy to watch the littles," said Toby, and Charlotte pretended to punch him.

Then she looked over at me. "Don't worry—I'll be careful about my insulin," she said.

"Thanks, sweetheart," I said. "Let me know if you need anything."

"So how was it?" I whispered to Paul as we trailed behind Shiloh and Charlie, who were chatting about soccer.

"To quote my son, better than a stick in the eye," he said. "But not by much."

"Have you told him what you told me when we got home from Puerto Rico?"

Paul's shoulders slumped. "Yes," he said in a low voice. "I've apologized repeatedly, and he's accepted each time, but neither of us seems to know where to go from there."

I didn't have an answer for that, and anyway, we were nearly at the booth where the hostess was seating us.

"What's new, you two?" asked Charlie. If he was uncomfortable, he didn't show it—though then again, the man was a professional actor.

Shiloh cleared his throat. "Um, the big update at the Ross-Velasquezes is that I have a lymph node in my groin that I have to get removed. It's possible I might have cancer again, so I'll be going in for a full-body scan in a couple weeks."

Charlie and Paul looked stricken.

"Sorry to be the bearer of bad news," added Shiloh.

"Hey, man, it's not bad news yet," said Charlie.

"Agreed," said Paul. "Do the girls know?"

"No, but we'll talk to them next week, before the tests." Beneath the table, I reached for Shiloh's hand. He squeezed it and smiled at me. He looked back at Paul. "I'm lucky to have Libby by my side."

I saw Charlie's eyes flit to Paul, who was looking at him. It happened so fast that I almost wondered if I'd imagined it. But no—a glance had been exchanged.

"And I'm lucky to have you," I told him.

He smiled. "That's the best part of marriage—in a world full of unknowns, you have a known. That's basically the holy grail."

I looked at Paul, not caring if I was being obvious. "Yes," I agreed. "Yes, it is."

~

The following morning, we were standing at the entrance of the cemetery with Paul, Charlie, and the boys. We'd awoken to the sound of rain beating down on the hotel room, but it had since slowed to a drizzle; we huddled beneath black umbrellas that Paul had the good sense to pick up at a drugstore on the way. "You ready?" he asked when I hugged him hello.

"No," I said, but then I corrected myself. "Yes, I am. I feel like he's been waiting long enough."

"I know. We should have done this a while ago, but . . ."

"We're here now," I said, and darn it, the dam had burst and here came the flood. Before I could even sniff, Paul was handing me a tissue. I wiped my face. "Let's go do this," I said.

The cemetery was located in a small Detroit suburb; our mother had been laid to rest there because it was where her parents and grandparents had been buried. I hadn't been to visit since Paul and I had made the trip thirteen years ago. As he took my hand and we made our way through the winding path down the center of the rolling hills, I was comforted that little had changed.

But one change was unmistakable: the gray granite headstone that was now beside my mother's.

PHILIP EDWARD ROSS, 1944–2018
BELOVED FATHER AND HUSBAND

Paul and I had decided on an informal event, knowing it was what our father would have wanted. After Paul spoke quietly with the gravedigger who was waiting for us at the plot, he took a spot beside the gravestone, holding the urn in his hands, and began to speak.

"They say the mark of true character is what a person does when no one else is looking. But growing up as a gay boy in a time and place where that was considered shameful, it was what my father did when everyone else was looking that showed me who he was," he said. Like me, he already had tears streaming down his face, but he didn't bother wiping them away. "Dad loved and accepted me and made sure everyone knew that. He never asked me to change a thing about who I was, and because of that, I was able to learn to love and accept myself, too." He sniffled and paused for a minute before continuing. "I know it was so hard for him after my mother died, and though he didn't pretend that he wasn't tired or that he always knew what he was doing, he never once made Libby and me feel like we were a burden to him. Instead, he acted like we were what made his days bearable. He was such a good man." Paul looked up at me and managed to smile. "Libby, remember what he'd say whenever he screwed up and we called him on it? 'Gosh darn it, you two, don't make me turn this life around!'"

I nodded, laughing through my tears.

"Philip Ross was the best man I've ever known," said Paul, his voice barely above a whisper. "And I will miss him every day of the rest of my life, even as I know those days are sweeter because I had the luck of having him as my father."

He was weeping, but before I could go to him, Charlie took him in his arms. Then Toby and Max put their arms around their fathers, and the four of them held each other and cried.

Please, I thought as I watched them. *Please let them figure this out.*

"Libby?" said Shiloh, touching my arm softly. "Do you want to say anything?"

I turned to him, which was when my neurons started making all kinds of terrible connections. What if the next funeral I attended was my husband's? I looked at Isa and Charlotte, who were standing somberly beside Shiloh. All this time I'd worried about myself dying, but I'd never considered that they might spend part of their childhood without their father. And their father was the kind that my own father would be proud of. *Had* been proud of; he'd treated Shiloh like his own son and had boasted about him to anyone who'd listen. He'd loved to tell people how Shiloh switched between Spanish and English without missing a beat and flew planes and was the kind of husband he'd "always hoped my daughter would have." He'd loved Tom, but he'd never once said that about him.

I swallowed hard, even as the tears kept flowing, then went to stand behind my parents' headstones, where Paul had just been. I'd prepared something to say, but now it felt all wrong. I decided I would just share what was in my heart.

"I don't know if everyone has a soul mate," I began, looking at Shiloh. "Like the afterlife, I think it's one of those concepts we all have to work out for ourselves—and even then, we're probably just guessing. But if I know one thing, it's that my father loved my mother more than life itself, and her death didn't change that even the slightest bit. I keep thinking about this photo he sent me right after I was first diagnosed with cancer. The two of them were on the beach in Vieques. They were newlyweds, so in love that you could feel it beaming right out of the photo. My mother was pregnant with me and Paul then, actually, and she and my father had no idea about the difficulties that lay ahead."

Paul was handing me another tissue, which I accepted, and I took a moment to compose myself. Already, the sun was breaking through the dark clouds, and I could tell that the sky would soon be as blue as if there had never been rain at all. In a few short hours, the stars would appear. But I didn't need to watch them glitter to know that my mother and father were out there somewhere, somehow, smiling down at the legacy they'd left behind.

"Even if they'd had a crystal ball and had seen every single thing coming, I'm willing to bet that they still would have been glowing like the world was their oyster. Because that's what it feels like when you love and know you're truly loved by another person." Shiloh was holding my gaze now, and I smiled at him softly. I might lose him before I was ready, just like my parents. It was a risk I would have to take. "See, that's the thing about love. You know it can't last forever, and that no matter what happens, you're going to have to say goodbye before you're ready. But that doesn't mean you don't do it. It means you just try to love even more and even better, while you still have the chance."

I took a deep breath and looked around at the wonderfully flawed people I had the good fortune of calling my family. Paul and Charlie, who were holding hands and standing between their sons. Isa and Charlotte, who were huddled together and smiling softly at me. Shiloh, whose warm eyes were still resting on me.

Then I looked at the granite headstones that were but mere placeholders for my parents. I would always wish they were with me; I would always want more chances to love, to laugh, to take one more spin around the sun. That was what it felt like to be fully alive. But this day, this moment, was a gift.

And it was more than enough.

EPILOGUE

Three weeks after we got back from Vieques, the girls and I were returning from a walk in Prospect Park when I saw a bright yellow butterfly resting on the wrought-iron fence outside of our apartment. Sometimes you know before you know; I wasn't surprised to find Shiloh sitting at the table, waiting for me. When he looked up at me, his eyes were brimming with tears. "Milagros is gone," he said. "I'm sorry, Libby."

Oh, how I was, too. But now, finally, I knew that trying to pretend otherwise would only make it hurt worse.

Several days later, a FedEx envelope arrived for me; Hector's name was on the return address. That night, after the girls went to bed, I turned on the patio lights and went outside to open the envelope.

Inside, there was a handwritten letter paper-clipped to a stack of legal documents. I waited a second for my eyes to adjust to the dim light, then began to read.

> *Dear Libby,*
> *If you're reading this, I'm winking at you from the sky.*
> *Hola, mija!*
> *I've had hundreds of people stay at my guesthouse over the years. You could have been any one of them—someone*

who had a friendly chat or two with me, then let me fade into the memory of their time in Vieques.

But I knew from that first day when we had drinks that you weren't just another traveler. Even though you were hurting, you had a spark that reminded me of myself. You and I—we know that two people can have the exact same experience and walk away with two different stories. This life is only ever what we make of it.

I know you've had a rough go of it lately, and that you feel guilty about that. Don't. Having a roof over your head and a family you love and a body that works the way you need it to doesn't make your pain any less valid than anyone else's. And life is pain, mija. Not always, but often enough—and gracias a Dios for that, because without it, how would we ever truly appreciate all the good that comes alongside it?

Entonces! This is a long way of saying that you are very important to me, Libby. I treasure our friendship and all the smiles you've put on my wrinkled face over the years. I love that you love Vieques and the people of Puerto Rico—and not just because you married one of them.

Which is why I'm leaving my home, and my guest home, to you, Shiloh, Isa, and Charlotte.

I know it's a lot. But I don't have a relative who deserves it—or even wants it, unless it's to sell to a developer, ay. And Hector already has two homes, not including Flor's! He doesn't need or want it. I didn't tell you I was going to do this when you were in Vieques because I didn't want you to spend your whole trip thinking about it—or feeling guilty because you felt you didn't deserve it. You do.

*I'm sure you're wondering how you're going to man-
age to take care of a place that's far from your own home.
I don't have that answer. But I've read your palm and
seen your lifeline—remember that time when you first
arrived in Vieques?—so I know you have time to figure
it out. And isn't that the best gift of all?*

*I know you miss me, and believe me when I say I
miss you, too. But remember—once you love someone,
they're with you. Always.*

Te quiero siempre,
Milagros

"Libby?" said Shiloh, opening the sliding door. "Are you okay?"

"Yes," I said, wiping the tears from my eyes. I stood and handed him the letter and waited for him to read it.

"Wow," he said when he finished. "I . . . I don't even know what to say."

"Right?" I said. "Even after she's gone, Milagros manages to surprise us."

"What do you think?"

"I think we have a retirement plan," I said, breaking into a smile. "I think it's generous and amazing and completely crazy. What about you?"

"I have to admit, I love the idea of living there, at least part-time." He wrinkled his nose. "But what if it's back?"

He meant his cancer; we still had a few more days until he went in for his follow-up tests.

"Then we'll work around that," I said. "This isn't our first rodeo— we know how to handle it."

He wrapped his arms around me. "You're absolutely right."

"Say it again," I said, and he laughed and put his lips to mine.

As I closed my lids and kissed him, I could see my favorite beach, where tiny shells dotted the sand and calm waters stretched for miles. I saw a patio, too, where a hammock hung between a pair of palm trees and orchids grew wild. And I saw a home filled with love, where a family—and yes, their small, one-eyed dog—was ready for whatever came next.

AUTHOR'S NOTE

Dear reader,

The storm that Libby and her family experience is fictional, though loosely based on a storm I experienced while in Vieques in the summer of 2019. But as you may know, Hurricane Maria was all too real. It struck Puerto Rico in September 2017, and as I write this, the island is still recovering from the devastation that impacted its residents, infrastructure, and economy.

One way to support Puerto Rico's recovery is to visit the mainland or one of its smaller islands, such as Vieques, if you have the chance. I've been traveling to Puerto Rico regularly with my husband, who is Puerto Rican, for the past twenty years; now we spend part of each summer there—not just to give our kids a chance to know their heritage, but also because it's my favorite place in the whole world. If you do go, I'd love to hear what you think. My contact information is on my website, www.camillepagan.com, and I read every email.

All my best,
Camille

P.S. If you enjoyed *Don't Make Me Turn This Life Around*, please take a second to write a brief review; reviews make a world of difference for a novel's visibility and success. If you already did, thank you! Either way, I appreciate you taking the time to read my latest. You, dear reader, are why I write.

ACKNOWLEDGMENTS

Writing and editing a novel in the middle of a global pandemic was a challenge I hope I'll never have to accept again, and it's no exaggeration when I say I couldn't have managed it without the support of my family and friends. Thank you to my husband, JP, and to our children, Indira and Xavi, for giving me the time and space to craft this book. Lauren Bauser, Shannon Callahan, Ann Garvin, Stefanie and Craig Galban, Kelly Harms, Laurel and Joe Lambert, Stevany and Tim Peters, Katie Rose Guest Pryal, Alex Ralph, Sara Reistad-Long, Pam Sullivan, Mike and Michelle Stone, and Darci Swisher: I am so lucky to have you in my corner.

Likewise, my deep gratitude to my editor, Jodi Warshaw, for helping me shape this story as well as my writing career; Tiffany Yates Martin for her wise and witty editorial guidance; my agent, Elisabeth Weed, for being—well, the absolute best; Danielle Marshall, Mikyla Bruder, Gabriella Dumpit, and the entire Lake Union team for their continued support; Michelle Weiner at CAA for championing my work; and Kathleen Carter and Ashley Vanicek for helping my books find their way to readers.

I'd especially like to thank my youngest sister, Janette Noe Sunadhar, for being gracious enough to answer my endless questions about what it's really like to live with type 1 diabetes.

And thank you to the Lizarribars, Pagáns, and Rodriguezes for making Puerto Rico my home away from home for the past two decades.

Read more about Libby and her family in *Life and Other Near Death Experiences* by Camille Pagán.

ABOUT THE AUTHOR

Photo © 2017 Myra Klarman

Camille Pagán is the #1 Amazon Charts and *Washington Post* bestselling author of seven novels, including *This Won't End Well*, *I'm Fine and Neither Are You*, and *Life and Other Near-Death Experiences*, which has been optioned for film. Her books have been translated into nearly two dozen languages. Pagán has written for the *New York Times*; *O, The Oprah Magazine*; *Parade*; *Real Simple*; *Time*; and many other publications. She lives with her family in Ann Arbor, Michigan. Learn more about her work at www.camillepagan.com.